THE MURDER INVESTIGATION OF ADOLF HITLER

THE MURDER INVESTIGATION OF ADOLF HITLER

A MUNICH MYSTERY

PETER CLENOTT

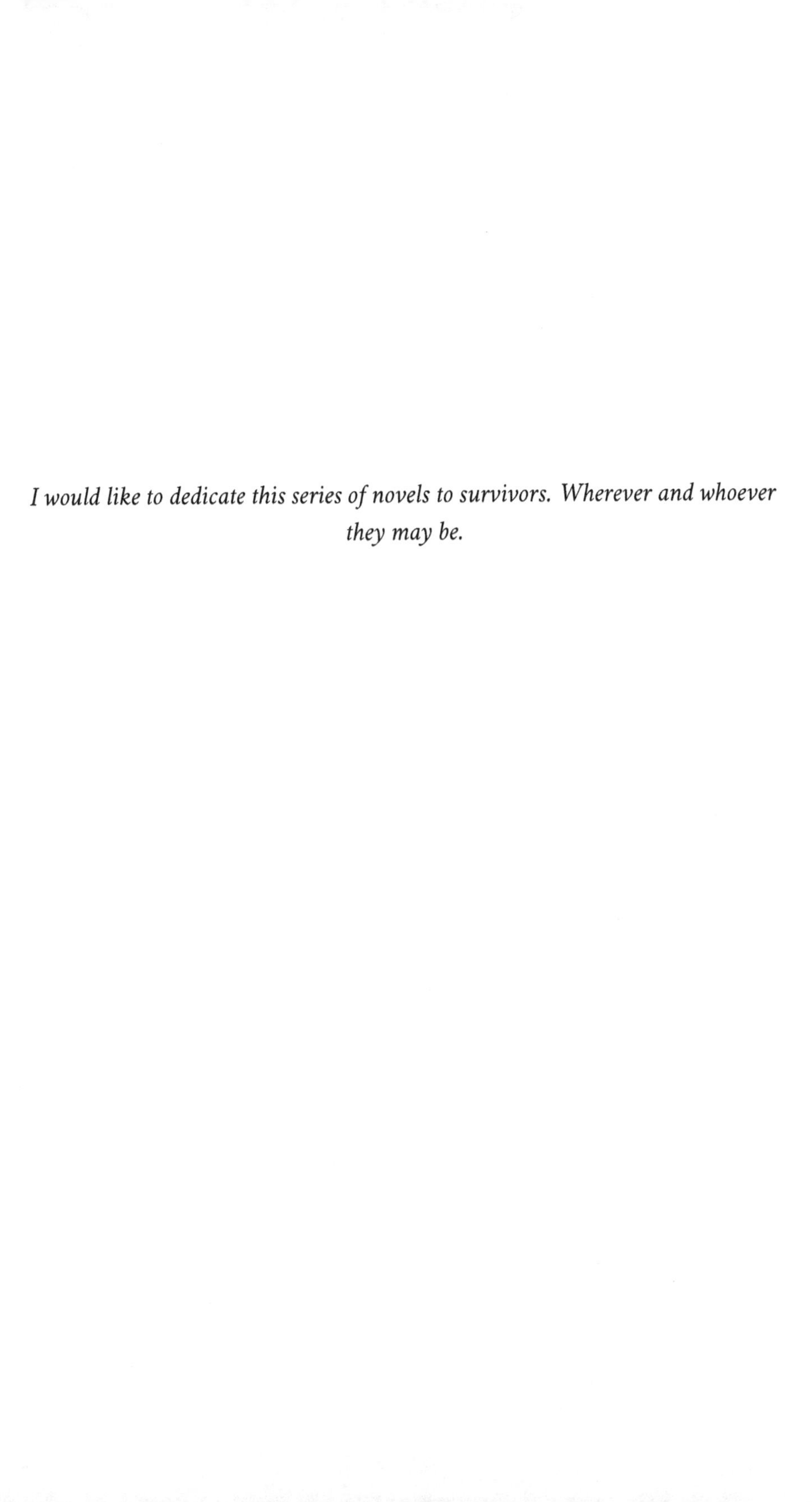

I would like to dedicate this series of novels to survivors. Wherever and whoever they may be.

Prologue

September 4, 1931

The last woman she would compare herself to is Helen of Troy, the Greek queen whose beauty launched a thousand ships. She's a country girl, after all, born in poverty, having survived a difficult childhood. When she studies herself in the mirror, which she does with frequency, she sees what most people see. A good-looking young woman of twenty-three, some say beautiful. Not everyone. Curly brown hair and brown eyes, always gleaming with anticipation. She's a tall girl at five feet seven, athletic. Charming, confident, bubbly. When in Munich, she likes to pretend to be cosmopolitan, attend the opera, dine out at the fanciest of restaurants, and shop at the most elegant of boutiques. Out here in the high Alps at Obersalzberg near the Austrian border, Geli Raubal can let loose and become the gay, carefree, and guileless girl she really is.

"Munich can be so confining," she admits to her companions. "But at least he let me come."

"Your uncle."

"I practically had to get on my knees. He doesn't trust me anymore."

"You are the master, Geli. He, the unwitting puppet."

Surrounded by the majesty of Europe's tallest mountains, they are trudging downhill for a swim, she and her accompaniment: her younger sister, the quiet and diffident Elfriede; her best friends Hennie Hoffman, eighteen, and the intentionally Bohemian Klara Fries; and, of course, her uncle's ever-present watchdogs, Julius Schaub and Martin Kaspers. *Schutzstaffel.* SS. But at least they are dressed as Bavarian mountaineers rather than in their SS uniforms. Uncle Alf will not let her out of his sight if he can help it. But due to the rising political tensions not only in the country at large but within his own party, Adolf Hitler is away much of the time, and he suspects what his niece, his half-sister's daughter, might be up to while he is gone.

She never stumbles as she takes the steep descent. Small rocks careen down the slope toward the valley floor. Some she intentionally kicks as if they are impediments her famous Uncle Alf has put in her path to keep her on the straight and narrow. She's certainly pretty enough to have earned the attention of men, young and old. Including, as an example, Emil Maurice, Uncle Adolf's former driver, who had proposed marriage to her before being unceremoniously canned. He saw in her what many around Hitler see. A desirable young creature, willing and available, to the right hero.

"He needs to understand," Klara says, "that you have a right to your own life. He's old enough to be your father, for God's sake. Your fucking uncle. Tell him."

"It's not so easy." This remark comes from Hennie, who ought to know Geli as well as anyone. Her father is Heinrich Hoffman, Hitler's personal photographer, who has never been so prosperous thanks to the patronage of the Nazi Party leader. As such, Hennie has entered Geli's life as her closest intimate despite their five-year age gap. "He loves her," she explains. "In his way."

"Like a dog in heat." Klara is disgusted, looks around to make sure her remarks have gone unheard. If Elfriede has an opinion, much like her and Geli's tolerant mother, she keeps it to herself.

"Do you actually, you know, do it with him? Or does he just watch?"

"Klara."

"Seriously. If he were my uncle, I would call the cops on him."

"He is the 'cops,'" says Hennie. "Isn't any subject off limits to you?"

"No."

"It's not at all what you think," Geli says.

Or is it exactly what Klara thinks? What girl wouldn't be tempted by the affections of a man who could someday rule Germany? He does love her, adores her, actually. He is ambivalent about all other women. Prefers the company of men. Only she arouses him to physical and emotional passion, degrading though it can sometimes become. Up until the past few months, she has known how to manipulate him and keep him in her thrall. What she is afraid of is that the world is moving too quickly. Uncle Alf is impetuous, and even her strings may get snarled soon enough.

"Pray for me," she says. "I'm going to ask him to let me go to Vienna when I get back to Munich."

"Vienna. I envy you." Klara takes a long study of her friend. In her mind, she is preparing a portrait that will outlive them all. Even Geli's uncle, the failed artist, should appreciate that.

"Don't envy me, Klara. I have much on my mind."

"I have no doubt, *Liebchen.*"

As dear as she holds her friends, there are some things Geli keeps close to the vest. The beauty of Obersalzberg is that she can release all of her pent-up anxiety into the clean, clear mountain air, hike for miles, swim, eat, drink, and be merry. She has the best of friends, she thinks. One particularly in Austria whom none of them know about. A young man. An actor. Someone her attentive uncle would detest.

Toting a picnic basket in one hand, she carries the Rollieflex camera that Uncle Alf presented her to commemorate days such as this. Hennie is a diarist, and Klara is an artist who has brought her etching pad and pencils. In her heart, Geli, hard G, soft heart, fears this may be the last time she will be able to be so uninhibited. Change is brewing. Germany is on the edge of chaos, and her uncle is in the middle of it all. On the one hand, she doesn't want to be a petty domestic thorn in his side. On the other, Klara is right. She should have the freedom to be happy, and since her uncle will never propose marriage to her, well...

They reach the spring beneath the home, Haus Wachenfeld, that Uncle Alf rents and that Geli's mother Anna tends. Geli and Elfriede will help with the cooking and other housekeeping needs, but such domesticity can entertain such a young woman only so long. Obersalzberg is a favorite picnicking spot for her uncle whenever he accompanies her. Today, he is in Nuremberg or Hamburg or Berlin jousting with his political rivals for power in the

Reichstag. Today, she is free to breathe.

At the bank of the stream, Geli and her friends unpack. She gazes about. Her two male guards, Schaub and Kaspers, stroll at a short distance behind, probably wishing they could be elsewhere but are forever obedient to the demands of their boss. Long ago, she had a brief fling with Martin. If he remembers it, he shows no indication that he ever kissed her.

"Hey!" she shouts at them. "A little privacy, if you don't mind."

She and Hennie undress behind a bush. She didn't pack a swimming suit. Neither did Hennie. The men will have to trust that they aren't going to fly off like Wagner's Valkyries. Elfriede is reluctant to join them. She will distribute the food while Klara begins to sketch her favorite subject: the female nude.

"No peeking!" Geli yells.

She is a flirt; no one can deny that, a scholar at the art of catching the male eye. The men pay her no mind. They keep their distance, knowing that Uncle Alf will throw a tantrum on the Richter scale of ten if he should find out they betrayed his trust in them and sullied his niece. Hitler loves her in a way that most Germans, certainly those he is courting for their political support, would find appalling. It is not such a secret among those in the know, Hitler's most intimate circle. Even so, the drama must keep to Hitler's script. Geli can have her boys, but the leash is only so long.

After a half hour of working up an appetite, Geli grabs a sandwich from her sister, then lies down on a blanket to tan her naked body.

"What's in Vienna, by the by?" asks Klara, continuing to draw in between bites of lunch. Julius and Martin are sitting on a rock in the distance, eating dessert and seeming to ignore the two sunbathing German beauties.

"I told Uncle Alf I'm not happy with the singing lessons I'm getting from Herr Vogl," Geli says, half asleep. "If you want to learn how to sing opera, you must go to Vienna."

"I wouldn't know. Your canary sings better than I do." Klara holds up her drawing of Geli. Germany opened up after the Great War. The Roaring Twenties swept aside the prudish nineteenth century, barreling through cities like Berlin and Munich. Queen Victoria's era chased away by the poet, author, scientist, and a healthy twentieth-century libido. Uncle Alf might not approve of Klara's rendition of his niece, but Geli does.

"Uncle Alf draws me sometimes," she says.

"Like this?"

"Yes."

"I'll bet."

Hennie, lying beside Geli, warming her belly, eyes covered by a towel, wisely keeps her counsel. Adolf Hitler may be a prig in many ways, but he makes Geli do things unmentionable even in the unflappable Twenties. His renditions of his niece are not for public consumption.

Geli lifts herself off her blanket and makes sure that the Alpine breeze can't carry her secrets any further than Hennie's ears. "That's not why I'm going to Vienna," she says. She speaks so softly, even Klara and Elfriede are kept in the dark.

Hennie leans in closer. Two schoolgirls sharing the unthinkable. "So, what then?"

If the photographer's daughter expects something truly juicy, her friend Geli doesn't disappoint.

"I'm pregnant," Geli says. "By a Jew."

Chapter One

A short history of Germany, 1931. Necessary to understand why a young woman should be murdered.

Flash back thirteen years to the end of the Great War. Germany is humiliated. Not only has it lost a war, the reparations imposed upon it are nothing short of calamitous, impossible to fulfill. We Germans will be paying until the next millennium. And who is to blame? The Communists and the Jews who now run the Weimar government. The people of Germany call it The Great Stab in the Back.

Deutschland is a divided land. It isn't even a hundred years old, the product of that Prussian Bismarck. There is Prussia in the north, Bavaria in the south, and every other state and palatinate in between. One third of the population is Catholic. There are five hundred and five thousand Jews. Luther was born here, but superseded by Hegel and Nietzsche and Goethe. Marx, Engels, and Max Schmeling are German. So are Einstein and Himmler. It is a nation of warriors and artists, of Freud and Wagner. Thomas Mann, Marlene Dietrich and Bertolt Brecht. The Three Penny Opera, All Quiet on the Western Front, the films of Fritz Lang. And, oh, yes, Mein Kampf and Adolf Hitler.

In 1929, the stock market crashes and whatever hope the Weimar regime has of staying in power vanishes. It still exists. For a bit longer. Unbeknownst to the world, it is a moment in history that ultimately will doom millions of people. It is a moment to be taken advantage of, where a charismatic, energetic man, a former army corporal from a broken family, can force his way through a gap in the power vacuum and take control.

If his luck continues, that is. But luck is a funny thing, Herr Hitler. A frivolous thing.

* * *

Those who are resolved to probe the city in darkness, to navigate its most forbidden precincts, to investigate what lies beneath the apparent, should come prepared. There's an odor to murder unlike any other, a grim sensation that sticks to the surface, snags your clothes, sinks its claws into your flesh. Suspects lurk behind every door, peer from parted curtains as you drive past, daring you to look, challenging you to guess when, what, who, why.

Avi Kreisler doesn't cringe at the prospect of what he might find. He has a cop's nose for decay, a detective's eyes for detail, the morbid curiosity of a bloodhound. There is just one problem. For every murder that is brought to the attention of his superiors, there are a dozen more that escape assignment. The dead pile up. Manpower is deficient. War and revolution will do that to a city.

Death belongs here. In Munich. One war down. Another to come. A nation tearing itself apart. Death is life's partner, perhaps even its better half. During his abbreviated childhood, thinks Kreisler, an avid reader of Conan Doyle and Poe, death was more bourgeois Victorian, circumspect and remote, feigning disinterest. Old age. Chronic illness. Poison. A slip and tragic fall. Death never used to be so pernicious, so vindictive. A political beast set loose on the occupants of this city. At least, Kreisler doesn't remember it that way. Then again, he's twenty-eight years old and has only been a detective a few days short of a month.

These days, death is defiant. It brays with the shout of a trumpet, stormtroops out in the light of day, glorifying its brazen ability to bludgeon the life out of someone on the open sidewalk, only to elude justice in the courts of law. But not tonight. Tonight, the death of a young woman, a prostitute, perhaps, has brought Kreisler and his division associate chief into the heart of madness.

Kreisler's job is complicated for many reasons. There is another sort of murder going on in these latter days of the Weimar Republic. Sanctioned and tolerated even by the course of German history, assassination is a child of the Great War and of the revolution that followed it. Its powerful instigators ignore the law with the nonchalance and pomposity of aristocrats. Its scruffy soldiers expect the courts to be lenient. It is a frustrating time to be a detective. And yet, Kreisler chose this path. Chose it despite being the most suspect of all: a Jew.

"Hungry?" Fritz Langer asks him. Langer, his immediate superior, is driving as if they are fleeing the Cossacks. He's a fifteen-year veteran of the Munich police, yet when behind the wheel, he is like a giddy child. It is an important lesson for Kreisler, who thinks it may be time for him to get his own driver's license.

"You're asking now?" Kreisler holds onto his armrest, breathless with each wild turn.

"I don't know what it is about me," Langer says. Blowing cigarette smoke out his window, Kreisler's senior considers the death they are hurrying to investigate. He is completely blasé about it, exhibiting the interest of a *schwuchtel,* a fag, watching a beautiful woman take off her clothes. "The moment I'm assigned a case, I get the urge for a huge steak. A thick, juicy American steak from Kansas. I was there once, you know. Kansas. An uncle." Needless to say, Langer is short and heavy set, Oliver Hardy to Kreisler's Stan Laurel.

Except, Kreisler is in no mood for a pie in the face. He takes his job seriously, has to. He is as religious as a sardine, but that doesn't alter the facts. He was honest in filling out his application to become a cop six years ago. What religion do you practice? Back then. being a Jew wasn't so awkward. Neither was being forthcoming. If he wants to work his way up through the ranks, he must prove his worth every day with every case. Against the tide was his father's motto. Kreisler has adopted it, having come up with nothing better.

"I grabbed something an hour ago."

Langer takes a sharp turn around a corner that flattens Kreisler against the passenger side door.

"Jesus, Fritz! Whatever it was," Kreisler says, holding onto his hat, feeling his insides roll, "it's going to end up all over your windshield any second."

"Must develop the stomach, Kreisler," Langer shouts with a laugh. Then they are there. AugustBebelstrasse 12. The disturbing scene of death and all else is forgotten.

A crowd of gawkers has already gathered, some on the sidewalk, some in the busy street blocking traffic. Working men and women coming home after a long shift, going to or coming from the nearest tavern. The gallery at a soccer match, oohing and aahing every turn of events. Langer's sudden swerve, the braking of his car, nearly into the startled audience, with an accompanying blare of the horn, gets more out of them than the enthusiastic sounds of diners enjoying a lavish if bloody meal.

"That's how you scatter the vultures," Langer says with a second gleeful beep of his horn. "Out of the way! Crime scene!" he shouts.

Kreisler reaches into the back seat. Before he has even seen who the heights have deposited on the ground below, he is grabbing his camera. Exiting the police car, he steps onto the sidewalk and immediately turns his attention to the crowd. He snaps a photo, then a second and third. Some of the crowd back off, hide their faces. Others pose with a smile and wave. Pure Hollywood. Except that it isn't.

"You think they're all guilty?" Langer asks, chugging up beside him. "We don't even know if a crime has been committed."

"Just in case," Kreisler says. "Before someone decides to run."

If anything about this incident can be considered Hollywood, it is the young Jewish detective. Kreisler is considered a sharp dresser among the detectives of the Munich Homicide Division. As a new member of the force, Kreisler might be scolded for showing up his betters, but that doesn't stop him from declaring his style. An expensively tailored gray suit with matching pants, pale blue tie and white fedora. If Sherlock Holmes and Auguste Dupin and Hercules Poirot can have their style, so can a Weimar man. Langer, on the other hand, merely looks chubby.

Kreisler's eyes take in the crowd, too, more slyly than the camera lens. He has an Eidetic memory for the trivial. It is only when he turns that he sees the prone, shattered body of a woman drenched in a spray of blood that has congealed outward as far as the curbstone in one direction and back toward the entrance of the building the other way. She had to have impacted hard to have created such a frightful human mess, he thinks, meaning she must have fallen from a great height.

A street cop arrived on the scene earlier and called the DOA in. He's done as well as he can, managing the crowd. It is an ugly scene, a violent death, and Kreisler wonders, 'How curious do you have to be to stay this long and stare so hard at something so grim?'

"*Schulerselbstmord*," Langer says, giving his opinion. He is standing on the far side of the body, writing in his notepad.

"Pardon?"

"We've seen a run on these. Students committing suicide because they can't make the grade. Though the beginning of the school year isn't typical. It's mainly around exam time they jump."

Kreisler gazes upward toward an open window on the fifth and top floor of the building. It is slightly to the left of the spot on which the victim landed. The awning protecting occupants of the building from the elements juts out into the sidewalk, but not so far that it might have somehow broken her fall and saved her life.

"Are we in agreement?" Langer asks. He has spoken briefly to the street cop to get the preliminary details.

"That it's a suicide? She's definitely a faller." Kreisler steps cautiously to avoid getting his shoes covered in blood and bends over the body.

"That much is obvious, Avi. Officer Hartmann says he was a block away when he heard someone scream."

"The victim or one of these people?"

"I assume one of these people. Someone must have seen something. Or heard it. Splatter, you know. But no one has been questioned yet. We made pretty good time getting here."

Kreisler pulls a handkerchief from the breast pocket of his suitcoat and holds it over his nose as he places a gentle hand under the dead woman's face and turns it his way. There isn't much left for identification purposes. She clearly landed head and face into the concrete, forehead caved in, teeth forcefully torn from the gums or shoved into her jaw. Was she pretty once? Who can say? Clearly, there was no attempt at bracing her descent with extended arms.

"I was just wondering," he says, "if she screamed on the way down or if she was silent. There's a bruise, a lump, on the back of her skull."

"What does that mean? She fell."

Kreisler shrugs. "I don't know. You'd think even a jumper would yell something, wouldn't you? Out of fear. A last-second change of heart. You'll order an autopsy?"

"I wasn't planning to. A jumper's a jumper. We'll talk to some of these people. Unless someone saw something significant, we can call in the wagon and head home. I'll turn in our report tomorrow."

"What about the owner?"

"The owner?"

"The landlord. I'd like to inspect the room she jumped from. Don't you want to find out who she is?"

Langer closes his notepad and takes a gander toward the open window overhead. An evening breeze is swirling a curtain. "If she were anyone important," he says, "she wouldn't be here on the sidewalk. But suit yourself. *Streifenpolizist* Hartmann and I will talk to these schmucks. You go find the landlord. I'll be up. Let me know if you find anything."

Kreisler, with reluctance, releases the young woman's face to rest back in the grime of the world. Whoever she was, she deserved better than this. He rises, tucking away his handkerchief, but snaps a few photos of the deceased before heading to the entryway.

"She was a fucking Red!" someone in the crowd yells. A male.

"She was a whore. Ask anyone."

And another. This time, a female, with what Kreisler considers a complete non sequitur. *"Juden, raus!"*

He is tempted to turn to try to locate the spouter of such hatred in the wake of such tragedy. Jews! Get out! *Ein bahnstrasse nach Palastina.* Go to Palestine. How many times has he pretended not to hear words like this? Out on the street. Among his fellow cops. 'A Jew can't be a real German.' It comes with the territory, he thinks, but like many of those who follow the religion he was born into… he, himself, is a non-believer… he doesn't expect it to go as far as it will. An Eidetic memory is of no use to an improvident mind.

As soon as he enters the foyer of the building, he can start making assumptions about the dead woman. Munich's neighborhoods are divided not only by class, upper and lower, but often enough by political association. Communist neighborhoods. National Socialist neighborhoods. The most violent neighborhoods are those whose residents' loyalties are divided. Don't wander where you don't belong unless you're with a dozen friends, armed friends.

Posters line the walls of the front hall. There, a red fist. There, a portrait of Lenin and Marx. A flier has been taped to the wall at the head of the stairs going up, announcing a rally of the Spartacists, the radical branch of the Communist Party, scheduled tomorrow afternoon. If the dead woman was planning to attend, she won't now.

Kreisler knocks on the first door to the left of the staircase.

"Munich Police!" he hollers.

A head pokes from a room down the hall. "She's deaf. Gotta bang a little harder."

"The landlady?"

"Yes. Bang harder."

Kreisler tries two, three, four times until the young man from down the hall comes to his aid and rattles the landlady's door, shouting, "Frau Becker! Frau Becker! *Es ist die Polizei!*" Still, no answer. The young man, perhaps a student, lifts his shoulders. "Oh, well, maybe she's dead, too."

"You know what's going on outside?"

"I heard the commotion."

"Not curious yourself?"

In his elegant upper-crust suitcoat, Kreisler contrasts with the young man who is dressed only in underwear, undershirt, and ratty slippers. Several things catch Kreisler's eye. A Star of David pendant hanging around the young man's neck, heavy eyeliner, and dark black hair still damp, a towel wrapped around the shoulders.

"I looked, came back inside and threw up. I hate the sight of blood," the young man says. Kreisler has seen the type before, coming out of the bars with an older male in tow. He notes the pierced ears and the delicate way of speaking.

"So, do I. Do you happen to know who the deceased is?"

"She goes by many names. Pick one. Maybe it'll stick."

From down the hall, a voice interrupts. "David! Hurry up. I need the sink."

"Can you wait five fucking minutes! I'm talking to the cops." The young man with the Star of David does his own careful study of the police detective. "You're Jewish," he says.

Kreisler is thrown. "You can tell?"

"Liebchen, if I had laundry that needed drying, I could hang it from your nose."

Though he doesn't bat an eye, Kreisler wonders if it's true. About his nose. "And you," he says, trying to break even, "you're an actor."

The young man bows. "Something like that," he says with a grin. "We all are one way or another, aren't we? Doctor Caligari at your service."

Kreisler doesn't take the bait. He looks toward the staircase and up to the next floor. "Was she? Having so many names. An actress? Did she have many men?"

Before the young man, David, can say anything, Frau Becker's door opens, and an elderly woman appears. Unlike David, readying for bed, Frau Becker is dressed as if prepared to go clubbing with Kreisler. Early Twentieth Century, but still...

"Pardon my tardiness," she says. "My late husband warned me always to dress well for the police."

"Frau Becker." Kreisler bows. "You're aware of the 'accident' outside?"

"Accident?"

"5-B falling out her window," David explains, "landing unceremoniously on the sidewalk. I suppose Kurt and I will have to clean up the mess."

"I deduct two pfennigs a week for you to help around here, Daveed."

"It's Rosh Hashanah. The Sabbath. It will have to wait."

"For what? The last time you went to synagogue, Moses was parting the Red Sea. Red Sea. Not to be confused with a Communist body of water, *Inspektor*."

"I thought not."

Kreisler inserts himself between the landlady and her tenant. Ordinarily, he likes interviewing people. He acted himself in his college days, appreciates a good character. But tonight, he is unsettled. Murder, he is convinced of it, has happened here, and no one seems to care, the crowd of onlookers, the deceased's fellow tenants, even Kreisler's superior. She deserves respect. All dead do no matter how they pass into the next plane. If there is a next plane.

"I need to get into the young woman's apartment," he tells her. "Can you show it to me? A name, too, would be helpful."

"Klara. Klara Fries," David says, at last surrendering what he knew all along. "Now there is an actress."

"How so?"

"Wait'll you go through her costumes."

Frau Becker has to recover her tenant's keys from her apartment. Then she leads Kreisler and David up the staircase, pausing at two landings to catch her breath before reaching the top floor.

"I don't own the building, you understand," she says outside Klara Fries's apartment. "Herr Waldmann does."

"Waldmann?"

"He's the publisher of *Der Weg*," David elucidates.

"That's the Socialist newspaper, isn't it?"

"One of Klara's many costumes. She'll tell you she's Lenin's kid sister when she's really a fascist social climber. I liked her, actually, I did. But she could hang out with the wrong people, if you know what I mean."

"Not entirely."

To Kreisler, these days, everyone is the wrong people. He is aware of the weekly Socialist publication. Munich has dozens of newspapers, all attached to one party or another. *Der Weg*, The Way, represents the radical left in Munich, the Spartacists, once led by Karl Liebknecht and Rosa Luxemburg, Red Rosa, dead by assassination these thirteen years. While Kreisler tries to stay above the political fray, he has been called on many occasions during his foot patrol days to protect the offices of one newspaper or another from the vandalistic intents of its rivals.

The door swings open without the need of a key, another clue that murder, rather than suicide, occurred here. If Klara had decided to end her life, surely she would have wanted privacy. He asks his two companions to wait in the hall before taking out a police-issued revolver and cautiously entering 5-B.

Klara Fries's apartment is small. Three rooms. Front, kitchenette and bedroom. It is the single window of the main room that is open. A worn couch has been moved aside to give access to the opening to the street below. Klara could have moved it herself, but Kreisler has long since abandoned that thought.

He quickly perceives that there is no other occupant, but keeps Frau Becker and David outside. He doesn't want anyone accidentally tarnishing potential evidence. Or being shoved out a window. He is about to question them further on the landing when Langer joins him, huffing and puffing to the top floor.

"Why do they always have to jump from the top?" he manages to say.

"More certainty of success, I should think. Anything from the crowd?" Kreisler asks.

"Nothing revealing. Only one witness from across the street saw her fall."

"Heard her scream?"

Langer rolls his eyes. "Sorry, Avi. Forgot to ask. He was drunk, heard a thunk, didn't see her come out the window. Even if there are other witnesses, no one's going to say anything. There's a Nazi beer hall down one block, a Communist one down the other. They fear retribution."

"Klara had enemies," David says. "She was out there, if you know what I mean."

"Once again, not entirely. Please explain."

"Some would call her fearless. I'd call her a big mouth with big ideas. A queen in search of a court."

Kreisler glances at Langer, who is peering at his watch. "Did either of you see anyone leave the building in the past hour, hear anything unusual? Arguing. Fighting."

Neither David nor Frau Becker did. Langer sighs. "We'll have to pound on every door, you know that. The two of us. Why do you think she didn't just jump?"

"Well, one thing in particular," Kreisler replies. "If no one else noticed, I did." Kreisler, being the former actor, pauses ever so briefly, getting his timing just right. "What woman would jump from a window wearing only her underclothes?"

* * *

It is after midnight before Kreisler and Langer finish interviewing the building residents. No one heard a thing. Though Klara was new to the building, she had made her presence known as an outgoing party girl, party having two meanings. She was both a loyal Communist and a loyal National Socialist, depending upon who the detectives talked to, and a woman who enjoyed the *kabaretts*, the Weimar music halls. She was an artist and a musician. A painter and a violinist. In short, a working-class product of the Weimar social revolution. Langer is all for stationing one of their cops at the door to keep out nosy-pokes so he and Kreisler could go home for the night and come back tomorrow. But Kreisler is insistent.

"You go home, Fritz," he says. "I can't sleep. I'll see what I can dig up, meet you back at headquarters in the morning."

Langer leans against the doorframe of the apartment, smoking. One month on the Homicide Unit under his wing and already the novice detective is driving his mentor to early retirement. Pushing out one final cloud of tobacco, he drops the butt on the floor and stamps it out under his shoe. "Suit yourself," he says. "I'll make sure an autopsy is conducted. Anything in particular you want to suggest?"

Kreisler has his camera out and is once again taking shots. "Yes. The contents of the stomach. I'm thinking, if she didn't scream coming out the window or going down, then she was already unconscious, or dead, and the fall was a cover-up for what really happened. She was practically naked, so I'm thinking she could even have been asleep, or knocked unconscious, then tossed out the window. If she'd jumped, she'd have gone straight down. She didn't. Maybe she picked someone up at one of the clubs who had it in for her. We'll have to check all of them out."

"Maybe, maybe, maybe." Langer grunts, shakes his head in wonder. "They said you had brains. Just don't go spilling them on the walk home. The night. This neighborhood. You being a Jew. Good luck."

Once Langer is gone, Kreisler shuts the apartment door so that he can be alone with the ghost of Klara Fries. He takes his time in each of the rooms, digging through drawers and cabinets, under pillows and mattresses. If someone did kill her, they may have already emptied the flat of all evidence. Still, there are items of interest. In a shoebox beneath her bed, he finds numerous letters of a personal kind. These he will take with him for further reading. One on top captures his attention because it was written by one Helmut Fuchs. It is both business and romantic in nature. The Fuchs name also appears on music sheets next to a violin case as publishers. Kreisler's interest is generated by the fact that Helmut Fuchs is his cousin, and it was the Fuchs family that raised him after both of his parents died.

He tucks the letter away in a pocket. This, he thinks, is the last thing I hoped or expected to find. The Fuchs family is a wealthy Jewish family that converted to Catholicism in the last century to aid in their rise in German society. They did his parents a favor, but not him. He has not seen them in at least two years and has no interest in renewing contact. Perhaps he can convince Langer to interview them. He doesn't want to do it.

Back in the main room, Kreisler lets his feelings for his distant family subside. He needs to merge with Klara Fries again. One gets a sense of one's fellow human being, even if the other person no longer exists, if you stay, percolate, reside with them for a while in the place they felt most at home.

All the senses come into play. Standing in the middle of the main room, he listens to the traffic outside, the night air rattling the window pane, an apartment door closing. He experiences with his eyes how Klara Fries made this small apartment her home. She wasn't a complete misfit. She was a skilled artist who etched, drew, and painted in the Weimar spirit, freed from the frigid grip of emperors and empires. Perfumed and flowered though the rooms were, the primary odor Kreisler smells is that of paint. After he pokes his head out the window to take in the parting crowd and snap yet another photograph, he closes the window to lock in the atmosphere.

Either Klara had spread a new coat of fresh green paint on the walls of her main room herself, or Frau Beckman had paid to have it done. Kreisler suspects the former. On her foot, on the sidewalk, he had seen dried green color. She wasn't planning on going anywhere. She was making this her home. Maybe David had her wrong. Not surprising. Maybe she was an art student. His guess, he believes, is validated by the renditions of people, portraitures, that adorn the walls of her bedroom. A more careful inspection of her lone bureau reveals pen and ink sketches. He picks up and studies the most intimate portrait: the nude likeness of a woman lying on a blanket, her ravishing face turned toward the artist.

"Well, well…" he thinks. She put her heart into this…gift? A girlfriend? Was she a lover of men and women? Perhaps she was killed out of jealousy. If so, if this is murder of passion, there must be other things to find. Other proofs of love gone awry. The letters. Helmut Fuchs.

Klara Fries was a woman born for the freedom of the Weimar Republic, a woman of the Roaring Twenties. Kreisler has changed his mind about one thing. If she had been murdered, her murderer had conducted a search of her apartment. Not a violent, violating search, drawers ripped open, contents strewn across the floor. Rather, a more cautious one. Don't tip the police that someone was here going through her things, searching her things. This is evident to Kreisler after his own brief search. The drawers of her bedroom bureau and of her kitchen cabinets, while not left open, have visible signs that someone sifted through the contents. Unless Klara was unlike most women Kreisler was familiar with…neat, ordered, as if they expected and so prepared for another woman to invade her most private areas…this investigation was conducted by a male. The drawers had been searched, the articles within lifted and put back, but not in a manner of respect. Did the killer find what he was looking for? Clearly, he forgot to look in the most obvious place. Under the bed.

Kreisler continues to conduct his own, more feminine search. Into the early morning hours, under loose floorboards or cavities in the walls. Even out on the ledge of the death window. Inside the pillows of the couch, for which, he is afraid, he has been more masculine, leaving behind a trail of feathers. In the bags and cans of food. Among the tools of her paint trade.

He is about to give up, surrender to fatigue, thinking that maybe he has gotten Klara wrong. She wasn't a neatness freak. She was a Bohemian who didn't care what people thought of her own personal appearance or that of her rooms. The clutter was her doing. The fresh layer of green paint a cover for something she wanted hidden from the world. This was simply a matter of domestic violence. Or robbery, pure and simple. Brutal. Typical. Mundane even. Nothing more. He could already see the satisfied smirk on Fritz's pudgy face.

In the end, what catches Kreisler's eye is the curtain, now at rest since he had shut the window. Rolled up and hidden by the curtain is a window shade. And it is as if God, annoyed by the detective's obtuseness, at the very last moment thrust a bolt of brilliant understanding Kreisler's way. Launching himself at the only spot in the apartment that he hasn't searched, he lowers the shade and, at first, disappointed, doesn't see anything worth collecting. Until he looks at the far side facing the street below. There, taped to the shade, is a letter.

"Gotcha!"

Joyfully, carefully, he unpeels the letter from the surface of the shade. So, there was something to David's unfavorable opinion after all. But what? Why would Klara hide this document so carefully? Carefully enough that her killer didn't find it.

The monogram AH at the top is significant enough. But it is the contents of the letter, written by the leader of the National Socialists to his niece Geli Raubal, that causes Kreisler to drop to the floor in shock.

'Oh, my,' he thinks. 'Oh, my.'

Chapter Two

September 12

Charlotte Leinsdorf loves Avi Kreisler. This statement of fact is not etched into the trunk of some tree in the Englischer Garten. It has adorned her heart since the two met at university almost ten years ago. They were both, ridiculously, enrolled in the pre-med program. Ridiculously, because they were both following in the path of a parent, in his case his father, in her case her mother, in a field in which neither had the slightest interest.

Charlotte, Lotte, preferred the arts. Specifically, the theatre. A young German actress named Marlene Dietrich was her idol. Blonde, blue-eyed Lotte certainly had the talent and the looks, and Weimar Germany the opportunity. But Lotte is from an aristocratic German family that makes certain requirements of its young ladies. The theatre is not one of them.

Avi not only dropped out of pre-med but university entirely in his junior year. His father and mother were both dead long before then. He had no siblings, so the choices he made were his own. For a while at least, he encouraged Lotte to follow her heart, and they both joined a Socialist theatrical group performing meaningful plays for the entertainment of the German left wing. They moved in together, against her family's permission, subsisted as best they could, and enjoyed a life of youthful excess. For a while.

Lotte has fallen asleep in a chair in the main room of Avi's flat in the

Schwabing section of Munich. The Bohemian section. In the ten years that they have known each other, their relationship has become of the on-again-off-again variety, though their feelings for each other have never waned. Or so Lotte likes to think.

She is dreaming now of a road trip they once took to the Bavarian Alps. They made love beneath a tree on the shores of a beautiful blue lake. She became pregnant, and he proposed marriage. The infant in her dream is fiction. The real baby was miscarried. She has not become pregnant since. The proposal, as well, as it turns out, was also fiction.

When she stirs, it is because Avi is returning from his investigation of Klara Fries. It is three in the morning, still dark outside. She has left the lights on, and there is a book in her lap. Rousing, calling out his name, she lets the book fall to the floor as he enters.

"Avi? What time is it?"

"Lotte? What are you doing here?"

Whatever their relationship is currently, she has a key and is welcome anytime, but he is not expecting her. Certainly not after what he has just witnessed.

"You're not angry with me, are you? You said I could come whenever."

"Of course. Yes. It's just…"

He remains standing in the doorway, holding a briefcase filled with evidence taken from Klara Fries's flat, his camera hanging from a cord around his neck. He looks the way he feels: exhausted. She waits for him to approach. Her shoes are off and she is wearing a knit sweater over a green blouse, her hair recently done up in the fashionable page boy style, a flirtatious look. Perhaps she had hoped to catch Avi earlier in the evening in a more promising mood.

"Someone died," he says, moving into the apartment after shutting and locking the door behind him. "A woman."

"Oh, God, I'm sorry."

"No one I knew."

"No, I didn't think so. Your job. Was it so bad?"

Avi takes off his hat and suitcoat, the prized fedora set on a shelf in a closet, the suitcoat on a rack. Only then, loosening his tie, does he come over to give Lotte a kiss on the cheek. He drops into the chair she had been sleeping in and, after a moment of uncertainty, she settles down in his lap, resting her head on his shoulder. In many ways, an old, affectionate couple.

"Fritz thinks she just jumped," he explains. "A student suicide. But it wasn't. She was murdered, tossed out a window on the fifth floor in her bra and panties."

"The poor thing. Why? Do you know?"

"It's pretty early in the investigation, but I have a clue." Kreisler yawns. "You were cooking," he says.

He can smell the aroma, he thinks, of tomato sauce. He and Lotte and some of their friends often hang out at an Italian restaurant on the corner of his block. He will cook once in a while. Lotte isn't a great cook… she was raised in a family that employed servants to do the menial work… but she likes to play housekeeper and wife and will shop for food and do her best when she is in the mood.

"I started to," she says. "Then it got later and later, and I just turned off the stove. If you're hungry, I can heat up the spaghetti."

The offer is worth considering. Kreisler is a child in certain ways, the product of an early, unanticipated, mortal divorce from his mother and father. For example, he has never gotten his driver's license. He owns a bicycle and, instead, will pedal for miles for exercise and the pleasure of getting out of the crowded city. Lotte can't accompany him on those trips. She has her own automobile but never learned how to ride a bicycle as her parents deemed it too working-class. Besides, she suffers from heart palpitations, so has to exclude hard physical activities, while Kreisler prefers the occasional solo expedition to clear his mind of the complexities of the world. Since Langer left him at the crime scene, he had to walk several miles to his own flat. Hungry as he is, though, fatigue wins out.

"The thought was spot on, darling, but I have to be up in a few hours."

"You're exhausted."

"Beyond. And I have to face Fritz with what I found in the apartment. He won't be happy."

Lotte doesn't ask, and Kreisler doesn't tell. But it is hard to sleep knowing what he knows and not being able to share it. He washes in the kitchen sink before depositing himself in his bed. Lotte strips and joins him. She has no shame, and he is not in the least averse to having her snuggle naked against him and even kisses her behind her ear.

"You've been drinking again," he mumbles before sleep overtakes him.

"Just one," she admits. "Out of worry.

"Good. Good."

She is still sleeping when he wakes up in the morning, sunlight streaming through a skylight in the ceiling over their bed. Talk about living on the top floor. He has that in common with the woman he has taken to calling Klara. He will need to return to the flat sometime today. He remembers the many black and white photos Klara had arranged around her flat. The avant-garde painter, the jazz vocalist, a champion of the working man. She reminds him of the days when he and Lotte performed on stage. The wine, women, and song. It had all ended, for him, if not for Lotte, during the Beer Hall Putsch in 1923.

Back then, at the age of twenty, much as he might have denied it, he was still under the sway of his beloved father, a frontline doctor who died during the Battle of the Marne. His mother lasted only a few months longer. When Hitler launched his attempt at overthrowing the German government in Munich, Kreisler decided he was taking life too frivolously. He had no real goals. He was drinking, partying, taking the Twenties for all it had to give. His father would have been ashamed. So, he broke off his engagement with Lotte the Regal Leinsdorf, took the police exam, and became part of the force that kept the political thugs, left and right, from destroying the country. Truthfully, if he will look back on it, he will admit that he never intended to marry anyway, and the right-wing insurrection was merely his out.

He tries not to awaken Lotte. It's only half past six. He's had approximately three hours of sleep. Not enough, but he's survived on less. Gazing at her prone and gently snoring, he is greatly tempted to wake her up and waste away the morning naked with her. Guilt has its role in their relationship, but not enough yet to pry them completely apart. Memories and loneliness hold them together.

"Avi?"

She seems to intuit that he is awake, standing over her and staring at her. She graces him with a gorgeous smile.

"I have to get going," he says.

"Immediately?"

"They'll be doing an autopsy this morning. I want to be there."

"So…" She sits up and reaches a hand for him to take. "…you would rather spend time with a dead girl than with me, is that what you're saying? Give me fifteen minutes, and I'll change your mind."

Kreisler pauses, dips his head. A smile follows, then surrender. They have never and probably will never completely part. "Ten," he says.

"Twelve. I have to open my bookstore, too."

"Done."

In a sudden outburst of laughter, all is forgotten as Kreisler reverses direction, drops his pants, and jumps into bed. Lotte's arms and legs encircle him, capture him, and make sure that she gets her full twelve minutes of paradise. It is a half hour before she lets him go.

"Damn you, woman," he hollers when she finally rolls off of him. "Look what time it is."

"Damned and happy," she replies. "So are you. Admit it."

"Damned, yes. Happy, yes. Late, obviously."

He quickly belts up. Grabs a shirt from his closet.

"I'll heat up breakfast."

"No time."

"Eggs. Toast."

"I thought you had a bookstore to open. Later. Tonight. Italian. With Anni and Anton. I promise."

"Does Anni have to be there?"

"Yes. Why not? Jealous? Don't be."

Shirt buttoned, the tie follows. He never leaves until he is properly attired. "One thing," he says, as he grabs a kiss and his briefcase and camera. "Do you know the name Klara Fries? From the theatre perhaps. Or the art world."

"Not offhand, but I'll give it some thought. She's the…?

"Yes."

Kreisler keeps his bicycle in the hallway outside the flat. Hopping on it, he heads to the main police headquarters, home of the Homicide Unit. A slight drizzle tickles his exposed flesh. He doesn't mind. It helps to wake him up. Already, he has forgotten his morning dalliance with Lotte. His mind is the organ of the day, and it is brimming with plans and ideas.

Hurrying past the elevator, he jogs two flights of granite stairs to his office, where Langer is lying in wait, with coffee and a strudel.

"You didn't sleep with her, did you?"

"Sleep?" Is he talking about Lotte?

"With the vic. How long did you stay at the flat? You look like you've been up all night."

"Close," Kreisler says. "You'll see why when you see what I found."

Kreisler places his briefcase on Langer's work desk. Above it hangs the blue and white lozenged flag of Bavaria, the Wittelsbach flag, and a photograph of Rupprecht the Crown Prince standing awkwardly among a group of police cadets, presumably including Langer. Before opening his case, Kreisler shuts the door to the office.

"I think Klara Fries was blackmailing someone. I think that's why she was killed," Kreisler says. "Can you do me a big favor?"

"Depends."

"I found a letter. It involves the Fuchs family."

"In the vic's apartment?"

"In a shoebox under her bed."

"The music people?"

"Yes, them. I am distantly related. After my parents died, they took me in. We hardly speak anymore. Would you mind interviewing them for me?"

Langer glances at his watch. "Today? I can't. I have some important business to take care of."

"Related to the case?"

"Related to my career, if you must know. So, the case, and everything to do with it, I'm afraid, is all yours."

Kreisler gives that unanticipated consequence some thought. "You might think twice about that after you read this," he says. From his briefcase, he withdraws the letter he had found taped to the window shade. He hands it to his superior. "Read this."

"Do I want to?"

The letter is lengthy, intimate, filthy, and makes quite clear the ugly desires of its author. It's impact on Langer is immediate and complete. He balls it up and tosses it in the trash.

"No one must see this," he insists. "You didn't see it, Kreisler. I didn't see it. Klara Fries died by suicide. End of story, got me?"

"What if she had a partner?"

"I don't care." Langer growls, the fat Tabby becoming a lion. "You hear me, Inspektor Kreisler? My career, didn't I just tell you? She was trying to blackmail fucking Hitler! Do you see what she is accusing him of?"

"Coprophilia. Urolagnia. In his own words."

"Seriously? What are you? A fucking Urologist?"

"I was pre-med."

"With his sister's fucking daughter!"

By now, Langer is yelling so loud, he has gained the attention of detectives beyond his office. Red-faced, he has to take a seat behind his desk, take a drink of his coffee, possibly laced with something stronger, and brace himself to calm down.

Unperturbed, Kreisler states the obvious. "The problem, Fritz, is that this may not be the only letter Hitler wrote with such clarity, perhaps to other women, as well."

"No, no. It is well known that Herr Hitler has strong feelings toward his niece."

"Well known to whom? There might still be other letters out there somewhere. Perhaps the person who killed Klara has them."

"And perhaps," Langer says, "in case **you've** missed the obvious, Hitler has recovered these letters, having sent his henchman to deal with the matter. This is no Farmer Franz butchers his sow of a wife murder, my friend. Hitler is no man to fool with. Me, I'm no fan. You know my political leanings. I supported Eisner and the Bavarian Socialist Republic. But there are plenty of men in this building who think like Hitler does. Drop it. If other letters come to light, well, that's none of our affair. Let it go, Avi. For God's sake, you're a Jew. Think of the consequences for you if this is found out. Think of the consequences for all of your people."

He didn't. He hadn't. Thought as a Jew, that is. Rather, he was thinking as a realistic, educated German. Whatever political backdrop there is to this story, a murder has been committed. It doesn't seem right to Kreisler that he should just drop it. Then drop other cases as well that he doesn't find palatable for one reason or another? What if Klara hadn't been murdered for her improvident behavior? What if she had been tossed unceremoniously out of her window by a serial rapist? At the very least, the police should investigate. Let them drop it if they find they can't take the political heat. But Kreisler knows now that if he is to do this thing, he will have to do it alone.

"They fished a body out of the Isar this morning," Langer says, convinced that he has convinced his young protégé to lay off the Fries murder case. "Probably just some poor drunk. He's in autopsy now. Get the details, write it up, and get me the report by lunch. Then go home. It's your Sabbath. Shouldn't you be at the synagogue or something?"

"Rosh Hashanah. I don't really celebrate."

"You should. A day to purge yourself of sins, something like that, right? A way to reconnect with your past. Do that, Avi. Promise me you will, and forget this other matter. Leave me your information, and I will deal with it."

* * *

Impossible to forget about the matter. The Institute of Forensic Medicine is Kreisler's next stop. Well, after all, Langer told him to go there. After that, regrettably, he will have to reconnect with a part of his past he would just as soon deposit in the trash with Hitler's provocative, pornographic letter. The Fuchs family.

Dr. Johann Müller greets the young detective in the basement of the building. Kreisler first visited the facility as a pre-med student. In fact, that was where he and Lotte met. He was the one to vomit. She was the one to offer him a silk handkerchief to wipe off his mouth. Since then, he has built up a resistance to seeing the formerly alive carved up, dissected, then stitched back together so that the nearest of kin won't have to view the viscera.

Müller is an accomplished forensic specialist who has been with the institute since shortly after it was founded in 1909. He's a man in his fifties, tall, graying, serious. He is not one to make jokes of the cadavers. He attended his own wife when she died unexpectedly on their twentieth anniversary. Kreisler has come to know him well over the years. Their relationship is professional, cordial. The one thing that they never talk about is politics. Kreisler is a Jew. Müller is an early member of the National Socialists, a supporter of Herr Hitler.

"Inspektor Kreisler," Müller says by way of greeting. "Who are we here to see this morning? The tides of battle have blessed us with a half dozen bodies since yesterday."

"It never stops, does it?" says Kreisler, offering his hand to the older physician.

"It never will. Those who think the Great War ended in 1918 are mistaken. It will persist until rights are wronged."

Kreisler looks past the doctor's shoulder to the autopsy chamber. It smells of formaldehyde and bleach. A bank of drawers to his right contains bodies already or yet to be examined, or who have not been claimed by family. There are eight autopsy tables in the room, chilled to prevent decay. Six of them contain bodies under sheets. Müller has two assistants who are prepping for dissection.

"I believe a young woman came to you last night," Kreisler says. "A jumper named Klara Fries. Is she here?"

"Indeed. Table One. We were able to begin already. I like to do things in order."

"Also, a man pulled from the Isar. Inspektor Langer wanted me to view the body and file a report."

"That would be Table Six, a fresh one. Do you prefer one to the other?"

"The girl first," Kreisler says.

They move into the room, and Müller pulls out a chart and gives it a brief scan before lifting the sheet off the torso, bottom first.

"No point looking at the head," Müller says. "I assume you got a good look last night."

"Yes."

"Your conclusion isn't a suicide?"

Kreisler bends to study the broken legs and hips of the deceased, who was trying to blackmail the leader of the Nazi Party. He wonders if Müller knows this. "As I told Inspektor Langer last night, I have my reasons. A woman, a young woman who cares about her looks, her reputation, will not commit suicide in such a public way, dressed only for sex. She was thrown out her window."

"But not first," Müller says, raising a gloved finger. "First, she was raped."

Taken aback, Kreisler glances from the forensic pathologist to the exposed crotch of Klara Fries. "Raped or had consensual sex?" he asks. This is important to him. "How can you tell?"

"Well, I suppose I can't. The way the young engage in sex these days, anything could be possible. But there was much damage done during penetration and in the vaginal area. Possibly with an object other than the one men are gifted with naturally. Whoever did this to her, and we have found semen, he was particularly violent. For her, I can't imagine much pleasure. Rather, I would think, pain, torture even."

Kreisler has to take a step back. Not since his first encounter in a morgue ten years ago has he had this kind of nauseated reaction.

"Well, then, I was right," he says, steadying himself. "Murder, not suicide. Stomach contents?"

"Too soon. We haven't opened her up yet. This much I can say. She didn't put up a fight. There are no bruises or scratches other than what we can attribute to the fall itself. She may have been unconscious when he attacked her and disposed of her. We'll have a better idea when the test results come back."

"One happy thought, at least," Kreisler says. "Her being unconscious. No one heard her scream coming out the window, so this would corroborate my theory." He will not discuss the case in any greater detail with the doctor, though. "Anything at all that might tell us something about who did this to her? Beyond the fact that he was a male."

Müller chuckles, hand to jaw in thought. "Well, if you're asking me if he was well-endowed, I can't begin to calculate. But she weighs in at one hundred and fifteen pounds. He must have been big enough to pick her up and hurl her from the window. He is also brown-haired. He left pubic hairs. And, if I might be a bit presumptive, he may have been left-handed."

"Left? How could you possibly tell?" Kreisler wonders. He wonders, too, how he could have missed that.

"Her left breast," Muller says, "has the marks of being squeezed tightly. I made the mistake of telling you there was no bruising outside of those caused by the fall. There was one area of interest. Not the right breast. Only the left one. I am thinking the fall did not cause the damage. A hand did it. A rather large one."

Kreisler begins taking notes. He is developing a picture of the killer. Large man with big hands and brown hair. And a violent disposition. If a loyal follower of Hitler, his name may be found on the list that the National Socialists keep of their members. Satisfied that he has as much information as he can get, he turns to leave.

"Wait." Müller touches Kreisler's arm. "What about the male we got this morning? From the Isar."

"Oh," says Kreisler. "Right. The male. Show me."

His disinterest couldn't be more obvious, but Müller likes showing off his cadavers as if they are pieces of granite he is about to sculpt into some Olympian statue. At Table Six, he lifts the sheet head-first.

"Bludgeoned to a pulp," Kreisler says. "Both ear lobes are torn. He was wearing earrings? I don't suppose you found them."

"At the bottom of the Isar, probably."

"And a hint of lipstick, do you see? Very telling. Did he come to you naked? Were there any artifacts at all?"

Müller shrugs. The young detective is stealing his show. "He was fully clothed but with no identification. There were, however, two revealing facts." At this point, Muller becomes the sole master of ceremonies, flourishing his evidence. The first is a tattoo of a young man's face.

"Recognize it?"

"Nope. You?"

"No. But lovers do such things, don't they? Boys who love other boys?"

Kreisler doesn't respond. He recognizes the apparent glee in the pathologist's voice. "And?"

The second fact is revealed when he lifts the lower portion of the sheet.

"Voila!"

"Yes?"

"You don't see it, Inspektor Kreisler? I'm surprised at you." Müller now thrusts a pointed finger at the dead male's crotch. Only then does Kreisler see the obvious. "He's circumcised," Muller proclaims. "He's a Jew."

Chapter Three

Not only is the body on the autopsy table Jewish, he is a familiar Jew. The tattoo was the biggest giveaway. He had seen it before, very recently, in fact, though he didn't reveal his suspicions to Dr. Muller. From an Institute phone, Kreisler contacts Langer back at the Munich Police Headquarters.

"You're sure?" Langer asks when Kreisler tells him who belongs to the Isar River body. "He lives in the same building as Klara Fries?"

"Lived. I interviewed him myself, and please don't tell me he was a suicide, too," Kreisler says. He is sitting at Müller's desk just outside the autopsy chamber and gazing at David's covered body as he speaks. "Or a coincidence. He was either Klara's partner in crime or witnessed more than he told me. The killer, fearing he'd been seen, came back to take care of the witness."

On his end of the line, Franz Langer is none too happy with Kreisler's report. He is not alone in his office. Word has leaked somehow. Klara Fries's death has become common knowledge among those who would take an interest. One of those is Franz Gürtner, the all-important Bavarian Minister of Justice, every cop's boss.

"What is he saying?" Gürtner asks. He is a fifty-year- old man who looks at least a dozen years older, stern, humorless. A bureaucrat with a pedigree and places to go. He, too, knows Hitler.

"He says there is a connection between the Fries woman and the body pulled from the Isar this morning. I hate to admit it, Sir, but I would have to agree. Whoever killed the first killed the second."

"And this Kreisler, he's a good man?"

"In what sense, Sir?"

"Competent. Capable."

"He's fairly new on the job."

"I didn't ask that." Gürtner is smoking a cigar. He taps the ashes into a tray on Langer's desk. "Tell him he can continue to pursue the culprit, but to keep you and me both apprised every step of the way. When I say 'stop', he stops. Make sure he understands that. No arrests are to be made without my consent. He is not to confront Herr Hitler."

"Of course, Sir."

Kreisler gets the message, hangs up, and rejoins Müller in the autopsy room. Müller has already opened up David's chest cavity and done some exploration, removing the lungs.

"I thought you'd like to know," Müller says, looking around. "He was dead before he went into the water. Whoever killed him probably hoped the victim didn't wash up as soon as he did. You've seen the signs of the beating he took. Enough to kill him, almost certainly."

With a grunt of acknowledgment, Kreisler bends over the corpse. The face had been brutalized to the point of unrecognizability, but Kreisler has an eye for details, such as hairstyle, the earrings, lipstick, purple. The tattoo.

He says, "I notice that most of the facial blows have been delivered on the right side of the face. The left side is bruise-free. Delivered by a lefty?"

"Possibly," Müller says, taking a closer look. "Probably. The killer just kept hammering away until the boy was dead. And in case you weren't going to ask, there was anal penetration."

"Another rape?"

"It would seem our killer doesn't play favorites." Müller steps aside, satisfied with his opinion. "Whoever did it, Inspektor Kreisler, enjoys killing. Enjoys killing homosexuals, Jews, perhaps?"

"That is mere speculation, Doctor. In a world such as this, it is more likely he enjoys killing anyone. Everyone."

Kreisler takes a final scan of the body in case the killer left a part of himself somewhere, then offers his hand to the doctor.

"*Danke Schön*, Herr Doktor. I don't envy your job, but I respect it. This has been very helpful."

"We try. Just be careful out there. *Dein Mörder zieht den Tod dem Leben vor.* Your killer prefers death to life."

* * *

It was August Fuchs, the patriarch of the Fuchs musical empire, who chose to transfer his religious affiliation from that of Abraham, Isaac, and Jacob to Jesus, Mary, and Joseph. This change of loyalties came in the preceding century. Bernays did it, Heinrich Heine, Felix Mendelssohn. It was such a common enough practice that none took any shame in it. Even their fellow Jews just shrugged their shoulders with tolerance. Why 'next year in Jerusalem' when Berlin and Munich were right at hand? Blood is still blood, isn't it?

In the case of Abraham Fuchs, he also relocated and moved his family into a mansion in a row of similar mansions in the finest neighborhood of Munich. He expanded his business from the manufacture of musical instruments to the founding of symphony orchestras and operatic theaters. The Fuchs name was synonymous with music in Germany. It was Abraham's son who took in the orphan Avi Kreisler after Kreisler's mother died in childbirth. It is to that house that Kreisler pedals now, recalling the day he had it out with the then head of household because he refused conversion to the Christian faith.

"Why should I, an atheist, convert to anything?" he yelled at Eduard Fuchs.

"Because I tell you to," was the scion of Abraham's reply. "It is that or see if anyone else will take you in."

"I don't care if no one else does. I'm no traitor!"

Kreisler was only thirteen years old on that momentous morning. The elder Fuchs refused to allow him to have his bar mitzvah, so he refused to be baptized. In the end, cooler heads prevailed. Fuchs's wife, Kreisler's adoptive mother, Christine, a born Catholic, convinced her husband to let the recalcitrant boy stay. Which Kreisler did until university, when he left home purportedly to study medicine, but instead set off on an unknown journey that has led him today to wonder what Helmut Fuchs, Eduard's heir, has to do with Klara Fries.

He parks his bicycle against a wrought iron fence that protects the Fuchs mansion from prying eyes, gazes at its five stories of elegance and wealth, and thinks, 'Lotte lives in a place like this.'

He doesn't hold it against her. He never did. He might easily have entered the ranks of the leftist revolutionaries like his friend Anni, but even they, unbeknownst to themselves, have become conventional, predictable, unreliable. Kreisler makes his way up the brick walk to the front door of the Fuchs home much as he perambulates through life. Down the middle, trying not to veer off too far either to the left or the right. Just the straight and narrow.

He rings the buzzer under an ornate bronze plaque that reads simply FUCHS. Naturally, a butler in full livery opens the door.

"Yes?"

"Inspektor Kreisler of Munich Homicide." He holds up his police credentials. "I must speak to the head of the house about a matter that affects his family."

He knows the butler, an old man now, who has served the Fuchs family for at least thirty years. The butler knows him, too. There is no love lost between the two. Which is the reason Kreisler moves past the butler into the front foyer before the butler can slam the door on him.

"Sir, you have no right…."

"Just get Helmut, Louis. Now. I'm in no mood."

He waits then with a thumping heart, wishing he could be anywhere else but here. Not much has changed since his departure ten years before. Music is represented in the decorative pattern of the house. There, an oil painting of the great composer Mendelssohn, above a marble bust of Mozart. To his left, a mahogany cabinet containing the personal musical instruments once owned by some of the great performers of the day. To his right, photographs of the first Fuchs music store, daguerreotypes from the mid-Nineteenth century. Straight ahead, covering an arch leading into the main hall, a carved rendition of Da Vinci's Last Supper centered by a gold cross.

Kreisler rolls his eyes in disgust. Every decoration has been placed to show the world that the Fuchses are not Jewish, never have been. Overdone. Obvious. What next, he wonders? The National Socialist swastika? A plea that ultimately will fall on deaf ears.

"Inspektor Kreisler."

He turns when he hears his name being called. Eduard Fuchs is still alive, somewhere in his seventies, a tall silver-haired man who towers over his shorter eldest son, Helmut.

"I hope I'm not disturbing," Kreisler says, lying.

"Of course, that's exactly what you hope," Eduard says. "We are, in fact, quite busy."

"We're in charge of the Oktoberfest activities this year, Avi," Helmut says, extending a hand. For the younger of the two Fuchs males, it seems as though ten years has not passed and that they just lunched together yesterday.

Kreisler stands straight, stiff, with his hands folded behind his back. He does not doff his hat. Nor does he bother to take Helmut's hand. "There was a death yesterday," he says. "A young woman. You've been implicated."

Be blunt. Be direct. Show no mercy. See how they like that.

"What do you mean?" Eduard asks. He is stern, determined not to react.

Helmut is less composed. "What woman?" he asks. His cousin's face has gone so pale, Kreisler doesn't have to jot down 'guilty' in his notepad.

"Klara Fries," Kreisler says. "Do either of you know her?"

"Not me," Eduard says. "You have a hell of a nerve to show up here after all these years, tossing accusations at us." And yet, as his uncle makes this charge, Kreisler also notes the way his eyes quickly turn toward his son and protégé. Note number two: Guilty.

"She was thrown out a window, died instantly," Kreisler persists. "In inspecting her apartment, I discovered a box of letters under her bed. I had the chance to read through them last night. I brought one…"

As Kreisler reaches into his coat to reveal the mystery missive, Helmut grabs his arm and pulls him away into a side room. "Why do you hate us so much?" he snaps so his father, who they have left behind, can't hear.

"You tried to corrupt me," Kreisler says. "Do you want to read the letter?"

"Do I have a choice? Don't tell my father. Please."

Helmut takes a few moments to read the letter that he sent to Klara Fries not two weeks ago. In anger, he crumples it up. "That bitch was going to tell the world."

"She was blackmailing you?"

"Ten thousand marks. My father would disinherit me if he found out. You must keep this between you and me, Avi."

Kreisler extends his hand, palm up, to recover the letter, crumpled but still readable and usable in a court of law. Helmut reluctantly gives it back. "Sex?" the detective asks.

"You need to know the details?"

"Did you kill her?"

Helmut is shocked that such a question should be directed to him. "Of course, not. She said she knew people in the National Socialists. She even knew Hitler. She would have revealed our past to him."

"That you have Jewish blood in you."

Helmut looks to the floor, embarrassed, though he was born a Catholic and never entered a synagogue or uttered a word of Yiddish or Hebrew. It is all the answer Kreisler needs.

"Where were you last night?"

"Here. My fiancé can vouch for me. I'm to be married in a few months, Avi. To a lovely woman. This would ruin everything."

Kreisler straightens out the letter and files it away. The Fuchses live in a world entirely alien to him, though he lived in their household for next to a decade. He wonders how he came out of it the man he is.

"Come to our wedding, Avi," Helmut says. "We'd be so glad to have you come. Let's let go of the past."

He can't. He won't. He doesn't give his cousin any reason to hope that the investigation will end here, now. Kreisler turns away toward the exit. "I intend to find the killer of this woman," he says. "However it comes out. And, I guarantee, a lot is going to come out."

* * *

Kreisler sags against his bicycle outside the Fuchs mansion. He had posed as the tough, no-nonsense detective. But the interview, short as it was, has enervated him. He had only a few hours of sleep last night. Pedaling around the city has not only fatigued him but made him remember that he turned down Lotte's offer of breakfast. He's starved, and before he can set off on his next stop, he has to grab some lunch at a local cafe.

Kreisler is considered by the few Jewish peers he knows as a non-practicing secular Jew. His parents were intellectuals, his father a surgeon, his mother a musical prodigy who could play Mozart and Brahms when she was six years old. When she died in childbirth, taking with her what would have been a sister for Kreisler, he stopped going to synagogue. This was due, both because the Fuchs family wouldn't allow him to go, and because even without their permission, he had no further desire to worship God. His desire to have a bar mitzvah had only been an inspired challenge to his new parents, his Catholic cousins. It has only been in the past few years that he has attended services during the High Holy Days, only then, and only occasionally. He is on a search. For what he doesn't quite know. Lotte went with him once but didn't like being set apart with the women.

He bicycles to a stop outside the main entrance to the Great Synagogue on Herzog-Max-Strasse, the Ten Commandments raised high off the pavement. Husbands and wives with their children are coming and going. A morning service, scheduled for the second day of Rosh Hashanah, is letting out. Kreisler has spotted a friend engaged in passionate debate with a man Kreisler recognizes as the chief rabbi.

"Hey, Birnbaum! Dov," he calls. Birnbaum works as the all-around maintenance man. Younger than Kreisler, he sports a dark black beard, curly hair with a yarmulke on top, and a white prayer shawl wrapped around his shoulders. He is in constant motion, which would explain his thin frame. His five children are reportedly as active as he is, making life exhausting for his wife, Rachel.

"Birnbaum! Over here. Two minutes. A favor, then you can drive the rabbi deaf."

Birnbaum is delighted to see Kreisler. He's always delighted to see anyone.

A Jew returning to the brotherhood, even better. Always a smile even on the darkest days. Kreisler doesn't understand him, but Kreisler can't help liking him. Who wouldn't?

"Dov," he says, careful not to offer his hand lest he lose it in an overly enthusiastic greeting.

"You're not staying?" Birnbaum asks.

"Can't. The job calls."

"God calls."

"Not to me. Not today. If He exists at all, He is calling for a dead Jew named David Sussman."

"Sussman?" Birnbaum's face loses its smile. "I know the family. The son, not so much. How many Sussmans are there in Munich?"

"That's what I was hoping," Kreisler says, still perched on his bicycle seat. "He washed up in the Isar this morning, brutally beaten. He's part of an investigation I am pursuing that involves a young woman, as well. A Klara Fries."

"That is not a name I am familiar with."

"Not surprised. It is this young man I need to know about. Contact his family for me, will you? Have them reach out to me or let me know how I can reach out to them."

"Come to services."

"No time." Kreisler places his feet back on the pedals. Starts to push off. "It's murder, Dov. Murder. Anything you can come up with will be greatly appreciated."

In daylight on a late summer Saturday, Munich is truly beautiful. The rain clouds have departed. The hate that stalks it at night is replaced by excited shoppers, strolling mothers with their newborns, people relaxing in the parks, swimming in the ponds and streams. It is a vibrant city, innocent enough if you can ignore the political flags, banners, and posters. Right, center, left, there are more political parties and more political infighting than anywhere else in Europe.

At the moment, Kreisler chooses to see the spontaneous side of the city, the innocent side. Once he reaches Klara Fries and David Sussman's apartment building, however, the shadows come out. There is still a police presence. Kreisler flashes his identification to an officer on guard duty, then steps into the building.

Frau Becker is awake, alert, and sweeping the front hallway. Her smile greets Kreisler, a sign that she is unaware of the circumstances he is about to impart.

"Herr Inspektor Kreisler," she says, as if he is a man calling on her for things other than police matters

"You remember me."

"I'm not that old," she says, "that I would forget such a face. You dress so beautifully. You must have the frauleins wagging their tails at you."

"Well, one that I know of," he says. He removes his white fedora and lowers his eyes, saddening them for what he is about to say. "I'm afraid I've come on some terrible business."

"More or the same?" she asks. She leans her broom against a wall beneath a framed portrait of the former Kaiser of Germany, Wilhelm.

"More, I'm afraid. Your tenant, David from down the hall...he was found this morning. He had been assaulted, killed, and his body thrown into the Isar. I've just come from the autopsy. I don't suppose you saw..."

Before he can ask whether or not she saw David leave the building or noticed any stranger coming in, Frau Becker collapses. He is lucky enough to catch her before she hits the floor. The broom topples, making a loud knock. She lands in Kreisler's arms, weeping into his suit coat.

"Why?" she pleads. "You must be mistaken."

"I'm afraid not. I must speak with his roommate, anyone else who might be able to help me find out who did this to him, to Klara Fries, too."

Frau Becker composes herself. Perhaps she is overreacting or simply enjoys being embraced by the much younger man. Still in his clutches, she looks up at him with moist eyes.

"Daveed was such a harmless boy. Why should anyone want to hurt him? If he dressed up sometimes, looked like one of my daughters, well, what of it? He had the right. Do you think one of the men... Even those Nazis, those terrible men...Ernst Röhm, you know of him? I've seen him, with Daveed.

They would go to the *kabaretts* together. Röhm, the pig."

Kreisler wasn't expecting Frau Becker to be so cooperative; she would fill up his notebook with facts, relevant and irrelevant. Gently, he releases her from his arms and takes out his notepad. Röhm is an interesting name to be brought up, the chief of staff of the Nazi Party's paramilitary organization, the *Sturmabteilung,* the SA. Kreisler, of course, knows of the man, but was unaware until now that he might be homosexual. Could that be an issue? Röhm, as an ally of Hitler, killing David and Klara not only to protect Hitler's reputation but to protect his own, as well?

"Do you have any idea, Frau Becker, when David left the building? Last night? This morning?"

"I sleep soundly, Inspektor. No, I heard nothing. With all that is going on, I will have to consider bringing in a locksmith. People come in all hours of the day and night here, friends, of course, mostly. Comrades in arms."

"You're a Communist?"

"I knew Rosa personally," she replies, speaking in a conspiratorial whisper. "Red Rosa, they called her. You know the name? They killed her and threw her into the river, too, the monsters. The *Freikorps.* Röhm was one of them. I'll never forget."

"How about Fuchs? Does that name ring a bell?"

"Daveed had many friends. Klara, too. The young are like that. I would have been in my day, but my parents were very protective of me. I didn't ask any names. I let my tenants live their lives."

Kreisler nods. Polite. Understanding. "Have you had any problem with the Brownshirts coming in, harassing you, harassing your tenants?"-

"Not yet, thank God." Frau Becker says. She bends and picks up her broom, begins a desultory sweeping right around her feet. "If they did, I would sweep them out." Then, just as abruptly as she began to work, she finds a chair in the hallway and sits down in it, exhausted by her labors, not of the past five minutes, but of the past three decades. "You must be careful, Herr Inspektor," she says. "I fear bad times are coming. Very bad times."

Kreisler leaves her with a promise he will speak to her again, and he will heed her admonishment. He isn't sure he can get anything of value out of her, not at the moment anyway. Instead, he heads down the hall and knocks on David's apartment door. He calls back to Frau Becker.

"Do you know if…"

Kurt, David's roommate, opens the door before Kreisler can finish his question. Perhaps it was a case of opposites being attracted to one another, but Kreisler finds Kurt to be a solid athletic type, blonde, Aryan, and young, quite young. Still in his teens, Kreisler thinks.

"You're that cop," Kurt says with a broad yawn. "David's not here. He went to work several hours ago."

"Where would that be?" Kreisler asks, postponing the inevitable.

"He's a waiter at the *Bratwurstglöckl.* He does prep work for the chefs, so he has to be there early in the morning."

"On Frauenplatz. I know the place. Do you know when he left? What route he takes to get there?"

Kurt stops wiping his eyes and gives Kreisler the look of suspicion intertwined with fear. "Why are you asking this? Is David all right?"

Lowering his notepad, Kreisler gestures with his hand toward the apartment. "Perhaps we should speak inside," he says. "You will need to sit down, I'm afraid."

"He's dead?"

"Let's sit, please."

Kurt backs into a cluttered room. The yawn and the unkempt hair and the fact that Kurt is bare-chested indicates to the detective that the young man may have fallen asleep on the couch in the front room. It is the only open space with an upturned sofa pillow serving for the head and a ragged gray army blanket on the floor.

"Pardon for the mess," Kurt says. "Sorry. I'm just…"

"You're an artist."

Kreisler notes the easel by the window and the sheets of artwork on the dinner table in the center of the room. The window doesn't draw in much light. It faces out onto a dark courtyard barely lit. An opened sketchpad lies on the floor, revealed once the blanket is picked up, and Kurt offers the detective a seat. Kreisler guesses Kurt was working on the sketch of a building when he fell asleep.

"An architect, actually," Kurt says. He is shivering, holding himself, arms folded across his chest. He refuses to look at Kreisler directly, as if this is a way of denying the truth. "A student, that is. I've applied to the Academy of Fine Arts in Vienna. I'm just waiting to see if I'll be accepted."

"Well, from what I can see of your work," Kreisler says, "you're a shoo-in. But you'll want to know about David."

Kurt starts to cry. He doesn't want to hear about David, but he has to. Kreisler pats him on the shoulder.

"I think it has something to do with the death of Klara Fries," he says. "I know this is difficult to hear, but your friend's body was found in the Isar River this morning. He was assaulted, killed. I've seen him. Is it possible he was rendezvousing with someone? Did you actually see him leave the apartment?'

"Maybe. I don't remember. I was half asleep. I'm still..." With an abruptness that startles Kreisler, Kurt leaps off the couch, banging into the table and tearing loose one of the pages of his sketch pad. "You know, I'm tired of people bad-mouthing David. He was a trained singer, an entertainer. He loved people. He loved performing. People just don't understand. He wasn't rendezvousing with anyone. He wasn't going to have sex, if that's what you're saying. He was just going to work. That's all."

"I apologize," Kreisler says. "I didn't intend..."

"He's Jewish. He really took the holidays seriously. Especially the part about sinning. He was harmless."

Kreisler lies back into the sofa cushions, regrouping. Kurt is hyperventilating. Instead of pursuing the normal line of questioning, then. Kreisler picks up the sketch book.

"I can see that you were two struggling artists," he says, "just trying to make your way in a world which, I can totally agree with you, is unfair. Youth is thrown away in war, in revolution, in the everyday conduct of people vying for success. Unhappy people. Angry people. Perhaps David, unfortunately, ran into one of these. I admire your work."

"Thank you."

"David will want you to succeed."

"I know."

"You were close."

"Yes. But not in the way you're thinking."

Kreisler sits up, unfolds the sketch pad on his lap, and browses the pages. "I must apologize again, because that is exactly what I was thinking. But please trust me. My interest is in finding who killed David and Klara. I have suspicions but little else. Perhaps you know things that will help me."

Kurt is calming down now, enough to take a seat at the table. "Suspicions about what?"

"I shouldn't be giving you information about the case, but I think I can rely on your discretion here." Kreisler lifts the sketch pad to show a particular page to the budding architect. "I like this one," he says. "It's the Great Synagogue. The detail is magnificent, completely professional. And you haven't even begun your studies. Amazing. You're not...."

"Jewish? No. I try to get out every day to sketch something."

"You know what I like about it the most?" Kreisler pauses for effect. "The people. You haven't drawn just a building, an edifice. You've drawn the people who go there to find God. You've given the sketch the human touch. The synagogue is not just a structure mathematically perfect. It is a place of warmth where people in desperate times go for comfort. You feel that in the drawing. Congratulations."

"Thank you." Kurt smiles, wipes his nose on his arm, and gazes at his own drawing. "They say that Hitler tried to enroll at the Academy but failed— twice—because his sketches lacked just what you said. Humanity. They were exact sketches, true to what he was drawing, but they had no life."

"Interesting," Kreisler says. "I didn't know that about Herr Hitler. May I keep this drawing?"

"Of course."

"I have a friend who will love this properly framed." Kreisler grasps the boy's hand. "Maybe two? One for myself, as well?" They are friends now. Whatever is said here will stay here. "Now, if you would, can you show me the way David would usually go to get to his job. If he was accosted, it wasn't here. It was somewhere on that route. Perhaps there'll be evidence."

"Maybe, maybe," says Kurt. "The restaurant isn't that far away. He would walk it, unless he had something to do first, some place to go before he got to the restaurant."

"Show me," Kreisler says with outflung arms. "I will worry about the rest."

But first, Kreisler wants to take a look through David's personal items, so he gives Kurt the opportunity to wash up and dress and grab something to eat. But nothing in David's drawers or anywhere else gives any proof that he had any sort of relationship to Klara Fries. Kreisler rejects cruel coincidence as a factor in David Sussman's death. His death was most certainly due to the fact that he witnessed something he shouldn't have.

Leaving his bicycle in Frau Becker's front hallway, Kreisler escorts Kurt through the streets of Munich on the route that may have led to David's capture and murder.

"Think carefully," Kreisler tells him during the stroll. "Did David ever speak about anything that troubled him, anyone who bothered him, something he saw or experienced, no matter how slight that might be of help to me?"

"Maybe at the Brat," Kurt tells him, referring to the restaurant's more familiar name. "There are fights there all the time between the Reds and the Brownshirts. Hitler goes there."

"He does?"

"Yes. I've seen him there myself with a young woman about our age."

"Geli Raubal?"

"I don't know. It's him, the girl, and his bodyguards. He never goes anywhere without someone from the SS."

Kreisler nods in satisfaction. The SS. The list of Nazi Party membership. He will have to get a hold of that. Perhaps, as well, a night out on the town with Lotte at the Bratwurstglöckl might be in the offing.

"The Bratwurst, you say."

"Yes. Saturday night after the theater. Count on it."

"I will, Kurt," Kreisler says. "Birnbaum will kill me for desecrating the Sabbath, but who can resist a good sausage?"

Chapter Four

Lotte can't resist a night out on the town with Kreisler, no matter the purpose. Tonight, they will be joined by two other friends of Kreisler's: Anton Maier and Anni Leeuwenberg.

Maier is a playwright, a would-be playwright. He has had little success in staging his work. In the meantime, he teaches grammar at a Catholic boy's academy. Kreisler and Lotte have both acted in some of his one-act dramas. They have known each other since their university days. Anni is a von Leeuwenberg from Belgium, who dropped the 'von' upon aligning herself with Lenin and Stalin. Well, there's more to her story than that. She claims the "von' was part of a scam her parents used to fleece ignorant locals. A hammer-wielding Marxist, she writes articles for Oskar Waldmann's far-left newspaper *Der Weg*.

The weather has turned by ten in the evening. The theater crowd has exited into a cool autumn wind and a downpour of chilling rain. Lotte, alone among the four friends, owns a car and has pledged to drive everyone home after their late supper. Anton and Anni, having dashed from the closest tram stop, are soaking. Anton shakes the rain off his fedora onto the foyer floor of the restaurant where they have met.

"A long line," Anni says.

"It's Saturday night. There's a movie theater around the corner," says Kreisler.

As they wait to be seated, Anton hands Kreisler a bag. "I stopped off at the library and got the book you wanted. Classical architecture? I didn't know you had an interest."

"I do of a sort." Kreisler examines the thick, hardcover book on ancient Greek and Roman buildings and feats of engineering. He flips through the pages. His plan is taking shape.

"We're lucky we even got here," Anton says. He is shorter than Kreisler and Anni, prematurely balding, with bifocals, more the academic type than his friend. "We saw a man getting beaten up. Right in front of us on the tram."

Anni claims, "I wanted to intervene."

"She would have jumped the lot of them. But I told her we'd only get ourselves hurt, and, besides, we were late coming to meet you."

"Fucking Brownshirts."

"For all we know, they might have been off-duty cops, sorry to say, Avi, and a lot of good that would have done us."

Lotte lights a cigarette, offers it first to Anni, whose imagination is on the beating she would have given Hitler's minions had Anton not held her back. Taking a single puff of Lotte's cigarette, Anni hands it back.

"You've got to pick your battles," Kreisler says. "Live to fight another day, right?"

The line is longer than Lotte expected. From the main hall, she can hear music and laughter, gaiety Weimar style, a lively enough place, a place to escape what goes on outside. "You did the right thing, Anton," she says. "You're not the police."

"Well, we know where one off-duty cop is," Anton says, elbowing Kreisler in the ribs. "Will there even be a table?"

"In this city, there's always a table," Anni says, "if you belong to the correct party." Dressed to shock the casual observer, she is wearing a man's golf cap perched six feet off the ground atop her dazzling red hair. Her uniform of the day is a veteran's army jacket with a concealed nightstick, pants, and military-grade boots. If a fight is to be had with the Brownshirts, she's ready for it. Hence, her annoyance with Anton.

"You know this place?" Lotte asks her. "Avi and I have never been here."

"That you know of," Anni replies. She winks at Kreisler, then repents. "This is a BVP place. Bavarian People's Party. Really not the sort of establishment any of us should be seen in. I feel like Mata Hari just stepping through the door."

Impatient, Anni grabs Anton's hand and jumps the line to scout the dining area. With a shrug, Kreisler follows with Lotte.

"Are those two a thing?" Lotte wonders.

"Ask them."

"She is so much taller and, if you don't mind my honesty, a bit too abrasive. Anton is a sheep. Anni's a wolf."

As they enter the main dining area, jammed with sound, Kreisler's eyes investigate the scene, the dining tables, the stage where nightly performers entertain a drunken audience. Nobody sits still. Everyone is in motion. Dancing couples. Waiters slipping through the crowd carrying platters of food and steins of beer or glasses of hard liquor. Musicians swaying to the rhythm of their own beat. It is deafening.

"Anni's an orphan," Kreisler says, bent close to Lotte's ear as they maneuver through the crowd. "Like me, only she wasn't raised by humans. She was raised by a movement."

"She's a Communist."

"She's a Viking. An interesting mix. A Jewish berserker."

"Only partly." Anni has made her way back through the crowd, having located a table for them that Anton is holding. "My father's name was Erik. The Red. You get the joke?"

"A Communist, too?" Lotte asks as they slip through the crowd toward an open table.

"A grifter. A dime store novelist whose most profitable venture was Victorian pornography. My mother was one of his models. The first woman to refrain from wearing anything at the beach. Quite the couple."

"And yet you turned out to be so well-grounded," Kreisler kids.

"Indeed. The world needs to find a place for people like my parents rather than discard them."

The Brat is an old, turn-of-the-century beer hall with a hearty menu and entertainment. While few restaurants or taverns are aligned with a particular political party, the dozens of parties that are vying for power once Weimar collapses will adopt their favorite watering hole as their own. Hitler's Beer Hall Putsch in '23 began at the Burgerbraukeller.

Anton waves to them from a round table situated at the end of a long hall near the stage where poets are allowed to step up and recite their latest work and where singers are invited to show off their jazz, blues, or opera. On stage at the moment as a band plays swing, a juggler has moved into the spotlight, tossing up knives and forks.

When one of the knives leaves the act and lands on the floor near Anni, Lotte whispers, "Belay the Billy club, Anni. It was an accident. If he was really out to get you, he couldn't have missed from there."

"You never know," replies Anni with a smile. She is demure when she wants to be.

Kreisler pulls out a chair for Lotte before grabbing the attention of a waiter. He orders rounds for everyone. "Four beers. Stout."

"You know," Anton says as soon as he has everyone's attention, "I have been thinking, seriously, of the priesthood."

"What?" Kreisler is stunned.

Anni says, "Like you, he thinks he can avoid the storm by becoming the next pope. I've been trying to talk sense into him. Who ran the Inquisition, Anton? Who instigated the Crusades? Your church won't keep you safe. It will demand you follow Holy Writ."

"I can be my own man. I can help people. My plays are pablum. I need to face facts."

"Give it time," is Kreisler's input. "Rash decisions are usually bad ones. Take me as an example. Who tells the dean of students to kiss his ass?"

"You were young and foolish," Anni says with a grin. "And in the right, as I recall."

"Right off campus." Kreisler smiles back. "My aunt and uncle were furious."

"Your aunt and uncle shouldn't have sent you to a Catholic university."

Kreisler shrugs, takes a long swallow of his beer. "Catholic or otherwise, I wasn't ready to be a scholar in those days."

"We like your plays," Lotte says. She has decided to change subjects. "Playwrights often don't find success until they're much older."

"Or dead. Well, we'll see," says Anton. He gazes around at a bawdy hall filled with people whose last thought is likely to be religious. They pray to God on Sunday. On Monday, they beat each other to a pulp.

The waiter brings them a menu. Kreisler puts in the order.

"What made you choose this place tonight?" Anni asks. "We usually do Italian."

"There's always the possibility of meeting new people." Although, there is no guarantee that Hitler and his entourage will show up, Kreisler sits so that he can keep an eye on the entrance. "I happen to be starved. I trust we are all meat eaters here."

Anni gives a thumb's-up while taking her first gulp of beer. Anton pats his belly, which is growing robust. Lotte leans over so Kreisler can hear her over the crowd.

"Do you really think he'll show up? What will you do if he does?"

"I haven't thought that through yet," he says, though he is keeping the architectural library book on the table in front of him. "A writer needs time to build up the drama."

"Just don't do anything crazy."

Kreisler's face suddenly opens up with a smile, and he whisks Lotte to her feet. "Like this?" he says, and hauls her onto the dance floor to show off his dance moves. A photographer making her way from table to table, earning her pay by snapping portraits of the jovial customers, catches Kreisler's eye, and he dances Lotte over so they can get their shot at immortality.

"Smile for the camera," he tells Lotte.

She does, lifting her skirt, kicking off her shoes, and rotating her hips as she jives to the rhythm of an American jazz classic. She is a beautiful woman, Kreisler thinks, when she dares to let go. Everyone notices the young couple swinging to the beat. They must be in love, they think. Only when the music stops do Lotte and Kreisler stop. She collects her shoes. They are both out of breath when they return to the table.

"That's how you do it," Lotte tells the table.

She leans into Kreisler and gives him a big kiss on the cheek, before saying something into his ear that makes the usually unflappable detective turn red.

The intimate exchange doesn't go unnoticed.

"What are you two whispering about?" Anni, the journalist with the eye of a detective, notices everything. "Don't tell me Avi has proposed marriage?"

"Not yet," Lotte says, but can't help casting a sideward glance at her date to see his response. "I believe I have convinced him to enter rabbinical school. He and Anton can spend time, while the rest of us are trying to survive, arguing theological bullshit."

Lotte laughs again. The crimson of Kreisler's face has not disappeared. "I'm a Jew by blood only," he says.

"Not a *mischling*, but a real full-blooded Jew."

"Just don't tell my friends that. Once a year at temple, and they buy into my solidarity with them. A non-believer can't be fully Jewish. Not that I ridicule their beliefs. But what century do we live in? How can we believe that God created the heavens and earth in seven days?"

"Six."

"Really? I thought it was seven."

"No," Anton says. "He rested on the seventh day."

"Well, even more ridiculous, then. I see death every day. Murder. People falling out of windows. People drowning. We've all witnessed things we detest. And where is this God the religious speak of?" Kreisler's face is still red, but now more in anger than embarrassment. The book in front of him, the product of an idea that came to him while interviewing David Sussman's roommate, sits open. Hitler was an architectural student? No wonder he failed, Kreisler thinks. What he would build would only fall apart in an instant. It's the lack of humanity that's the issue. Not the math.

"Which is why," he says, "you should remain secular, Anton. Join the Red Cross if you want to help people. Write a play about the hypocrisy of man. It might not sell, but it will be the most real thing you've ever written."

Anton sits back, hurt by his friend's sudden, unexpected critique. "You must be very hungry," he says. "When the belly grumbles, the spirit mumbles."

"I know. I apologize, Anton." Kreisler gets up to embrace his friend. "It's not your pen. It's my vision that's lacking."

"It's this case he's working on," Lotte says. "Forgive him."

"A case, Avi? Is that it?"

"Don't be coy," Anni says. "Anton needs material for his next piece. And me, if you've got something I can write about for Der Weg."

"I'm really not allowed to say much about it." Kreisler certainly won't talk about it as the waiter brings over a platter of sausages and sauerkraut with a refill of beer. Once the food is distributed, Kreisler speaks with his mouthful of bratwurst. "Suffice to say, there **is** an ulterior reason for being here."

"Murder?" asks Anton.

Kreisler shrugs.

"Well, what else?" says Anni. "Avi's a homicide inspector. Spill."

"You'll just feed it to your Red newspaper," Kreisler says. "You know what that means, Anni. Biased journalism. You'll take what I tell you and spin it the way you want."

Anni lifts her stein as a toast. "For the cause! Yes. Absolutely. Lotte..." She turns her green eyes on the other woman in Kreisler's life. "The fact that your man is reticent tells me that the Brownshirts are involved with this. He doesn't want me to print the truth. He thinks that he can stand above the fray and not be struck when the bullets fly. Tell him he is willfully failing to realize what is going on in Germany today. Unless the good people do what they must, we will all end up being swallowed by the beast."

"The beast can always be taken down," Kreisler sincerely believes. He takes a sip of beer, eyes fixed anew on the entrance. "That's my job."

"Your job is to obey orders," Anni says. "Like a priest. Half the cops in this city are National Socialists or Iron Helmets or phony socialists. They all answer to someone." At this point, unconcerned by who hears her, Anni launches into a popular worker's song.

"Politicians are magicians

Who makes swindles disappear

The bribes they are taking

The deals they are making

Never reach the public's ear."

Lotte says, "Avi would never take a bribe. Shame on you for thinking that, Anni."

"Only time will tell. Hitler's not the only beast. He's just the toilet brush that scrapes the shit off the bowl."

Halfway through the meal, Kreisler signals the photographer to come to their table to take a portrait of him and his friends. Then, as director of photography, he places his friends for a shot.

"Pull your chairs in closer," he says.

"I'm not dressed for it," says a reticent Anni.

"Sure you are."

"Sure, for a Nazi wanted poster."

Kreisler is standing beside Anni, behind Lotte and Anton, when he sees Hitler arrive. On the Nazi Party leader's arm is a lovely young woman, Kreisler recognizes from Klara Fries's sketching.

"Jesus Christ," he says.

"Avi?"

"They're here. They came. Geli Raubal," he says to himself.

"What?"

Anni's attention is drawn to the newcomers. Hitler's arrival has not gone unnoticed. Much applause greets him. A smattering of *Heil, Hitlers*. Lotte reaches for Kreisler's hand. He can feel her quiver and senses a change in the entire atmosphere of the restaurant. Ever the detective, he maintains focus, spying a group of four SA men, dressed in their full regalia, coming in behind Hitler and Geli. Hitler is given a private table in a side room, with the four guards taking a table directly in front of the entrance, guarding their leader's privacy. Could one of them be the killer of Klara Fries and David Sussman?

"Give me your camera," he says to the photographer. "Better yet, come with me. Lotte…"

He extends his hand to Lotte, who rises uneasily from her chair. "What are you doing, Avi?"

"Photo op," he says, at the last second, retrieving the architecture book.

"No." She pulls away. "Not here, Avi. Not now. It's not safe."

"You're crazy, Avi," Anton says. He, too, looks nervous, checking out the hulking SS men who won't let anyone who appears in the least bit threatening get within ten feet of Hitler.

But Kreisler isn't deterred. Rejected by Lotte, he takes a hold of Anni's hand and drags her across the crowded restaurant. He is so intent on accomplishing his mission, he doesn't hear the singer on stage, whom the photographer is supposed to be photographing.

Hannelore lives with a flower-seller

At Hallesches Tor.

Hannelore sings in the choir at a

Revue, you can't really make her out

But wherever she goes and wherever she stands

The men go wild, especially in May.

"Just go along with me, Anni," he says. "They won't attack a couple, especially someone like you."

"What's that supposed to mean?"

"Just keep the club out of sight."

As anticipated, the four Brownshirts spot Kreisler and Anni long before they reach Hitler and Geli's private room. Kreisler studies the faces as if he can discern murder in one of their countenances. He whispers to Anni, "Be flirtatious."

"That's beneath me."

"It didn't use to be."

The wall of SA tightens as Kreisler and Anni confront them. Kreisler is sporting the foolish grin of an eager sycophant. Anni is trying her hardest to look enticing.

"This is a private party," one of the SS men says. "Herr Hitler doesn't wish to be bothered."

"One picture," Kreisler begs. "One. With my girl and me."

One of the four guards steps forward, hand up as if he is a traffic cop holding up traffic. "No further."

The hand raised is his right hand. This does not necessarily mean anything, but Kreisler automatically eliminates him and eyes the other three. With the tip of his shoe, he nudges Anni's ankle, and as if on cue, she lowers her red hair so that it falls gracefully and long down past her shoulders, almost to her waist. The movement is pure Hollywood. A starlet posing for the cameras. Each one of the SS men redirects his gaze toward her. One in particular seems to stare with lurid intent, his focus trailing from Anni's face down the six-foot length of her body. He is also the burliest of the four men, so Kreisler writes this in the notepad of his mind.

Whether or not this sultry move will alter the minds of Hitler's guards becomes moot when Geli Raubal appears at the door in a fancy white gown in heels that take her almost to six feet herself. She is definitely the girl in the sketch by Klara Fries.

"Ich brauche das Badezimmer," she says to one of the guards. I need the bathroom.

Instantly, Kreisler steps in. *"Ah, du musst Geli Raubal sein, das Mädchen auf Klaras Zeichnung."* You must be Geli Raubal, the girl in Klara's drawing.

The effect is immediate. Geli stops and eyes Kreisler. "You know Klara?"

"I am one of her neighbors. We live in the same building," Kreisler says. He ignores the dour looks the men are giving him. "You didn't hear?"

It is at this point that the burly guard steps in and grabs Kreisler's arm. "It is you who haven't heard. You must leave the Führer and his niece alone."

"No, wait, Wilhelm," Geli says. "What do you mean?"

Apparently, Wilhelm hasn't read the screenplay or heard the director yell, "Action!" Kreisler, the actor, has taken over. The play, however, is unwritten, so he must ad lib.

"Well, it was a terrible thing," he says. "The police call it a suicide."

"A suicide!"

"She did a drawing of you. The police have it."

"A suicide?"

Geli is visibly upset. So is Wilhelm, who shoves Kreisler so hard, he drops the library book. Anni stoops to pick it up, but is pushed back by one of the other SS men. Kreisler gives her a not-so-subtle look to warn her not to throw a punch, just as Hitler, in a fashionable blue suit himself, appears in the doorway to the private room with a look of consternation and annoyance.

"What is going on here, Julius, Martin? Why are you roughing up this lovely couple?"

Ever the politician, Kreisler thinks. Not a bad move. A good one, in fact, that creates an opening for Kreisler to take advantage of. He grabs the book on classical architecture from Anni and shows it to Hitler.

Geli is trying to tell her uncle, "It's about Klara. Something about Klara committing suicide."

Kreisler has to talk over her. "We have much in common, Herr Hitler. Here, see what I have. We're both students of architecture. I was hoping you would sign this book."

"Architecture? Let me see."

Kreisler as Moses parts the wall of SS men to hand Hitler the library book. They are both ignoring Geli, so Anni steps in to console the younger girl. "Let's talk in the bathroom," she whispers, and Geli reluctantly follows with the guard called Martin, stepping in behind them.

"I tried to enroll at the Vienna academy like you," Kreisler tells Hitler. "I was rejected. They said there was no humanity in what I drew, but I simply drew what I saw."

"Those people are talentless *schweine*," Hitler says. "They are all into this Bauhaus *scheise*."

"We need a new architecture in Germany. One that reflects the glory of the past and the glory of the German future."

Hitler's eyes go alight with joy. Where has Geli gone? Why is she so upset? Who cares? In the moment, Hitler has discovered a fellow architect who appreciates what has been and what will be. Someone of such comprehension must be rewarded.

"You read Mein Kampf?" he asks.

"Cover to cover five times. A magnificent piece of literary architecture if I may be direct."

"Not everyone in Germany appreciates that, my boy. Are you a member of the National Socialists? You must join if you haven't already."

"Tomorrow, sir," Kreisler pours it on.

"Your name?"

"Kreisler. My girlfriend Anni is with your..."

"Niece. My sister's daughter. My half-sister. Angela has artistic dreams, too. As a singer. She wants to go to Vienna. But as you can imagine, my thoughts about Vienna aren't the highest. Who needs to go to Vienna when we have everything she could possibly want right here in Germany?"

Hitler glances around as Geli returns with Anni. Hitler's niece is sobbing, so the Nazi leader takes her in his arms. "Now, now," he tells her. "What is this all about, Franks?"

"A suicide. A girl jumping from her window. A friend of Fraulein Raubal," the SS man named Martin says. "I told her we would investigate and find out what happened."

"Good, good," Hitler says. "These things happen, Geli. Suicide is common among women. Mustn't ruin our dinner plans. You have many friends."

"I want to go to Vienna. I insist upon it now after this."

"That, my dear, is no way to mourn a friend."

Have to hand it to him, Kreisler is thinking. Despite the embarrassing position Geli has put him in, making demands in front of his men, in public, with gawking strangers standing around, Hitler maintains an avuncular calm.

"Take her back to our table, Franks," Hitler says, before turning back to Kreisler with a smile. "You wanted me to sign something."

"I will cherish it forever." Kreisler knows better than to offer a hand to Hitler, who does not like to be touched. He proffers the book instead and a pen he happens to have on hand. Hitler scribbles his name on the inside front cover and hands back the pen.

"Are we done, Herr Kreisler?" he says. "My niece…"

"One more thing, if at all possible?" Kreisler may be pushing it. Then again, such an opportunity may not arise a second time. He turns toward the photographer. "One photo. With all of us. For my father, who, like you, was a runner in the Great War."

"A runner? I suppose I'll have to sign that, too."

"Only if you will be so magnanimous."

Hitler agrees. The great man cannot resist the blandishments of a fellow architect who sees the future as he does. Kreisler finagles the SS men in a line, two on either side, with himself and Hitler in the middle. He inserts Anni beside him, then gives a single command to the awestruck photographer.

"Smile."

Chapter Five

September 12-13

Lotte is not happy with Kreisler. She has hesitated to speak until now, as she drives him back to his flat. She has already said goodnight to a supercharged Anni and a more restrained Anton.

"You're playing with fire, Avi," she tells him. "Why do you do that? We were having such a lovely time. Hitler, of all people."

"I'm a detective," Kreisler says. "Don't you want me to find out who killed Klara Fries?"

"No. Honestly? No. Not if it gets you killed."

She turns onto his street. The car, a black 1932 Duesenberg, isn't usually seen in this working-class neighborhood. It gathers some attention from pedestrians walking outside Kreisler's building.

"It won't," he says. He cracks a smile to put her at ease. "I'm Hitler's best friend. Why would he kill me?"

"Those people will kill anyone."

Lotte parks but doesn't move, her hands still gripping her steering wheel. Kreisler doesn't move either. It is still raining, though not as hard as earlier in the evening, and Lotte's wipers have been shut off so that the rain coats the windshield, giving her and Kreisler a sort of protection from the gazes of the outside world.

"What we talked about back at the restaurant," she says, turning a nervous glance his way, "what do you think?"

"We talked about a lot of things," Kreisler says. "We live in a world on the edge. I appreciate that, Lotte, honestly I do."

"That's not what I mean."

"Klara Fries deserves an answer. So does David Sussman. Their killer…"

"I'm not talking about that either, Avi."

Kreisler returns her gaze, silently recalling the events of the evening and what they might have talked about that would have Lotte so visibly upset. She's crying. Now Kreisler is upset and leans over to give her a kiss on the cheek, but she averts her face, letting out a sob.

"Lotte, what—"

"The proposal!" she shouts. "Marriage! Is the thought just a joke to you? Have you ever considered it? With me? For us? Or do you intend to string me along forever?"

"Lotte, no."

"Then what is the answer, Avi? Is it because you're a Jew and I'm not? I've always wondered."

Kreisler lets out a breath to give him time to ponder that question. He sits back in his seat, looks from the passenger-side window to the windshield, each covered in rain. The Duesenberg has become a trap. He doesn't want to lose his temper. He does love Lotte. But life is complex, the human mind often unable to cope with the twists and turns thrown in its path, even for a detective as insightful as Kreisler.

"It has nothing to do with my faith," he says at last. "You know that."

"Your uncle and aunt converted to Catholicism years ago. You were raised by them. Maybe that's it."

Lotte has a hopeful look on her face. She can accept the lengthy on-again-off-again course of their romance as Kreisler has bedded other women while she has remained faithful. It is the way of most men, she believes. Certainly, her own father and brothers. She has always felt that Kreisler is worth the patience and that he would inevitably return to her.

"I would like to have children," she says to him softly. "A family. We can raise them any way you want. I don't care. But I must have an answer after all this time. If this Klara and this David have their rights, so do I. So do you, for that matter. I can make you happy, Avi."

Can anyone truly make anyone else happy, he wonders, if happiness isn't in the cards for anyone?

It is his turn to shed a tear. Lotte has touched a nerve, whether she knows it or not. The real issue, he knows, is happiness and whether such a thing is truly possible in this life. Perhaps somehow he knows what lies ahead. He can sense the shifting of the world to something so horrible, it can't be understood. How can he make her happy, how can he reassure her that he will remain true to her as she has been to him, true, that is, in the sense of being there for her one hundred percent of the time, when he knows he is incapable of such a thing?

"Let me finish this case," he says at last. "Let me do what I can to get justice for these people. Then I will do what you wish."

"Not what I wish, Avi," she says, touching his arm, squeezing it. "What is in your heart to do. If you can't do it, now or then, just tell me."

Kreisler nods. He smiles. So does she. Then they kiss. When he leaves the car, enters his building, and climbs the stairs to his flat, though, he does so alone as Lotte drives into the night. He will tell her. When he finds the courage. Just not tonight. He promises himself that he will do the right thing by her, even marry her. He just can't see where happiness will come from.

* * *

Sleep is impossible, and he knows tomorrow will be a slog. He should have known better than to entrust the Fries evidence to Fritz Langer, so all he has with him to fritter away the night are the photographs he bought at the restaurant. Laying these out on his dinner table, he studies the faces of those captured in black and white.

It is hard to look at Lotte. She appears so happy in the picture with Anton and Anni. Just off the dance floor where she cut a rug, sliced it up, and kicked it aside, she embodies bridal delight. The same gleam. The same joy. A future of wonder ahead with her new husband. Anton seems to almost hide under the table, shoulders sagging, a kid in the confession booth, guilty of something but not sure what. Anni is the skeptical one with hooded eyes and a smirk that questions the need to share happy memories. No one will ever pull the wool over that one's eyes.

"Bolshevik," Kreisler calls her. "My Red Giraffe."

And yet, she fell right into line as soon as he grabbed her hand and forced her to accompany Geli Raubal to the bathroom. He wonders how much Lotte knows about his equally longstanding demi-relationship with Anni. The thought of betrayal disturbs him, especially now during the Yom Kippur season, when God takes an accounting of everyone's sins committed in the past year. Despite his atheism and his lack of spiritual inclinations, Kreisler feels something more powerful than he peering over his shoulders and whispering into his ears, "Sinner, sinner, thou art a pitiable sinner."

Kreisler pushes the first group of photos aside to focus on the one taken of himself with Hitler. Nestled beside him, with her unfilmed hand pinching his back, Anni is wearing that eternal smirk on her lips.

What a fool I am, Kreisler thinks. *Lotte's jealous. That's what happened, and I didn't see.*

Four of the men in the photo are SA. He recalls the names of three of them: Wilhelm, Julius, and Martin. The fourth man is unnamed. Any one of them could be Klara's killer. Hitler, on the other hand, looks completely uneasy, a celebrity reluctantly wasting a moment of his time in the company of oddball strangers.

It is the person who is not in the photo that makes Kreisler suddenly sit back as if the Almighty had just injected him with prophetic vision. Angela 'Geli' Raubal never stood with them. After returning from the bathroom, she escaped into the private dining room of the restaurant by herself.

She is already a ghost, he thinks. She just doesn't realize it. She knows too much. Unless she remains pliant to Hitler's wishes, *der Führer* can dispose of her, too, no matter what his feelings toward her might be. Kreisler, himself, and Anni heard her threat regards Vienna. If she isn't careful, she could push Hitler too far, and that could put him and Anni in jeopardy, too.

Kreisler rises from the table, yawning. A sinner he may be, but a persistent, relentless one. Having made an important decision, he can now relax, sleep.

The first thing in the morning, he is going to conduct an interrogation of Geli Raubal.

* * *

It is Sunday, a day for communing with God. Kreisler rises with the sun and eats a quick breakfast of scrambled eggs and sausage that he cooks for himself. He is a svelte two hundred pounds on a frame six feet. He can look Anni eye to eye, something he can't do with Lotte, who is a half foot shorter than he.

On a more carefree Sunday, he might head over to the Englischer Garten and enjoy a stroll. If Lotte, or someone else, slept over with him, he would lie abed until noon. Today, he hops on his bicycle and rides the two miles from his flat to an address on Prinzregentenplatz 16 on the far side of the Garden. This is where Hitler lives with Geli and her mother. Are they church-goers? Can Kreisler approach them on the street? He doubts he can gain access to the apartment itself, not if Hitler is in residence. Will their guards intervene, be impossible to get around? These are all chances he has to risk.

Kreisler ponders the many possibilities as he bikes through the city. Power is a corrupting force, and Hitler is aiming for the very top of German politics. Love, under the circumstances, no matter how passionate and strong, takes second place. A distant second place. What Geli Raubal knows could topple Hitler from his high post. He is cozying up to the German bourgeoisie and the German industrialists, traditionalists who don't like violence and aren't particularly fond of uncles who enjoy having their nieces shit or urinate on them. A word from her, an admission of her participation in her uncle's debauchery, would end his career and, perhaps, drop the Nazis from history. Who wouldn't kill to stop that?

Geli's address is in a more expensive area of the city at a busy crossroads. The traffic is not so heavy this morning, so Kreisler can bike his way at a good clip through the main intersection until he finds a place to park his bicycle beneath a lime tree against a bench. This spot gives him a perfect view of the entrance into Prinzregentenplatz 16 across the intersection.

He is removing a backpack stuffed with his camera and his notepad and pencils when he notices that a neighboring bench twenty meters to his left is also occupied. A woman dressed in her social climbing finest is sitting alone, gazing into a hand-held mirror as she applies lipstick. Kreisler approaches.

"Stalin would be ashamed, Anni," he says. "He might even have you executed. What are you doing here?"

"Brilliant radical minds think alike. Take a seat, Avi. Pretend to be my husband."

"I've been doing that for at least ten years, haven't I?"

"On occasion." Anni finishes coloring her lips a bright red. Satisfied, she slides over to give Kreisler room. "I figured," she says, "that you were investigating Herr Hitler for some murder or other. Possibly the woman who drew that sketch of Fraulein Raubal. You were probing for a reaction."

"Which I got."

"You sometimes forget how well I know you, Inspektor Kreisler."

"Better than I do myself, probably." He grunts with amusement about something she admitted to last night. "Erik the Red's daughter. He never wrote porn."

"Sure, he did. Anyway," Anni continues, eyes turning to the house across the street, "if Hitler is somehow involved and his niece Geli knows something about it, who better to interview? And sooner rather than later. I misread you by an hour."

"I overslept, then made myself breakfast. I figure Fraulein Raubal to be a late riser."

Kreisler looks through the lens of his camera for a potential long shot. He is equally well-dressed, the actor poised to make his starring entrance. Side-by-side, they wait for ten, fifteen minutes, a half hour. Foot traffic picks up. Several trams pass by. The day is warm and sunny, good for a morning stroll. Kreisler is tempted to ask Anni if she'd like to get something to eat and bring it into the Garden for a picnic, only to have Lotte's face pop up condemning him to hell.

"Lotte got to you last night, didn't she?"

Kreisler is caught completely off guard. "What are you: prescient or something?"

Anni smiles. She pats his knee, gazes into his eyes. "Oh, you poor thing. No, I'm just a woman, though Lotte is more of one than I am. She wants what most women want. I don't blame her. I assume you didn't propose."

"No."

"Are you going to?"

"Do you think I should?"

"Not if you don't love her back."

Kreisler is silent.

"Ah, that's it."

Anni has the darkest eyebrows that make her even more lovely when she frowns in wonder. Nothing is obvious about Anni. Nothing ever has been. She is a mystery and likes being that way. Case in point, she takes Kreisler by surprise when she gathers his face in her hands, turns it towards her and plants a passionate kiss on his mouth. When she pulls away, she studies his face for his response.

"Your love is divided," she says.

Kreisler is blushing.

"There's no shame in that," she says. "Would it surprise you to know that I love you?"

"You've never told me."

"I've never told you many things about me."

Kreisler considers kissing her back but doesn't. "Don't you ever want to get married?" he asks. "Or is that too bourgie? Stalin's married. Lenin was married. I'd think they'd appreciate a dozen red-headed Communists overpopulating Germany."

"Are you proposing?"

Anni's eyes twinkle. There is a moment when they both think he really might do just that. There is a hesitancy on the part of them both, though. Hesitance to plow ahead. Hesitance to know how to respond. Hesitance that spoils moments like this. Instantly, they both break out into raucous waves of laughter, best of friends who just can't quite take the mundane plunge into happiness. Once they subside, though, Kreisler turns serious.

"Would you accept?" he wonders. "It would break Lotte's heart."

"Yes, it would. I'd have to think about it."

"How long?"

"Longer than today," she says, then nudges his arm and nods her head toward the apartment block across the street. "I think your girl has emerged."

Kreisler turns to look, disappointed, wanting an answer just the way Lotte did last night. "Your timing," he says, "couldn't be more opportune. Yes, that's her, with her mother, I'd bet." He stands but doesn't move right away, looking to see if any SA guards follow behind. Luckily, it appears Geli and her companion are off on a Sunday walk by themselves.

"You still haven't told me what you're doing here," he says to Anni.

"I am a journalist, after all," she says, proffering her hand. "Waldmann will be excited. I can see the headline already. Killer Hitler brought to justice."

"Yes, well," Kreisler says, "let's not jump ahead. This is an investigation first, a Communist takeover second."

Kreisler starts across the street, Anni at his side. They don't clasp hands. That performance won't hold water today. If he wants Geli to open up, he must be open himself. They catch up to Geli as she and her older companion turn left to head down the street toward, not a church, but a series of elegant shops.

"Pardon! Pardon, Fraulein Raubal! A moment, please."

Geli is wearing a pleated blue skirt, nothing too elegant, her hair done up in a single twisted braid. A blue bonnet festooned by a white Edelweiss flower keeps the sun off her head. The choicest thing about her are the sunglasses sitting on the bridge of her nose, making her look just like a young Hollywood starlet out on the town, hoping to go unrecognized.

The older escort turns first to see who has called out to them. A dour woman of about fifty, she is dressed more in the fashion of the old days before the Great War, frumpy and colorless, with a long gray coat concealing her heavier frame.

"*Wer bist du?*" Who are you? Suspicious. Protective. Motherly.

Geli immediately recognizes the tall woman with the red hair. "Oh, it's you," she says. "From last night."

"We're sorry to interrupt," Kreisler tells her. The first thing he does is show his police credentials. "It has to do with Klara Fries. Perhaps we can find a café or head to the park."

With her sunglasses covering her eyes, Kreisler can't fully read Hitler's niece's reaction. Geli has every right to be confused, even distraught. This is not helpful, although it is good for her to feel vulnerable in some way. But Kreisler doesn't want her to push him away before he gets to interrogate her.

"About last night in the restaurant," he says.

"You're a policeman," Geli says. "You lied to him."

"He had guards. It was the only way for me to get access. I apologize. You will understand why shortly."

"We needed to speak to you." Anni jumps in. She is sensing that the sisterly touch will help ease the concerns of both women, mother and daughter.

"You said you were an architectural student," Geli says. "Now you're telling me you're a policeman."

"I needed to get to talk to you," Kreisler says. "Without your uncle around, if possible. About Klara. I imagine you can understand how difficult that would have been under the circumstances."

"But you said it was a suicide."

Kreisler nods, remains silent, staring back into Geli's masked eyes, allowing the girl to grasp the terrible alternative herself. It is the older woman who responds.

"You're saying it wasn't a suicide? If not that, then what?"

"That's why we have to talk to you in private. You are Fraulein Raubal's mother?"

"I am. Herr Hitler's sister. My brother would be very unhappy about this. He watches Geli with a hundred eyes."

"It is a dilemma." Kreisler maintains his silence. He must be cautious about what he says. He doesn't know whether or not Geli will report back to Hitler and, if so, what she will tell him. He would rather have conducted his interview without the mother present but must hope she doesn't tattle either.

Coming to the rescue, Anni inserts herself between the other women and takes them both by an arm. "Fear not," she says. "You are among friends."

"You're a police officer, too?"

"What else would I be?"

"I didn't know they employed women."

"Only the daughters of Vikings."

There is a café down the block, but Kreisler would rather conduct his interview somewhere prying eyes and ears can't tune in. The park is several blocks away, but a more suitable place to talk in privacy, a more peaceful place that will put his interviewees at ease.

"My superiors want me to clear up this matter as quickly as possible," he states as he walks at their side but slightly ahead, as he has a longer stride. "You were a friend of Klara's, I believe."

"The name is unfamiliar to me," the mother says.

"We found a portrait of your daughter, Frau Raubal, in the deceased's flat. I could show it to you, but…"

"No, don't!" Geli practically shouts. "I know Klara, Mother, from university. She was an artist, a very good one."

"She made a painting of you?"

"A sketching. It's nothing. A doodle, when she was with me in Obersalzberg. Why would such a thing cause someone to kill her?"

Kreisler looks both ways at the main street dividing them from the park, then, when he sees an opening in the traffic, directs his quartet across the boulevard.

"I can only conjecture, Fraulein," Kreisler says. "The drawing was not the only thing we found in her apartment. That, in and of itself, is nothing. I could get it for you…."

"No. No, thank you."

"Or destroy it, whichever you would prefer."

On the far side of the roadway, there are benches under the shade of trees and a vendor selling Italian ice cream and German cider. Kreisler buys everyone something to help cool their thirst and finds a bench for the three ladies to sit on. He remains standing, occasionally spooning in a bite of strawberry gelato, unthreatening, a pastoral scene to fool any passersby.

"Tear it up, throw it away, I don't care," Geli says regarding her late friend's drawing. Her dessert sits in her lap, for the moment only nibbled upon.

"She had talent, I'll say that for her," Kreisler says. He glances at Anni, who, thankfully, is keeping her mouth shut except to eat her own cold dessert. Kneeling then directly in front of Geli, he follows up in a guarded whisper. "What we found is not something for public consumption. It was a letter written by your uncle."

"By Uncle Alf?"

"It was meant to be private. To be personal. To be very intimate. A lover's letter to one he must love quite deeply."

"My brother?" Frau Raubal says. "To whom? What did it say?"

"Those are only two questions that come to mind. How did Klara get her hands on it, when did she get her hands on it, and what did she intend to do with it?"

"I don't know," Geli stutters.

"A traitor in our midst?" her mother growls. "If I find out...."

"No, Frau Raubal, you must say and do nothing," Kreisler warns her. "We do suspect blackmail and that her death may have been due to her trying to blackmail your brother, Geli's uncle."

Here, Kreisler is being subtle. He is not openly criticizing Hitler and his niece for engaging in unnatural incestuous sex. A letter written by Hitler? To his niece? Graphically depicting his desires and what he wants her to do to him. He lets that sink in, though. Surely, he thinks, the mother must know what the daughter is up to. She can't be completely innocent. But where does her loyalty lie? With her child or with her brother, her half-brother?

"If such a letter became public...."

"That might be terrible," Geli says.

"Destructive to one's political career, in fact. And so, to prevent that from happening, someone, someone perhaps very close to you and your mother, first raped Klara...." Let that sink in, too, he thinks, "then killed her and tossed her out the top floor window of her building to crash to pieces on the sidewalk below."

Geli lets out a startled cry, a bird caught in a cat's mouth. But Kreisler doesn't let up.

"If you know someone in your own household, or close to you in some other way, who would have access to such a letter, who either has it in for Herr Hitler or who would kill to protect him, you must tell me. Someone who, perhaps, favors the left hand." He has caused Geli to weep, but he doesn't care. He turns his attention to the mother now. "Consider, Frau Raubal: if this Klara was killed because of what she knew, who else is in danger?"

Before she can answer, he rises now and takes a bite of his gelato. Nonchalant. An inquisitor with other, more important things on his mind. "I think," he says, "the letter was written while you were in the Alps. I believe that Klara had an accomplice. A boy was killed, too. A boy who lived in the same building as your friend. They found him floating in the Isar. Perhaps he saw something...the killer...and paid with his life."

"I'm so sorry," Geli says. Her mother lends her a handkerchief with which Geli wipes her eyes and her nose. "What was his name?"

"David Sussman. I see murder every day, Fraulein. I'm sure you're aware of the violence in the streets. It would be a shame if we let this killer get away with what he has done. I only ask your help in whatever way you can give it."

"Of course," she says. Her eyes turn to Angela, nee Hitler. "We must, Mother. In whatever way we can." Then she swivels to face Anni. "And you, you're really a cop, too?"

Anni shrugs.

"We'll try."

"Quietly. Secretly. Anything you can tell us, any tip you can give, anything at all suspicious among those who live with and work with your family, will be helpful in solving this case."

Kreisler smiles at the young woman. He feels he has gained as much ground as he can today. He has put the fear of God in Geli and her mother and turned them into allies, spies within their own home. They will serve as a buffer between him and Hitler. They know who the killer is. They just haven't pinned him down yet.

"By the way," he says, "Vienna is a lovely city. I haven't been there since I was a student. What does your uncle have against you going?"

"Singing lessons, that's all. Singing lessons."

His question is asked as much out of curiosity as out of any relevance to the murder case. Geli's reaction, though swift, brief, and, to Kreisler, telling, changes everything. As she was about to rise off the bench, her hands went over her belly in a reflex motion before dropping to her side.

Kreisler pretends not to notice and says nothing until Geli and her mother have departed.

"I never realized you could be so cruel," Anni tells him, taking his hand whether he likes it or not. "I'm impressed."

"Cruel?" Kreisler says. "Me? Didn't you see what Geli did when I asked her about Vienna? She put her hands over her middle."

"So?"

"So? She was protecting her baby. Geli Raubal is pregnant."

And that's not all, he thinks. The blackmail letter. The murdered friend. The argument over Vienna. Knowing way too much or not knowing enough.

"One way or another," he tells Anni, "Adolf Hitler is going to kill that girl."

Chapter Six

September 19

In future days, Rudolf Hess will become an important man in the Nazi rule over Germany, second in succession behind Goring, before he flies solo on a baffling mission of peace to England in 1941 and ends up the last Nazi prisoner of war at Spandau Prison in Berlin.

On this Saturday morning in 1931, he is just another nervous wreck.

"Who else is coming? Did someone contact Hoffman?" The question is asked of Hess because Hess was the first one here. The first one of importance, that is.

"He's already been here," says Hess, whose deep-set eyes and dark brows have been furrowed with worry for a good hour, ever since he'd kicked in the door to Geli Raubal's bedroom and found her dead of a gunshot wound to the chest. "Hoffman and Schreck have already taken him. He's on his way to Nuremberg to make a speech."

"He had one scheduled?"

"He does now."

"What about the mother?" Gregor Strasser was the second man of National Socialist significance to arrive, having been called in by one of Hitler's SA guardians. He is the thirty-nine-year-old manager of the Nazi Party's national organization in charge of propaganda. At one time or another, Himmler and Goebbels have worked for him.

"Weeping inconsolably as you can imagine," Hess says. He is pacing in the front hallway of the Hitler apartments, trying to keep everyone else out of the dead girl's bedroom.

"How did she do it?" asks a third man. Kill herself, he means.

"Does it matter?"

"For propaganda purposes, yes," Strasser says. The two men are joined in the hall by Baldur von Shirach, the head of the Nazi Youth programs; Franz Schwarz, a bespectacled Munich city councilor and the treasurer of the Nazi Party; and Max Amann, the publisher of Hitler's *Mein Kampf.* "Is it agreed? Suicide?"

"Yes, yes. I'll call Dresler and tell him what to write up," Shirach says. "Suicide, yes? Agreed?"

Hess shakes his head. What else is to be done, though? Dresler runs the press department at the Brown House, the Nazi headquarters in Munich. He'll run the story and get it out as quickly as possible. But people will want to know the full details. Why would such a lovely, young woman, the niece of Adolf Hitler, commit such a sin? In his own apartment?

Strasser pulls Hess aside. "It wasn't really suicide, was it?"

"How should I know? I wasn't here. What are you proposing we tell the world? That he shot his own niece?"

"But you were here when Hitler was. What did he say? How did he react?"

Hess's eyes move left, right, up, down, but never alight on Strasser's face. "As you would expect. He was distraught, beside himself. Do you want me to tell you he was weeping? Well, yes, he was. Apparently, he actually loved the girl."

"Enough to pull the trigger himself? You know the rumors."

Hess doesn't. As close as he is to Hitler, he does not discuss anything with his boss other than politics and strategy. How does he know, what does he care, about Hitler's social proclivities?

"I turn a deaf ear to rumors. We all have rumors. The Party will die because of rumors."

"Yes, but these," Strasser says in a whisper, "are particularly salacious and destructive. Regards the Raubal woman. And who would know better than these people? Secrets can leak out. They must be squashed."

"Are you suggesting we kill them?"

Behind them, down the length of the hall, are huddled the people who know more than they need to say. Herr and Frau Winter and the maid Anna Kirmair, the household staff; Maria Reichert, the landlady, and her elderly mother, Frau Dachs.

"I didn't say that. Where's the sister?" Strasser asks.

"Apparently, mother and daughter are in Obersalzberg."

"Apparently? We have to know these things. Have they been alerted?"

"I didn't do it," Hess says.

"Well, someone should. Kaspers or Schaub can do it. They're down there all the time with the family."

"Kaspers is here."

"Did I hear someone say something about killing someone?" Having taken a quick glimpse at the crime scene, Schwarz, the Munich city councilor, joins them. "*Was für ein verdammtes Durcheinander!* What a fucking mess! I just finished paying off one blackmailer. Now this. This goes beyond scandalous."

"Close ranks," Hess advises. "What do we do about them?" He looks at the household staff. "They'll have to be told what to say. Do you think they can keep it straight?"

"Frau Drachs has lost her marbles," Strasser said. "Have you ever talked to her? Ask her if she knows who Hitler is, she'll ask you what's for dessert. If she witnessed anything, she'll look you straight in the eye and say, 'He did it. The one with the ridiculous moustache.'"

"It is only ridiculous to you, Schwarz." Von Shirach now joins the scrum. "Well," he says, "I've called Dresler, told him it was suicide. Munich will find out all about it in our next edition. I'll relay further news as it comes in."

"You mean, as we make it up."

"Whatever."

"Not whatever, Hess." Strasser gathers the men closer as if anyone else can hear them. "I think we should call it an accident, not suicide. Suicide, people don't like. The Church will have a field day with it, won't allow her to be buried in a church cemetery. It will be a bad look for us. Maybe we should call Dresler back and tell him Fraulein Raubal was cleaning her pistol…she has one, right…and it fired by accident and killed her. That's cleaner. People will accept 'accident,' and it won't lead to the Reds publishing shit about Hitler and his niece."

The men hum and nod in agreement before turning their attention to the story they will create and try to have the household staff remember and repeat.

"I never liked that girl," Strasser said. "I told Hitler it was a mistake to bring her here, to move her into his fucking apartment, for God's sake. Now this. If he's to survive this, he must be told from now on, hands off the women."

It is now ten-thirty in the morning. Geli Raubal has been lying in her bedroom, drained of blood, for who knows how many hours. That, too, will have to be incorporated in whatever they invent.

Despite the strategy finally agreed upon, Hess is no less worried now than he was before his comrades joined him. With reluctance, he looks at his watch. "I suppose now," he says, "it's time to call in the police."

* * *

It is Saturday morning, the Jewish sabbath, and Kreisler rolls over in bed and right into Lotte. She stirs but doesn't waken.

Last night was make-up night. Lotte has let up and accepted Kreisler's statement that he must conclude this all-important homicide investigation. Too much beyond the murder is at stake, he has told her. The fate of the nation could be in the balance, something that Lotte frankly doesn't care about. But she will be a good sport. Like always.

Kreisler rises, yawns, stretches, pulls on his jockey shorts, and heads into the kitchen to prepare breakfast. Somehow Lotte remains slender, though she is a big eater. She loves his veggie omelets and potato dumplings. Coffee and a newspaper crossword puzzle, all done in bed, is the perfect way to enjoy a morning, as far as she is concerned. Who cares if she has a bookstore to run? Who cares what her damned parents think?

For his part, Kreisler has spent his past week avoiding other murders that invariably are tossed his way. All big cities generate death. In Munich, the victims are not sorted out by manner of death but by political persuasion of the victim. Class also is taken into account, the middle-class victim getting far more attention than the working-class stiff who probably got what he deserved. Nobody, unfortunately, kills the rich.

Midweek, Kreisler managed to make it to the Brown House on Briennerstrasse, the National Socialist headquarters three miles from Hitler's apartment. The list of Nazi members is maintained there. Kreisler, though a Munich police detective investigating an active murder, was not allowed access to the list unless he became a member of the party himself.

"And so," he told Lotte that very night, "I have become a loyal Nazi. I even have a pin."

"I suppose you didn't tell them your parents were Jewish."

"That I neglected to mention, and while they might eventually find out, I only needed the hour it took to see the full list and, of course, photograph it. I am number 9677. Hitler was only 555."

The most recent pages covered the year 1931, January to the present September. But Kreisler is curious enough to go back to the very beginning. Hitler's 555 is a product of early National Socialist marketing. At the time he registered, there were only five members. Strasser, the propaganda chief, inflated the number to five hundred members, so that when Hitler registered, rather than number five, he became number 555. Surprisingly, shockingly, only a few months later, Kreisler found an unexpected inductee. Klara Fries was number 2344.

"I'll need to dig more extensively into her past now," he told Lotte in bed. "Why was she on that list? Why become a party member? That early in the game. When she was so young. The first woman. This changes my opinion of her slightly."

"Only slightly?"

"Well, my dear, after all, I am number 9677."

What was Klara Fries up to, he wonders? Something. She was too Weimar to be a National Socialist. Was she an actual, passionate member of such a violent throwback-of-a-party? An artist who drew nudes? Or did she have, like himself, ulterior motives? She certainly was able to finagle herself into the most intimate corridors of power, becoming a close friend of the party leader's niece. Just a ruse, then, to make money? Kreisler didn't think so.

He was planning his next step in uncovering this growing mystery of the girl who committed 'suicide', frying Lotte's egg, when a loud rap on his front door startled him, causing him to flip hot oil onto his bare arm.

"Avi! Kreisler! Open up!"

"Fritz? Damn it!"

Kreisler opens the door, blowing on his injured biceps.

"Are you damning me?" Langer asks, watching Kreisler administer treatment to his burned flesh. "Because it's Saturday or because you genuinely don't like me?"

"Both, if you must know. I was cooking eggs."

"I can smell them. Unfortunately, you won't be able to finish them. Is Lotte with you?"

"She is," Lotte herself says, peering from the bedroom doorway. "What's the matter, Herr Inspektor?"

"That's *Erster Polizeihauptinspektor* Langer, to you, my lovely. I was given a promotion the other day from Justice Minister Gürtner himself." He doffs his hat and makes a hasty bow. "And so, in my new position as head of Homicide, I'm afraid I must call your spouse away from breakfast. Another murder, Inspektor Kreisler. One we can't avoid."

Kreisler can already detect the anxiety in Langer's eyes, the way he fidgets with his hat, shifts his feet about as if he needs the bathroom. Kreisler would offer it to him, but Langer leans in and whispers.

"Geli Raubal."

"What?"

All at once, the temperature in the room rises to Saharan levels. Kreisler gapes like a camel waiting to be led to the nearest water hole. His blood pressure soars, and he feels faint. He has to find purchase on a piece of living room furniture to prevent himself from toppling to the floor.

"This morning," Langer says. "At least, that's when they found her body."

"Hitler?"

"I don't know. We have to move. Now. Fast. Before word gets out."

It already has, thinks Kreisler, or Langer wouldn't be here. In his new elevated role.

Lotte steps into the room, unmindful that she is only wearing pajamas. "What is it, Avi?" Fear is pouring off Langer, careening off Kreisler, and striking Lotte square in the gut. "Is something wrong?"

Kreisler gathers himself, switches on his professional demeanor facing Lotte. "It's Geli Raubal. She's dead."

"Dead?"

"Murdered."

"We don't know that. That's why we have to get over there as fast as humanly possible," Langer says. "Before this gets out of control."

"It isn't already?"

Kreisler is disrobing even before he reaches the bedroom. On go clothes, though not so fine as he would normally wear. Into his backpack goes everything he will need, though this time, for whatever reason, he decides to toss in his police-issued Walther.

"The car's out front," Langer says, as they take the stairs down. Kreisler didn't even have the chance to kiss Lotte goodbye. "First, the girl out the window, then the boy in the river, now this. Whoever said, 'Something's rotten in the state of Denmark' got the wrong country."

For Kreisler, as Langer drives like a tyrant through downtown Munich, his life isn't flashing before his eyes, but these cases are. It is as if someone has started an Alpine landslide that is cascading out of control, taking everyone in its path. He had predicted Geli Raubal's death at the hands of her uncle, but couldn't quite get himself to believe that it would really happen.

"I knew it, I knew it," he mutters, not in the least fazed by Langer's reckless driving.

"You knew what, Avi, what? That Hitler's niece would kill herself?"

Kreisler turns an angry glance at Langer. "You're already calling it suicide? That's twice you've done that."

"It could be, couldn't it? You'll need to mind your manners with this one, Avi."

"I had a bad feeling. She was a country girl walking into the lion's den. Maybe she thought she could control her uncle. Maybe she thought in the end she'd have her way. Maybe she's seen too many movies with her uncle sitting right beside her, feeding her candy, holding her hand, and doing God knows what else. Well, we do know, don't we, Fritz?"

Langer spins a turn onto Prinzregentenplatz. "Just keep in mind," he says, breathless from the exertion of racing his car and keeping it on the road. "We're dealing with the Schutzstaffel. Me, I'm no National Socialist, but I can read the tea leaves as well as anyone. Don't make any assumptions and don't open your mouth to anyone. Let me do the talking. Your job is to do what you do best. Observe."

Kreisler isn't paying attention. He's observing. His eyes are on the road ahead. With Klara Fries, a crowd had gathered outside her building. Of course, she had been unceremoniously hurled out onto the sidewalk. Even so, the fact that the sidewalk outside Hitler's lavish accommodations is practically empty of foot traffic troubles him.

"How long has she been dead?" he wonders aloud.

"Who knows?"

Langer pulls up with a squeal in a space usually reserved for taxis. He starts out his door.

Kreisler follows, lugging his backpack. "Where is everybody?"

"What 'everybody'? You want an audience, applause? Let's just do our damned job. And keep it, too."

Kreisler steps out onto the sidewalk and immediately hauls out his camera and begins snapping photographs of the surrounding area, including the cars parked along the street. One, as if not wanting to be captured on film, peels out of a space and disappears.

"Hess," Kreisler says.

"Avi, I told you…."

"What? I'm observing. I saw him. Rudolf Hess, Hitler's right-hand man. Driving away in that car. You saw it. What is he doing here?"

"What right-hand men always do. Shut up and get out of the way. Avi, take a hint."

Langer pushes ahead, forcing Kreisler to follow. There are no crowds, he thinks, because Hitler's men don't want them.

Up the stairs they jog until they reach the fifth floor. Awaiting them are four people, none of whom Kreisler knows. The lone male introduces himself.

"Georg Winter, sirs," he says. "I'm the one who broke in her door. It was locked from the inside."

"You the one who called the police?" Langer asks.

The four people exchange befuddled looks.

"Someone did," Langer says, but no one raises their hand. "Is the primary tenant here?"

"Herr Hitler?"

"If that's the primary tenant's name."

"No. He's gone. I think they said to Nuremberg."

"Who said?" asks Kreisler. His fingers clench and unclench. He is in the mood to commit his own murder at this point, and it could be just about anyone.

"Herr Hitler," one of the women jumps in.

"And you would be…?" Kreisler has at least found something to keep his fingers occupied: his notepad.

"Frau Winter, sirs."

"Would you show us the body then, Frau Winter?" Langer says, glancing behind him to check on Kreisler. "Nothing has been moved? Nothing touched?"

"No, sirs."

The Winters lead the two detectives through the apartment, which encompasses the entire fifth floor, past the outer rooms, down a left turn, ending up at the now open door to Geli's bedroom. She is still lying on the floor, face down, nose flat to the surface, the rug around her saturated in her blood. A gun lies clearly on the couch to her right. Nothing else in the room, none of the furnishings, appears to be upset or out of place, indicating no substantial battle before the fatal shot was fired.

Kreisler takes out his camera and starts snapping photo after photo.

"A gunshot," Langer says to the other residents of the apartment. He kneels beside the body. "Did anyone hear anything? You…" he points to the youngest woman in the group. "What's your name? What do you do here?"

"Anna Kirmair. I'm Herr Hitler's maid."

"And you?" Now Langer points to the oldest of the woman.

"I am Maria Reichert."

"And no one heard anything?" Kreisler looks up from writing the occupants' names in his notepad. He is wandering around the room, exploring and listening all at once. Observing with an intensity that Langer doesn't fully appreciate.

"I did," Frau Reichert says. "It was around three o'clock yesterday afternoon. I heard Fraulein Raubal's door shut. I saw Herr Hitler leave."

"By himself?"

Frau Reichert stumbles. It is clear to Kreisler that she is digging into her memory about either what happened or what she was told to tell the police what happened.

"Well," Frau Reichert says, "of course, Herr Hitler never drives himself. He has a chauffeur."

"Who would be?"

"Julius Schaub."

Kreisler has stopped moving and is standing in front of a writing desk. Lowering his camera, He picks up a piece of stationery.

"We can get into that later," says Langer. He is still crouched over the body, but has retrieved the gun off the sofa. The distress he is feeling may well surpass that of Kreisler. He has to wipe the perspiration from his brow with a coat sleeve. "So, Hitler leaves. Then what?"

"Well, not long after he left, for Nuremberg I believe…"

"You're sure Nuremberg?"

"I heard what I thought was a gunshot. I was in another room, so I can't be sure."

Equally upset, Frau Reichert rubs her arms and stares down at the body, trembling.

Kreisler ignores the woman and shows the stationery to Langer. "She was writing a letter," he says and reads from it. "When I come to Vienna…I hope very soon…we'll drive together to Semmering and…' Here she stops. Clearly, she was interrupted in the midst of writing to someone."

"Who?"

Kreisler peers at the letter heading. "It would seem a girlfriend. Perhaps a close confidante. Apparently, her uncle gave in to her desires. Or he didn't."

"Is that relevant?" Langer asks.

"I should think." Kreisler returns the letter to the desk and comes to crouch on the opposite side of Geli's body. "The mood of the letter is light-hearted, not something someone would expect from a person about to commit suicide."

"Fraulein Raubal and Herr Hitler were arguing. That much I heard." This comes from the maid who is quickly shushed by Fraus Winter and Reichert both.

"Perhaps everyone heard something different?" Langer does not like the path this interrogation is going and stands up to shoo the four witnesses out of the room. "Each of you find a room," he says. "A separate one. Don't say anything else to anyone else, including to each other. We will speak with each of you separately. See if we can sort this thing out."

"Too late for that, I'm afraid," Kreisler says. Carefully, he has tilted Geli's head up to gaze at her face. "Can you hold her like this, Fritz, so I can take a shot of her?"

"The nose is broken?"

"It appears that way," Kreisler says and takes a shot with Langer holding Geli's face up and toward the camera.

"She fell."

"Maybe. How far, though? From a standing position or a kneeling one? What height would be required to cause such damage? Can you help me roll her over?"

Langer looks up. He can hear a commotion outside the bedroom. "Those fucking people," he says.

But it isn't those people, the servants. Kreisler can hear the noise, too. A loud male voice giving out orders, getting louder and louder with each passing second.

"Quickly," he says. "Before they get here. Roll her over."

"We should wait for the ME, don't you think?"

Kreisler doesn't want to. He knows the fix is in already and wants to get as much information as he can before the fix can be fixed. But he and Langer haven't even lifted Geli's shoulders off the carpet, when a group of men bursts into the bedroom.

"Don't touch the body!" the first one in shouts at Langer. "Leave her alone!"

Langer recognizes the man, an important local politician, and bolts to his feet, dropping Geli back to the blood-stained floor. Kreisler is more reluctant to rise. He knows quite well three of the men who have charged onto the scene of the murder. Sauer and Forster are fellow homicide detectives. Doctor Müller is the forensic pathologist who oversaw Klara Fries's autopsy. It is the fourth man, the politician, whose bluster has caused the investigation to take a sudden halt.

"Schwarz," the man says. "Franz Schwarz. I'm on the city council. These two detectives with me will take over the case as of this moment." The balding, bespectacled fifty-six-year-old National Socialist treasurer interposes his frame between Langer and Geli. Kreisler doesn't budge.

"What is your interest in this?" he asks the politician.

"Kreisler!" Langer hisses. Back off.

"That is of no consequence to you. The Minister of Justice himself has asked these two detectives to handle this case. As you can imagine, extreme sensitivity is required."

"Sorry, Kreisler," Sauer says. "I was about to go fishing."

"Langer's been promoted."

"Doesn't matter," Schwarz says. "The Minister of Justice himself is running this investigation."

Doctor Müller also moves in, gazing at the corpse of the recently very young niece of Adolf Hitler. "Pity," he says. "Has Herr Hitler been notified of this tragedy?"

"He's been called," Schwarz says. "He was in Nuremberg making a speech."

"*In* Nuremberg or *going to* Nuremberg?" Kreisler inquires.

"Kreisler!"

Kreisler ignores Langer's audible warning. "It's just that witnesses here put Herr Hitler in the apartment close to the time of the shooting."

"We'll get to that," Forster says. "It's Saturday. Go home."

Kreisler does surrender his position to give the pathologist room to inspect the body, but he shakes off the hand that Langer has clasped onto his arm. Instead, he sinks into a chair that is situated by a window looking out onto the street, delaying his departure by pretending to find room in his backpack for his camera. He stops when a ruckus from the street below distracts him. Cheering. Heiling. The fanfare of an enthralled crowd that has gathered out of nowhere. One glance out the window tells him why. What was a practically empty street when he and Langer arrived has become a sideshow mob of fluttering moths drawn to the Fascist flame.

"It looks like Herr Hitler has made a quick return from Nuremberg," he tells the room.

"He's here? So fast?"

"My thoughts exactly."

While Kreisler makes no move to leave his position by the window, everyone else scrambles to greet the great personage about to discover the body of his niece. Schwarz leads the pack, followed by Langer, Sauer, and Forster. Only Doctor Müller remains behind.

"Quick thinking on your part, Inspektor," he says. "I assume you want a peek before the others get back."

"You're a mind reader, Doktor," Kreisler says. "Let me help you turn her over."

Lowering himself to the floor, he takes the far side of the corpse while the pathologist takes the near side, and they roll Geli onto her back.

"The bullet entered there," Müller is quick to point out the wound above and to the right of Geli's heart.

"It looks like she bled out," Kreisler observes.

"Indeed. Could have been lying here a good bit before she died. That will affect when rigor mortis sets in."

"And muddy the time of death."

"Possibly. From the looks of it…the bullet traveled south, through her lung, and, yes, I can even feel it. It never exited."

Müller shows Kreisler where the bullet ended its journey, just above Geli's left hip.

"I won't know for sure until I get inside her," Müller says, "but I think her life could have been saved if someone had found her soon enough. Was there no one else here?"

"Oh, they were here, all right."

Voices ascending the staircase from street level can be heard now. 'Shit,' Kreisler thinks. Once Schwarz and the other detectives return, his opportunity to get at the truth will disappear. Dropping his side of Geli's body, he trots to his backpack, grabs his camera, and hurries several shots, just as the parade of officials returns, Hitler in tow.

"Where is she? I must see her! She can't be dead. Not my Geli."

Kreisler takes a step back, instinctively, if pointlessly, hides his camera by his side, expecting Hitler with his entourage to rush ahead, pollute the crime scene, and make a mockery of Geli's short life. Instead, Hitler hesitates outside the entry as if he doesn't want to see what he knows full well is inside. He remains out in the hallway, surrounded by men reassuring him that he can do whatever he wants. Go in. Stay out. Give it a few minutes. Let the professionals handle it.

With that brief window of opportunity, Kreisler takes one last long scan of the entire room. Desk, floor, body, gun. She was shot, he thinks, from above with the pistol aiming downward. How else to explain the downward trajectory? She was on her knees, he posits, after having been in a scuffle and having had her nose broken. The gun goes off, accidentally or intentionally, and she topples over face-first into the floor. Then…

Then, who knows?

Hitler does. He may be the only one who does. And in he comes at last, shrieking, cursing like a madman, at first refusing to look at the corpse. Kreisler notices Langer among the horde, trying to get Kreisler's attention to get him the hell out of the way. Perversely, Kreisler takes a seat by the window, a front row to the drama as Hitler is held back by Schwarz and Sauer to keep him from sullying the body and the scene of the shooting. They manage after a brief tussle to sit the Nationalist Party leader in a chair just ahead and to the left of Kreisler.

"How could she do this?" Hitler moans. "How will I go on?"

"We have women on the way," Schwarz tries to comfort his boss. "They'll clean everything up, make your niece look presentable. She'll be in good hands."

"She's dead."

"Yes, she is, mein Führer. But she is with God now."

Schwarz looks up, notes Kreisler, wonders what he is still doing here. Kreisler, rather than take the hint, leans forward and pats Hitler on the shoulder. Hitler's response is to frown and wonder where he has seen this young man before.

"I'm the architect," Kreisler lies. "Last week at the Bratwurstglöckl restaurant. You signed my book on classical architecture. I said, once you are in charge of things, you will be the architect of all Germany."

"Yes, yes, all of it. That is the dream."

During his college years, before he dropped out, Kreisler took many courses in many subjects until boredom led him to cancel his education. One such course, taught by a Professor Freud, gave him enough insight into the human mind that he feels comfortable now in putting his studies to practical use.

Hitler smiles. Though his eyes are still wet with sorrow, Kreisler has opened the door for him into a tomorrow that, while absent one Angela Raubal aka Geli, will be a magnificent one filled with grand buildings and historic monuments.

"I do remember you," he says. Abruptly, his demeanor changes and he snarls, "All of you who are smoking, stop it this minute. What is the matter with you? Have you no respect for my Geli? The odor. The stench. This will be abolished in the future; do you hear me? An unhealthy practice."

Kreisler notes that Hitler is trembling, particularly his left side, his arm jerking almost epileptic. But the angry moment has passed, and, as all of the tobacco users in the room tamp out their smokes, Hitler resumes his interrupted train of thought.

"So," he says with interest, "you are a fellow reject from the Vienna Academy. Why are you here?"

"Well," Kreisler admits, continuing to ignore the marveling faces on his fellow detectives' faces, "I am a cop, too."

This fact does not seem to upset or unsettle Hitler, even when Kreisler shows his credentials. Rather, Hitler is delighted. "Put this man on the case," he orders. "He has a future with us."

"But…"

"He's a friend."

"I have even joined the party since we met. My number is 9677."

"Marvelous. You see, Schwarz. He's one of us."

Chapter Seven

Fritz Langer is furious. Franz Schwarz is furious. Kreisler's peers, Sauer and Forster, are amused. Hitler is relaxed and is now busy recounting his side of the story. He and Geli argued about Vienna. He left satisfied that she understood his position. More upset than he realized, she must have gone into his office to retrieve his Walther pistol. He can not imagine why she would take her own life, but now that it is done, he has a clear conscience.

"What are you up to, Kreisler?" Langer growls. He can do so now that they are back out on the sidewalk. "An architect? A medical student? Have you another degree you haven't told me about?"

Kreisler takes a picture of Langer cursing him. "Photography," he says. "Which may be the most important one of all."

"Well, you may joke now," Langer tells him. "Not so much when Hitler is told you are Jewish. And be sure, he will find out."

"By you?"

"Don't push me or I might."

Once back in his automobile, Langer can calm down. He wonders how such a smart detective like Kreisler can be so flagrantly stupid sometimes. There's a lot to admire about the novice homicide inspector. There's no doubt that, given the time and opportunity, he would crack the case. What Kreisler doesn't understand is that no one wants it cracked.

They drive by buildings from which Nazi flags and banners hang. Brown-shirts can be seen everywhere, Rohm's men, boastful in their SA uniforms. How many of them have committed murder? Even if they go to court, the courts treat them leniently. Poverty. Long memories of abuse at the hands of the Allies. Fear mongering. Germany is lurching toward oblivion or something far worse. People like Kreisler, Langer believes, will not be able to survive, no matter how smart they think they are.

"It isn't a suicide," Kreisler tells him matter-of-factly. "You do know that."

"It doesn't matter what I know."

"The gun had to be pointed down in order for the bullet to have entered above her heart and travel through her lung to her hip. You can't shoot yourself holding a gun like that. You'd point it right against your head or aim for your heart or stick it in your mouth to blow out your brains. If she had somehow managed to do that, she would have dropped the gun onto the floor. How did it end up on the sofa?"

"One of the help moved it."

"But didn't call for an ambulance. Then there's the letter."

Langer's head is pounding. What the hell has he gotten himself into, he wonders? Is this why he was promoted? To take the fall? He won't do it. "Do we know when the letter was written? Maybe she wasn't interrupted. There are no witnesses. No one was there when the gun went off. If there was a witness, they won't go to trial. They won't act for the prosecution. They'd be crazy. They'd be dead, and they know it."

"Then there are the cockamamie stories from the servants, each one contradicting the other. Who broke down the door to find Geli? Herr Winter? A locksmith? Frau Reichert says she's the one who notified Hess, whom we saw..."

"You saw."

"...outside the building. And *he's* the one who broke down the door."

Langer slows down his car as they approach Kreisler's flat. "You're missing the point, Avi."

"No, I'm not. I'm just telling you that, if we let this go, it'll be a grave injustice."

"Grave for you."

Langer parks, leans out his window as Kreisler departs the car and heads into his building carrying his backpack. "I'll support you as long as I can," he calls. "But that won't be forever. Just so you'll know."

Kreisler raises a hand in recognition of understanding. Oh, he understands, all right. Long before the police got to Prinzregentenplatz 16, Hitler's cronies did, cleaned up the scene, and provided a story for Hitler's help to digest and try to repeat. Any reasonable detective, looking at the evidence, would declare this a homicide, even if accidental. He knows full well that the National Socialists will actively undermine the investigation and that the Munich police will abide by their actions. But there's Geli to think about. And Klara. And David.

First, he thinks, build the case.

Climbing the stairs to his floor, Kreisler feels the fatigue of a long-distance runner beginning to accrue in his muscles. Despite all his bicycle riding, he is out of shape. But this will not be a physical race. It will be a spiritual one. Anton would understand. For him, the race against time began years ago in college. It is wearing him out, and he wants to be a priest. For Kreisler, the philosopher who prefers the heavenly view of the despicable earth but has chosen the cop view down in the dirt, the marathon is just underway.

At his door, he is surprised, first, to hear a tap-tap-tapping coming from his apartment, and, second, that someone has broken in and left the door wide open. He chooses not to grope his backpack for his Walther but flings the door inward, revealing Anni Leeuwenberg typing away, long legs curled up in a chair, cigarette smoke drifting from an ashtray at her side. She doesn't stop hammering on the ancient keys. Nor does she look up from her efforts.

"Spill," she says. "Tell me everything."

"Is Lotte here?" Kreisler is more anxious about a clash of the female type than he is of being ambushed by Brownshirts.

"Not when I got here. You don't mind my using your machine, do you? It could use a little grease."

Kreisler drops his backpack on the dinner table, loosens his shirt, then tiptoes toward his bedroom to make sure Lotte truly has left. "You know I can't talk to you about an ongoing investigation, Anni."

"I don't know that at all," Anni says, pausing to take a drag on her cigarette. "The Nazis have already hit the streets with the story that Hitler's niece committed suicide. Tell me otherwise."

"I wish I could."

"You can. He killed her, didn't he? You said he would."

"So, I'm the Prophet Isaiah, so what? Keep your distance on this one, Anni. Promise me."

"Anonymous is fine with me. But the truth must have a voice. Waldmann will want to shout this from the rooftops."

"Before he's thrown off. Like Klara Fries."

With a grunt of fatigue and skepticism, Kreisler takes a seat beside Anni, who proffers her cigarette. He enjoys a long drag.

"First, my dear," he says, "we were pulled off the case."

"What?"

"Fritz and me. Well, I was. Fritz is now the boss of the whole unit. Not that he's too upset about handing over the investigation to Sauer and Forster."

"The National Socialists want this wrapped up nice and sweet, don't they?"

"Of course." Kreisler hands back the cigarette. "If Stalin's daughter were found dead under suspicious circumstances in the Great Leader's bedroom, wouldn't you cover that up, too?"

Anni harrumphs, turning up her eyes to the ceiling, with a swish of her hair, a flirtatious move under other circumstances.

"I'm disappointed in you, Inspektor," she says. "You have no faith in me. My only obligation as a trained journalist is to set the people free, speak the truth from on high."

"As *Der Weg* sees it." Kreisler yawns, then is suddenly back on his feet, pacing under Anni's watchful, worried gaze. "But now I am back on the case. I have become Hitler's best friend."

"You're kidding, right? He fell for the architect line?"

Kreisler dismisses Anni's misgivings with a toss of his head. "I surprise even myself sometimes," he says. "Believe it or not, there was a moment when I almost felt sorry for the man. It was in his eyes. Like a child whose fondest dreams were crushed in childhood, suddenly finding someone who shares his sense of loss. Finally, he has a real friend. Everything that has happened since and that will happen going forward is a vindictive response against those he holds responsible for killing his dream, for denying his self-worth."

"Jews and Communists. Now you're just getting maudlin, Avi, *Herr Psychologie-Professorin*. This really matters to you," she says.

"Of course, it does. It's not just Geli Raubal. It's the others, too. Innocent victims of our German madness."

"Innocent." Anni gazes at the tip of her cigarette and at the smokescreen it creates between her and Avi. "In the future, everyone will say they are innocent. We won't need cops then, or courts. I don't want you to get hurt, you know. If you're going to pursue this, without Langer, you need to be careful, very careful."

Kreisler nods, smiles. "I know. Look who's giving me advice. The Leninist Joan of Arc."

"We can help you. Just tell me what you can. We'll be utterly discreet; only publish things we can corroborate. Your name will never appear. Poke the lion, Avi. See what he unleashes."

"A backlash. In-fighting *unter den Faschisten*. Dissolution."

"Self-destruction. The only good Fascist is a dead Fascist. Sound good?"

Kreisler shrugs, doubtful. He casts a look of wonder at Anni. Unlike himself, she is a true believer in something. It may not be the right thing, but she has thrown herself at the world like no one he has ever known.

"In which case, Don Quixote," he says, "it's you who need to be careful."

"Not careful, my love. Committed." Tamping out her cigarette, Anni leaves her typing and takes Kreisler's hand. "The bedroom," she says. "I feel a storm coming on."

* * *

A storm, indeed. Once aroused, Anni takes no prisoners. In bed, after exhaustion has forced her and Kreisler to lie together in deepest contemplation of what they have just undertaken, she tells him breathless, "I feel we have just forged an alliance."

"Typical Bolshevik," he says, no less worn out. "No love, just politics."

"No love? The great doctor of psychology has just made an incorrect diagnosis. A very wrong one." Laughing, tenderly, she rolls over against him, laying her head on his shoulder. "Bolsheviks do love," she says. "We just compartmentalize things."

"Good to know."

"But we have to be circumspect."

"Lotte will hate me if she finds out."

"Lotte already suspects. You can't be nice to everyone, Avi. The world doesn't work that way. What will you tell her?"

"That we've fallen head over heels after ten years of knocking heads? I don't know. Nothing right away."

"Coward."

"I can be. I have been."

"But not now. Not with Hitler."

Kreisler's mind becomes suddenly alert. "Aha. So, that's why you've suddenly left your senses and fallen in love. Because I'm going after your archenemy."

"Well, of course."

"Stalinist."

"Bourgeois romantic."

Kreisler turns to face her feet to feet, belly to belly, eye to eye, breath to breath. Absolutely reinvigorated. "I'm not afraid of Lotte. I'm afraid of hurting her. Hitler, not so much. And you, not at all."

Reaching between her legs, he places a hand on her bottom, scoops her up, and renews the battle. Gauntlet thrown, Anni accepts.

In sleep, after, Kreisler dreams of his mother, of all people, long dead, holding a wailing baby in her arms and running, fleeing something, perhaps, but running, on and on until she disappears over a hill covered in corpses. There is an iron gate at the top of the hill and a sign on the top of the gate. '*Arbeit macht frei*,' it says. The meaning eludes Kreisler. It won't forever.

* * *

He awakens with a start.

"I have to go," he says to Anni, who is half asleep.

"What?"

"I have to get up. It's Yom Kippur. Synagogue."

Tossing his sheet aside, he stands on wobbly legs. It's not just the exercise Anni has given him, but the disorientation of the dream and waking so abruptly.

"Avi, do you know what time it is?" she says, groggy.

"It's Saturday. There'll be an evening service."

"Really?"

Sitting up, Anni rubs her eyes and watches Kreisler get dressed in a hurry.

"You want me to come?" she asks.

"No. Stay. Better yet. Leave. In case Lotte…"

"I get it."

Anni isn't mad. Raising her knees, she rests her head on her hands, already planning her own Saturday. "You should meet with Waldmann," she says.

"Your publisher?" Avi pulls up his pants.

"He has contacts everywhere, so you don't have to worry about your pals on the force blaming you for leaking information about the investigation. But he'll want as much detail as you can give him. Embarrass Hitler, that's the point."

"I want to get all the photos I took processed, too, as soon as possible," Kreisler says, now tying his shoelaces. "And re-interview all of Hitler's staff. And follow up on Klara's and Geli's autopsies."

"That's a lot."

"That's the life of a cop, my dear."

"A good cop."

"One can only hope so."

With a kiss on the cheek, Kreisler leaves Anni in bed, grabs his bicycle from the hallway, and takes to the street for the Great Synagogue and Yom Kippur services.

Built in 1887, the Jewish house of worship, as far as Kreisler is concerned, is an architectural marvel even Hitler might appreciate. It could fill the entire

Jewish population of Munich. Kreisler would have been bar-mitzvahed here had his parents survived long enough to see him into adulthood. Their names are etched into a wall of small bronze rectangles, dates of birth and death. He pauses to read and try to remember what each of his parents looked like, sounded like. But it's been such a long time.

The *ma-arive* evening service has already begun when Kreisler arrives and sneaks in so as not to disturb the ongoing Amidah, the silent standing prayer. Taking his place in the back row, he opens a prayer book whose Hebrew writing he can't read. Halfway through, the man standing next to him elbows him.

"You're on the wrong page, Avi."

"Dov! I didn't even see you."

"Shhh. Some detective. I'm literally standing on your shoes."

Birnbaum, the synagogue custodian, returns to his silent reading. While everyone else is beseeching God to be good to them, Kreisler studies the large columned chapel. Any rabbi or cantor with a booming voice standing on the podium in front could probably be heard across the avenue or in the neighboring Catholic church. What Brownshirt or SS thug couldn't help but notice the odd Hebrew sounds emanating from the building? To them, it must sound like an alarum that the enemy has breached the gates, has entered the city, and is bent on conquest. A House of God to the Jews at worship is a magnet of evil to everyone else in the city.

Kreisler participates in the closing service of the holiday as an outsider. He is as Jewish as anyone in the hall, shares the same history, the same blood, but he feels every bit the stranger. What would these people think, he wonders, if they realized that this man raised by Jewish converts might be the golem that saves them?

After service, Birnbaum, who is accompanied by his wife and three small children, takes him by the arm. "You asked me about the Sussman family," he says. "Let me introduce you. They're here somewhere."

The death of Geli Raubal might have percolated onto the Munich streets by the National Socialist press, but the members of this congregation are unlikely to know about it. Birnbaum greets everyone as he escorts Kreisler through the crowd. He is the type of man who is greeted back with smiles and 'Good Yuntifs'.

"Hey! Mandel!" he calls when at last he sees the man he is looking for. "Over here! Spare us five minutes before you dash off to your palace."

Birnbaum shoves Kreisler forward like a father trying to foist his son off on an unsuspecting girl.

"Herr Sussman." Kreisler extends his hand in greeting to the man who has probably just buried his own child. "I'm sorry about your son, David. I'm the detective assigned to his case."

"Terrible things. Terrible things we see, we hear, every day." David's father is about the age Kreisler's father would be had he survived the Great War. His wife, at the mention of her son's name, breaks down in tears. "You, a detective, the things you must see. A Jew no less. How do you do it?"

"A lot of focus and an occasional beer."

Frau Sussman's sobbing draws the attention of everyone around them, so her husband, with Birnbaum, pulls Kreisler aside.

"Birnbaum tells me you want information about the girl, the one who fell out her window, David's friend."

"If you have anything relevant that might help in the investigation, yes. Whoever killed Klara Fries may have been involved in your son's drowning."

Herr Sussman leans in, whispers, as if the world could hear what he is imparting. "I knew the girl," he says. *"Ich bin Apotheker.* My family has owned the pharmacy for over a hundred years. I just put in an ice cream bar, like you see in the United States. All the children come in. She would come in, this Klara. Not the best of friends, if you ask me. But that was the life my David chose. The theater, you know. Those kinds of people."

"Non-Jews."

"Oh, no," Sussman insists. "We go to the Yiddish theater almost every week. I mean, the ones who come into my pharmacy and ask if I sell any cocaine, anything they can get high on, so they can sell themselves on the street. You know the kinds I mean. Me? Cocaine? What sort of business do they think I run? I'll tell you what kind. The kind run by Jews. At least, that's what the goyim think."

Kreisler shakes his head in phony sympathy. "What kind exactly was Klara?"

Sussman looks around to make sure no one is listening in. "She would come in every week for antiemetics, anti-nausea medication. She was pregnant. Unmarried and pregnant."

This bit of news, at last, gets Kreisler's attention. "You know this for certain?" Dr. Müller did not mention this at the autopsy.

"She discussed what someone might take if they wanted to terminate a pregnancy. I told her I believe in life, not death. She said she could always go to Semmering, in Austria. There, she said, you can find doctors who will perform abortions for a few pfennigs. Imagine."

Semmering. Kreisler visualizes the letter Geli was writing to a girlfriend about going to Semmering. Had she argued with Hitler about this? Had he refused her Vienna because she was pregnant by another man? Or could the child possibly have been his, and he refused to allow her to get an abortion? The king wants a son. Either was a motive for murder in the first degree.

"The father," Kreisler asks. "Did she ever tell you who the father might be?"

"No. David sometimes picked up the medication for her. She might have told him."

A dead end. Literally. Unfortunately. But Kreisler isn't fazed. "Anyone else? Any other friends David had who might also have been friends with Klara?" He would have to seek out the other local pharmacies to see if she got what she wanted elsewhere.

David's father pauses in thought. The crowd of service goers is thinning out. The great hall has become an echo chamber, but not so much that Kreisler can't hear what Sussman now whispers to him.

"The Schutzstaffel. She knew some of them. Go to the shop of Hoffman, the photographer. They'll know."

Chapter Eight

Anton Maier is more serious about taking his orders and becoming a priest than any of his friends realize. They kid him about it, but just this very morning, he dug into the attic of his parents' home looking for his old college Latin grammar book. Unlucky in his search, he knows where he can go to further his religious education. Lotte Leinsdorf's family owns a bookstore, the largest one in Munich. Lotte has taken over managing the business from her elderly parents and modernized it with Weimar sensibilities. She serves pastries and coffee or tea to her customers and hosts risqué poets and controversial authors to do readings of their latest works.

Lotte will also be sympathetic to his crisis of conscience. She is delighted to see him when he enters her store and immediately guesses what he wants.

"We have a section dedicated to Catholic authors, the Catholic church, religion in general. You're really giving up writing plays?"

"They're going nowhere. My cat uses my scripts to shit on when the litter box is full."

"Clean the litter box."

Anton chuckles. "See. That's what I mean. Even your jokes are better than mine."

"I wasn't joking."

After a half hour of browsing, Anton has pulled four books off the shelves to purchase. Lotte sets him up at a table by the window and gives him a free pastry and a cup of black coffee. Private school teachers in Germany are not paid well. She pours herself a cup of tea and nibbles on a vanilla biscuit, gazing out the window as she eats, and Anton relaxes.

"Avi's really into this case, isn't he? This Klara Fries," Anton says.

"Avi loves his work."

"He pokes fun at me."

"No, he doesn't. If you decide to enter the Church, he'll support you one hundred percent. It's just his way sometimes to be flippant."

Anton sighs, flips through the opening pages of a Latin grammar text. From outside, he can hear a clamor, like the approaching grumble of a thunderstorm. He disregards the noise, then, abruptly pushing aside his plate, leans forward to speak more intimately with Lotte.

"You're in love with him?"

"Yes."

"He, you?"

"One can never be sure with Avi. With men in general, I would say."

"Marriage?"

"We'll see."

Anton reaches a hand across the table to clasp Lotte's. "I hope it works out for the both of you. Can I entrust you with something?"

Lotte pauses mid-sip. The noise from the street is growing, but the fretful look on Anton's face commits her to concentrate on him. "Of course," she says. "What is it?"

Anton says, "I knew Klara Fries. I know why she was killed."

This was not at all what Lotte expected to be told. "You knew her?" She lowers her cup to the table. "How?"

"Since she was a child, the daughter of a neighbor. She was always a wild one. They were poor," Anton explains. "Who wasn't in those days? Her father was injured in the war; lost a leg. She always dreamed of being rich, of helping her family. It's been a strength of hers. And a weakness."

"How so?"

Lotte leans in, as well. She loves to read; will spend the day in her store doing her own browsing. Listening to Anton now is like opening the cover of an intriguing mystery. What will she tell Avi? Should she tell him anything? He'll want to know, and she'll likely want to tell him. Juice for their sputtering relationship.

"She'd do anything for money," Anton says.

"Many women will."

"She never showed me the letter. Klara is very artistic. She loves to draw. She can play the piano, sing. She has performed at the lesbian cabaret, you know, *Die Katze Katze*. Such a voice when she wants to belt out a tune."

"Yes, yes," Lotte says, "but what about the letter? What letter are you talking about?"

"The one Avi found. The one written by Hitler to Geli Raubal."

'He hasn't told *me* about the letter,' Lotte thinks. 'I wonder if he's told Anni.'

"Geli attended the cabarets, got to know Klara. Klara would play the piano, and Geli would sing. Hitler himself heard her play. Not at the *Katze Katze*, I'm sure."

"Hitler," Lotte says, lifting her cup for another sip. The noise on the street is growing, but she is too fascinated by Anton's story to give it any reflection.

"I thought *my* plays were decadent," Anton says, recalling the meat of the letter. "Klara likes, liked, the more provocative. It didn't bother her. She saw the potential for profit in it. It's like she had a devil on one shoulder and an angel on the other competing for her soul. She confided in me because I am like an older brother. She wanted to know what she should do with it."

"The letter."

"Yes. Filthy. That Hitler belongs in a zoo with the apes. And he calls himself a Christian."

"Many people do," Lotte says. "But what of the letter?"

"She wanted to know if she should, what is the word, blackmail Hitler. Blackmail Hitler! Do you hear me? She was asking if she thought she should blackmail Adolf Hitler!"

"And you said?"

"No! Of course, that's what I said. But did she listen to me? No. That's why she ended up tossed like garbage onto the street. My fault. I should have told someone what she was planning."

Lotte sits back in her wicker chair, shocked and titillated at the same moment. But she isn't about to interrupt the salacious narrative.

"What's more," Anton says, "she was pregnant."

"You know all this and said nothing to Avi? This is a criminal matter, Anton. If you feel so much guilt, why didn't you speak of this earlier? You couldn't have saved her, no matter what. She was bent on making money."

"Yes, money. That was her reasoning. Not for her family. For the baby. She was going to keep it, I'm certain." Anton throws back his head and groans. "She was treating this like she was in confession and I her confessor, don't you see? How could I tell Avi something I was told in absolute sacramental secrecy?"

"Because you're not yet a priest, that's how." Lotte looks up and through her window past the black lettering that reads *Leinsdorf Buchhandlung*. The first inkling that something isn't right out on the street is the cacophony of car horns that is an irritant to anyone trying to read. Several of her customers have already left the store to see what is happening.

Lotte says, "Did she tell you who the father is?"

"The father?"

"Yes. Don't be dense, Anton. A priest you may be, but even they know where babies come from. The father of the child might be her killer. Did you think of that? You have to tell Avi."

To be honest, he hadn't thought of that. But it was true. The likelihood that Klara's killer was the father of her unborn child was great. Unfortunately, she never told him who it was.

"All I know is…" he begins. Then a fire truck rolls by, clanging its horn, followed by a second truck whizzing past the bookstore, demanding a clear path. "All I know…"

"What is going on?"

Lotte abandons her seat to rush onto the sidewalk. From here, she can smell the smoke, even see plumes of it billowing above the buildings, a left-hand turn down the neighboring street. The curious are heading in the same direction, and Lotte, with Anton at her side, follows.

The crowd is halted at the next corner by police. Lotte is unable to make her way through to the front. Instead, she turns to a boy holding fliers that, despite the fire, he is passing around to members of the mob.

"Do you know what's going on?" she asks him.

"The pharmacy is on fire. The whole building is going up. Here. Take this."

Unlike the adults in the crowd, the boy is more intent on finishing the job he has been paid to do. Lotte gives the flier a quick glance. It is a National Socialist publication, a headline without a newspaper notifying the public of the suicide of Angela Raubal, the niece of Adolf Hitler. 'Herr Hitler,' the flyer states, 'will make a statement in the coming days. For now, he is too overwhelmed by the unexpected death of his beloved sister's daughter to comment.'

With a grunt, Lotte folds the paper but doesn't throw it away. She hands it to Anton, who takes one look at it and nudges her.

"Over there," he says, pointing to a man in a uniform with a red Nazi armband and the insignia of an officer of the Schutzstaffel. "One of them."

"Started the fire?"

"Is the father."

* * *

Kreisler is unaware of the fire, hears of it only later that night, back in his apartment, when his landlord comes rapping on his door.

"Kreisler! Avi! Wake up!"

The Munich police detective has never been a heavy sleeper. Lotte compares him to her cat, who will jump at the sound of a hair hitting the floor. Kreisler, the amateur psychologist, attributes this condition to being raised by parents who fought incessantly, usually at night. Fatigue set him to rest earlier than usual tonight while poring over his evidence file. He climbed into bed, alone, and fell asleep instantly. Though it only takes him two minutes to rise from sleep and open his door to Herr Greene, his landlord, Greene is reasonably annoyed that he has had to rouse himself at ten in the evening.

"When are you going to get a telephone, for God's sake?" Greene, dressed in pajamas, shouts at him. "What am I, your messenger service? Do I look like a concierge in one of those fancy hotels? You're a cop, for Christ's sake. You need a phone."

"For God's sake or for Christ's, Herr Greene?" Kreisler yawns, rubs his eyes. He is naked.

"What is this: a debate? Put on some clothes. Birnbaum's on my phone, invoking something only an Orthodox Jew can understand, which I, as you know, am not."

Intrigued, Kreisler throws on a shirt and pants and joins Greene in the landlord's apartment, where, once on the phone, Birnbaum is quick to the point.

"Did you hear?" the synagogue custodian yells into the phone.

"Hear what, Dov? Can you lower your voice? Herr Greene's walls are rattling."

"Mandel's pharmacy burned to the ground while we were at temple. A total loss. Another Jewish business destroyed by those fascists."

"Are you certain?" Kreisler is fully awake now. He knows how rumors spread. Nothing will be certain until he checks out the fire himself. "Have you seen it?"

"I talked to Sussman myself. Can you imagine? We just saw him today. On Yom Kippur. How's that for hubris?"

The SS. The SA. Nothing is hubris to them. "Thanks for alerting me, Dov," he says, "I'll look into it. How did you know to call Herr Greene?"

"I didn't. I thought that was your phone number. Maybe you should stop giving it out."

Kreisler hangs up, thinking the setting of the fire may have been more than hubris. Retaliation against a Jewish businessman wasn't unheard of. What about a Jewish businessman whose business may have contained records of interest in a police investigation? Klara Fries might have had prescription records at the pharmacy detailing who prescribed the medications she was taking. Perhaps there would have been records of anyone picking up and signing for her medications. An accident? Coincidence? Kreisler doesn't think so.

Tired as he is, wanting to get a full night of comfortable sleep, Kreisler thrusts his arms through the sleeves of a warm jacket and heads out into the night for the address of the pharmacy given him by Birnbaum. He rides his bicycle, as it turns out, past the Leinsdorf Book Store, where Lotte calls out his name from the sidewalk where she has parked her car.

"Avi!" Why does she think, as he almost rides past her, that he would have come to an abrupt jarring halt if Anni had called his name?

"Lotte, what are you doing out here?" he asks. "Why aren't you in bed?" Hopping off his bike, he gives her a quick kiss.

She is tempted to say, 'I would be if you would have me.' Instead, she tells him, "There was a bad fire." She's holding a broom and has been sweeping off the sidewalk. "The street was a mess. Rowdies came by. You know. Schutzstaffel. They don't care what they do. If they even think you're Jewish..."

"I'm sorry," Kreisler says.

What started with a fire in one building became an excuse to cause destruction and disruption in other local shops. Something had been thrown through the bookstore window. It is the shattered glass that Lotte is sweeping up and brushing into the street. Kreisler can't tell if the same ruffians got into the store itself. So, he gives Lotte a longer tender hug that she accepts as an apology for his not kissing her more deeply.

"I was just going to look at the pharmacy. Dov Birnbaum told me what happened. Do you want me to help here first? Have you had dinner?"

"This late? Is anything open?"

"I'm sure we can find something. I'm just worried that the fire wasn't an accident," he says. "I met the pharmacist. One of his customers was Klara Fries."

"I know, I know," Lotte says. She's excited because she has some of her own news to report. Laying her broom aside, she takes his arm and gazes into his eyes to capture his response. "Anton spoke with me this afternoon, just before the fire. He bought some books about joining the priesthood."

"He's not seriously thinking about doing that, is he?"

"I'm afraid so. But that's not everything we talked about." She lowers her voice, a conspirator with something to confess. "Anton was afraid to tell you, but I told him he must. He knew Klara Fries."

"He did? And didn't tell me?"

"Don't be mad at him. They've known each other since she was a child. He was taking her confession. At least, that's how he sees it."

"A confession." Kreisler rolls his eyes. His aunt and uncle made him say Confession once after they took him in. He admitted to the priest he liked to masturbate. The priest reciprocated. Kreisler squawked, and that was the end of that to everyone's eternal embarrassment.

"She was pregnant, Anton said. He thinks by a member of the SS. He doesn't think she was going to get an abortion."

"She was," Kreisler is convinced. "She and Geli both. In Austria. At Semmerling. An autopsy will prove the pregnancy. Unfortunately, it can't pin down parentage."

"She was blackmailing Hitler."

"Yes, I know."

"He tried to talk her out of it."

"Unfortunately for her, he failed."

Kreisler gets on his bike, pats the back. "You want to come?"

"My car is parked right here," she tells him. The rowdy mob didn't damage the Duesenberg. "Then I'll treat you to dinner. A nightcap?"

Kreisler warms up to that and gives Lotte a more respectable kiss. She is happy now, at least for the time being. Before he loses his nerve. Before he becomes the destroyer.

After taking his bicycle inside the bookstore, Lotte locks up, and together they relocate to the burned-out remains of a five-story building, the bottom of which was the pharmacy, the top being the Sussman home.

"A complete ruin," Lotte says as she exits her car.

The building is built of stone, but the insides have been blackened by the flames. The locals aren't as neat as Lotte, so the sidewalk remains caked in debris. Kreisler, the detective, isn't quite as ready to give up hope that nothing can be salvaged. Stepping around pieces of the wall that have been sheared off, he peers into the charcoal darkness of the pharmacy. He has brought along a small flashlight that he uses as he takes his first tentative step inside.

"God, Avi, you think of everything."

"I try. You wait outside."

"No," she insists. "I'm coming with."

At the entry, Kreisler shines the beam into the interior. The fire and the water used to kill it have brought down the ceiling tiles. The product shelves have been toppled, littering the floor with the remnants of over-the-counter medication, ladies' aesthetics, Jewish high holiday products. To step inside is to crunch on broken glass, blackened and broken pieces of timber, nails, predatory hazards of all sorts lurking in the dark.

"You sure you want to do this?" Kreisler asks.

"I want to be part of your investigation," Lotte says, heart betraying her excitement. Clinging to his arm, she is ready to take the lead. "Go on. Go on. This is like being in a film."

"Let's just hope the whole building doesn't come down on our heads. I'm surprised the place hasn't been padlocked. Why isn't there a guard posted out front? There has to be an arson investigation."

"Or not."

"Yuh, well…"

Kreisler moves slowly through the ruins. His goal is the far back, where the pharmacist, Mandel Sussman, would have dispensed his prescription meds and kept his vital records.

"I still smell gas," he says.

"Gas?"

"They weren't too careful, were they? Toss the accelerant anywhere, everywhere, and who cares who finds out? The shop's owned by a Jew. No one will prosecute."

Kreisler maneuvers around a melted metal display case, though not far enough to prevent Lotte from cutting an arm on a sharp protrusion.

"Ouch!"

"You get stuck?"

"Bleeding," she says, gazing at a trickle of blood staining her sleeve.

"You want to turn back?"

"Hell, no. *Wohin du auch gehst, ich gehe.* Wherever you go, I go."

Lotte pleads her determination well. Determination to follow. Determination to be loved. He isn't completely oblivious. Despite the perilous situation Kreisler has brought her into, or perhaps because of it, he allows an intrusive moment of shame to seep in. Perhaps they should turn back. He can return in the morning, if the authorities in charge will even let him in. Perhaps he should just level with Lotte right now, out on the sidewalk, and be done with his duplicity. He loves Anni. The pretense otherwise is a sin. He knows it. He agrees with Anni's assessment that he is a coward not to be honest with Lotte. And yet, here in the dark, among the ruins of a good man's business, brought about by the hatred of his neighbors, Kreisler can't help but feel love for Lotte, too.

'Scylla and Charybdis of a different sort altogether,' he thinks, then points the beam of the flashlight to his left at the far rear of the first floor.

"Over there," he says.

"What?"

"Cabinets. What's left of them. Wood and glass," he says. "Not much left."

Still, he drags Lotte along behind the counter where the cash register was situated. He wonders if the arsonists opened the register and stole the money before they torched the shop. Probably. The Brownshirts like to fundraise this way. It is a disheartening sight.

"Try over here," he says.

"Is one place any better than any other?"

Kreisler looks back toward the entrance. He thinks he has heard something move. Rats maybe, or an unsteady beam ready to fall and take the whole building down with it.

"I'm thinking," he says, refocusing the light on the damaged cabinets, "that the letter 'F' for Klara Fries would be in this general area."

"You want us to carry it out to my car?" Lotte is only being realistic. The cabinets, all of them, are too damaged, too heavy. "I don't see how you can even open them. Whatever's inside is probably ruined."

Much as he doesn't want to agree, he tries pulling on the one cabinet that seems redeemable only to wrench off the handle, leaving the drawer hopelessly shut.

"I could probably hammer it open."

"To take back in your apartment? How do we get it there? It won't fit in my car."

Frustrated, Kreisler tries one final option. He ignores sounds coming from the street. It is late, but this is Munich, and the city thrives on nighttime traffic of all kinds. Turning around, he crouches behind the ruined cash register. The items beneath were somehow protected from both the flames and the water hoses. Among them are thick books for maintaining the records of customers and what they purchased. Kreisler lifts one onto the filthy counter and opens it, shining his light on the pages.

"What is it?" Lotte asks.

"Sussman is a stickler for business," he tells her. "A who, what, why, and when of everyone who came into his shop. He said his family has owned this place for decades. There are so many books down here, he could open up his own museum."

Kreisler checks the dates. The first book he salvages from beneath the counter begins before the Great War started in the summer of 1914. Maybe if he researches long enough, Kreisler will find the names of his own mother and father, grandmother and grandfather, great-grandparents, part of a long line of Jewish customers the Sussman family served over the years. The sheer bulk of the dozens of books is probably what saved them from complete destruction.

He retrieves another and opens it on the counter, coughing up dust, as he flips open the front cover.

"Aha!" One page in, he blurts in relief, finding validation for his efforts. "January 1930 to September 19, 1931."

"Today!"

"On the hour." With renewed excitement, he skips through the pages until he finds the name he wants. Klara Fries. September 10, the day she died. "I don't know if this will tell us anything," he says, "but I don't think Sussman will mind my confiscating it." With a satisfied thud, he closes the book, hands the flashlight to Lotte, and hefts the heavy tome under his right arm. They don't make it past the counter when another flashlight beam strikes him square in the chest.

"Who are you? What are you doing here?"

Three tall human shapes form a barrier between Kreisler, Lotte, and the sidewalk. "Police," Kreisler says. "Who are *you*?" Gripping the book against his body, he takes the flashlight from Lotte and shines it into the face of the man closest to them. His pistol would have been more convincing. He can tell that the three men are armed.

"Neighborhood watch," the first and biggest of the three men says. "You cops should be out here."

"We are. I'm here."

Kreisler moves forward cautiously, keeping in front of Lotte in case the men decide to attack.

"You got proof you're a cop?" the lead shape asks.

"You got proof you're neighborhood watch?"

Boldness is the thing. Show no fear, no self-doubt. Up front and close, Kreisler recognizes the big man in the front. "You're SA," he says. "I saw you at the Bratwurstglöckl with Herr Hitler."

This causes the big man to pause and peer into Kreisler's face. "Oh, it's you," he says. "You get around. I didn't know you were a cop."

"Sometimes it's best to be judicious."

"You lied to him."

"Did I? I don't remember."

It's time to move on, Kreisler decides. This conversation is not going in a positive direction. He tries to step around, but the big man moves to block his path. He is wielding a club which he is knocking against his leg, anxious, no doubt, to put it to good use.

"You're not a fireman as well as an architect, are you?" he asks. "What's your interest in this fire? It's a Jewish pharmacy. *Bist du Jude*?"

"*Ich bin Deutscher.*"

Eyeball to eyeball now, Kreisler dares the SA man to start something. Then he remembers Lotte huddled against him. He can feel her shaking. "Come on, Lotte," he says and moves past the big man.

"You're looting," the man says.

"You put a hole through the window of this woman's bookstore." Anger suddenly reaches the surface, breaking through whatever fear or uncertainty Kreisler is feeling. It causes him to whirl around and defy Hitler's personal bodyguard. "*She* is not a Jew. I'll expect reparations. We'll be sure to send the bill to Herr Hitler in the morning. For this building, too."

Shaking himself now with rage, Kreisler somehow manages to direct Lotte outside without incurring any further bodily damage. At the car, he lets out a breath of relief. The Schutzstaffel or Brownshirts, whichever they were, could just as easily have ignored his official duty and beaten him and Lotte to death, and no one would have cared. The fire did it. As he slides into the Duesenberg, an equally upset Lotte, getting behind the wheel, he sees the three Storm Troopers stare them down. He'll see them again. Munich will insist upon it. One way or another.

Chapter Nine

They drive in silence, Lotte, every so often, turning her gaze from the roadway to the man sitting in the passenger seat, gripping the pharmaceutical log book in his lap.

She is uncertain what their destination is. Once they return to her bookstore, he will retrieve his bicycle. Then what? Should she drive home to her room in the Leinsdorf mansion, where her parents still live? Or should she follow him to his place to resume… what?

"What do you hope to find in the book?" she asks him as she parks outside her shop.

"I don't know," he says. "In a case like this, you're an archaeologist digging through the dirt, excited when you find the littlest thing which could reveal something much larger."

Her next question is asked in a subdued voice. "Can I help?"

His response is swift. "It's late. You've been working hard on your store thanks to those damned Brownshirts. You don't want to sleep?"

"Not yet. I feel my blood pounding through me. I've never been so scared. Those men. Threatening us like that. You were so brave standing up to them. Send Hitler the bill?"

Her merry giggle brings a smile to Kreisler's face. "Don't hold off paying your other bills," he says. "If you want to come up…"

He regrets the gesture the instant he makes it. The happiness he sees on her face at that moment, though, is undeniable. How can he reject her so brutally?

"I'd like to," she says. "You're tired, I know. Maybe just for a while? To see what clues the book holds?"

What can he say? "Just don't get too excited, Sherlock. There might be nothing."

If love can be etched into the contours of a woman's face, it is there in spades for Kreisler to see. He knows the book is only part of the reason Lotte wants to come up to his room. Sex is not the issue. She wants to share his love of the mystery, help him solve it, battle the villains, prove her worth. Even if he struggles with expressing his own emotions to her, she will have some piece of him in her heart.

Once in his apartment, he is quick to turn on the lights and open the book. He doesn't even take the time to undress or wash. Lotte does, begging him to hold off until she can clean herself of the charcoal filth and see to her wound. The book is an historian's treasure even if it uncovers nothing to do with Klara Fries's death. Kreisler wishes he could go back to the burned-out pharmacy and scoop up the entire trove traveling far back into the nineteenth century. The names he will find. The stories they will tell. The signatures of people long dead, who, when they wrote their names, were as alive as he is today.

Lotte, in the bathroom, finds a washcloth, wets it in warm water, and begins to wipe her cheeks of grime and cleanse her wound. Under the sink is a cabinet. It is there that she finds the lipstick that is not her color, hidden behind a box of silver IUDs that do not belong to her. This would be catastrophic if Lotte didn't know how to compose herself. This she does with exceeding difficulty, hands braced on the porcelain sink, over several perilous minutes, as she gathers her poise and wipes off the tears that threaten to undo her.

Back in the front room, Kreisler is waiting patiently for her return before diving into the pharmaceutical log. When he looks up, she is smiling.

"You know," she says, "I *am* tired. You were right. I should probably get going. I'll need to get to the book shop first thing. You can tell me what you find."

Puzzled, relieved, Kreisler rises. "You're sure? This can wait."

"No, it can't." Lotte heads for the door, turning her face away. "This is important to you. I'll just be in the way."

Still, Kreisler escorts her downstairs to her automobile. At the door, he kisses her. She smiles at him, but says, "Damn it, Avi, you're going to have to choose one day. You can't keep putting me off like this." Though she knows full well he has already made that choice.

He has no response for her, can only curse himself for his behavior as she drives away.

"Good job," Herr Greene says, peering from his doorway. "Some ladies' man. When are you going to put in your own phone?"

"When the ladies stop calling."

Upstairs again, however, he can regroup by studying Sussman's ledger. There is no sign of Klara Fries until June 1931, when, abruptly, her signature begins to appear on a weekly basis. She is purchasing, as he already knew, anti-nausea medication to treat the symptoms of her pregnancy. What is most interesting is a note, probably in Sussman's hand, beneath Klara's first purchase. He states that the customer, Fries, has been patronizing another pharmacy and doesn't want them to know she has switched over.

'She's hiding the pregnancy from the father,' Kreisler thinks. *'Only he found out.'*

Kreisler scribbles the name of the other pharmacy in his notepad. The first stop he will make tomorrow is the morgue to confront Dr. Müller. Then he must reach out to Klara's family, wherever they are. Then the second pharmacy. A busy day lies ahead, requiring sleep tonight. But that won't be the easiest thing to accomplish. Lotte is gone but not departed. He lies awake pondering the complexities of life before drifting into a dreadful dream of the dead walking the streets of Munich, heading into the rising sun in the direction of a place called Dachau.

The next morning, September twenty, is a Sunday. While it is a day of rest for the working man, it is a day for Kreisler to ride his bicycle around the city. At the morgue, he isn't completely surprised to learn that Dr. Muller is off, but one of his associates has a stunning revelation for Kreisler.

"Angela Raubal's body has been released for burial."

"Are you serious? Was an autopsy even performed?" Kreisler has pinned the unfortunate student against the cold wall of the basement. All the novice pathologist can do is hand over his clipboard.

"She was released to her mother," Kreisler reads.

"I assume so. I wasn't there."

"And there was no autopsy?"

"None that I am aware of. Why for a suicide? I heard that she is to be taken by train to Vienna for burial."

"Vienna?"

"Yes, sir."

"But not for singing lessons anymore."

Kreisler thrusts the clipboard back into the hands of Müller's fall guy. "What about Klara Fries?" he asks. "Has her body been claimed by anyone?"

The doctor checks his list and shakes his head. "No," he says. "She's still here. They have another week. If no one claims her, she'll be cremated."

"I'll claim her," Kreisler abruptly growls, startling himself as much as the pathologist. "What do I need to sign?"

"What are *you* going to do with it?"

"Give her a decent burial."

Actually, he hasn't a clue what he is going to do with Klara's remains. A cremation would be the simplest solution. But he feels she deserves something more respectful than to be burned like Sussman's pharmacy. Whoever killed her needs to know that death is not final, at least not in her case. It is still Yom Kippur. Someone needs to atone for their crime.

"I'll be back within a week," he says. "Tell Müller I'm displeased."

Now what? Back on his bicycle, he pedals to Prinzregentenplatz 16 in the hopes of speaking to Geli's mother, Hitler's half-sister. But the entry into the building is swarming with SS and SA, each in their own distinctive uniforms, competitors for power. Even short, stocky Ernst Röhm, the head of the SA, is outside policing the block, making sure no one gets in or out of Hitler's residence. The Nationalist newspapers are out on the street proclaiming suicide and Hitler's sorrow. The lie is taking shape. The killer is being protected.

Not if Kreisler can help it. A large lie has many holes in it. As Kreisler bikes away, looking for a rear entrance into the building, he spies two familiar faces hurrying along the sidewalk away from the building, eyes down, hoping, it seems to Kreisler, to get away without being spotted. Kreisler's not one to let the slightest opportunity escape.

"Frau Winter!" he calls, giving one of Hitler's household staff the shock of a lifetime. Tripping, she has to grab onto her younger female companion to keep her footing.

"This is Sunday, Inspektor," the companion says. "Should you be here?"

"If criminals don't rest, why should I?" Kreisler smiles, tips his hat, and indicates the bench his bicycle is leaning on. "I'm sorry if I startled you. I have some follow-up questions, and I noticed the front door was blocked, so I decided to look for another way in."

"To sneak in," snarls Frau Winter. She has regained her composure and her heavy handbag. "People say you don't think Fraulein Geli committed suicide. You think she was killed. By whom, for God's sake? By one of us?"

"Absolutely not," Kreisler insists. The ease has never left his face. He remains polite. He can't afford to alienate these women. "The rumor of my opinion is just that. A rumor. But it is my duty, my professional obligation, to pursue the matter to its correct conclusion. Herr Hitler himself has instructed me in this."

"Well, we all only want to help," the second woman says. Kreisler remembers her as the maid, Anna Kirmair. He notes the frown Frau Winter tosses her way.

"I was just at the morgue," Kreisler says, "and was told that Fraulein Geli's remains have been released for burial. In Vienna, if I have been informed correctly."

"You have," says Frau Winter, wintery. "Frau Raubal and Fraulein Raubal's sister have come up from Obersalzberg to accompany her by train."

"Which is confusing for me, because suicides cannot be buried in a Catholic cemetery, also if I am informed correctly."

This fact, which both women should have been familiar with, seems to catch them by surprise. Neither has an explanation for the detective. It is a vulnerable moment to be exploited.

"The fact that an autopsy was not performed, even under the circumstances, is problematic. It suggests a cover-up of some kind, not that I am accusing or blaming anyone. Perhaps, rather than a suicide, it was an accident. A struggle over a gun leads to a finger triggering an unexpected shot. Did either of you know that Fraulein Raubal was pregnant?" he asks.

No. Obviously. At least, that is what Kreisler infers from their stunned expressions.

"I know how sensitive a matter this is, especially among you women, but is it possible that Fraulein Geli confided in either of you? You needn't fear any repercussions if so. What you tell me will be kept in complete confidence. But it may go to the issue of motive. You see?"

Neither of the women speak for a good minute. Kreisler is patient, studying any change in expression. When it is clear neither will offer him an answer, he leans in for the kill.

"The shot that was fired, from Herr Hitler's Walther, was shot at an angle pointing downward. It could not have been fired by Fraulein Raubal attempting suicide. No," Kreisler says, with an innocent shake of his head. "One look at her body at the crime scene will tell any experienced detective that someone else fired the mortal bullet. Her nose was shattered, as well, indicating the possibility that she was in a fight for the gun, a battle, perhaps, for her very life. Which, regrettably, she lost."

Here, Kreisler pauses to let the two women, whom he guesses had some loyalty to the deceased girl, imagine the scene. Unless they were more loyal to the girl's uncle. He waits. Still no response. Just nervous swallowing and shifting of feet. So, he pushes on.

"I want to know who the father is. This might give us a clue to the true culprit. A man who would want her to keep the child, perhaps, who would not want her to travel to Vienna to see someone who might perform a terminating operation. Or someone who didn't want her to keep the baby, embarrassed by what the Leftist press might say. Or someone angry that the child was fathered at all. Not only that, but by someone else, God only knows who that person would be. A singer? An artist? All are motives to end the pregnancy in a way, if we can be more optimistic, that was unintended.

An accident. Yes? One could excuse such a thing, couldn't one? In a court of law? But still, wouldn't we want the truth to come out? For Fraulein Raubal's sake, if for no other reason, so she can truly be buried without hypocrisy in consecrated ground?"

Still, neither woman seems willing to give up what surely they know. But he can see, particularly in the countenance of the younger woman, the maid, that she is losing ground to her conscience.

Kreisler pounces. "Herr Hitler? They're seen together often. The theater. Restaurants. Or someone else? One of the SA, perhaps. Fraulein Raubal was a young woman. Was she a saint? Apparently, not. After all, Herr Hitler is her uncle."

Frau Winter is the first to react. With a curse representative of a trench soldier, she rears back and slaps Kreisler across the face as hard as she can. The strike knocks the hat off Kreisler's head, but he doesn't bend to pick it up. She spins on her heels and tromps away. The maid doesn't immediately follow.

"Frau Kirmair?" Kreisler says as if he has merely been offended by the soft autumn wind.

"Anna, *komm her!*"

The maid is torn between obedience and justice, turns, but stops all of a sudden and whispers to Kreisler. "Frau Dachs," she says. "Frau Reichert's mother. She heard something. She knows something."

"Anna, *komm her! Schweigen!* This minute!"

"But she's gone. I don't know where she went. She's gone."

With that bit of savory information slipped past Frau Winter's protective shield, Fraulein Kirmair turns around and leaves Kreisler with yet another mystery. Or, perhaps, another death.

"Thank you, ladies," Kreisler calls after them, retrieves his hat and bicycle. He is pumped. This is a good lead. He will have to catch up with Frau Reichert, the landlady, as soon as possible.

* * *

Frau Winter's slap to his face not only didn't upset him. On the contrary, it has acted as a stimulant. The Old Order didn't die out in the Great War. It is alive and well in conservative Munich. Frau Winter's angry rebuke is a reminder that the forces of rejectionism are thriving in today's Germany, represented by the politics of the National Socialists and one angry, repressive Adolf Hitler. Geli Raubal pregnant, out of wedlock, by an unknown man? What could be worse than that? Certainly not the fact that she was forced to shit and piss on her own uncle, be murdered for it, then denied access to a proper burial. Protect the Old Order at all costs.

For Frau Winter and her sort, Kreisler is Weimar, the opening up of the world to new things, to a new way of expressing what ought to be, a rejection of what never should have been. She can only deal with change by lashing out at it, even if that change, even if that monumental desire to be utterly open, would benefit her. Would benefit Geli Raubal.

Kreisler resumes pedaling with renewed vigor, feeling that he is on to something far larger than a murder mystery. The whole corrupt system needs toppling before it is allowed to come back to life and power. Should he pass along everything he's learned to Fritz Langer? He's not sure. Probably better to hold off and gather more definitive information first, something Langer can't easily dismiss.

During the initial interrogation of the so-called witnesses on Prinzregentenplatz, Frau Dachs's name never came up. She wasn't present then, though, according to the maid, Frau Dachs *was* there at some point during the confrontation between Geli and Hitler. 'She heard something. She knows something.' Crucial. So much so, Kreisler suspects, that Hitler's band of angels scooped her up and took her away. Based upon Frau Reichert's age, Kreisler guesses that her mother must be in her seventies or eighties. She could have been placed with other relatives, ordered to keep their mouths shut, somewhere as far from Munich as possible. Or a nursing home or a home for the elderly.

Kreisler makes his next stop the *Bayerische StaatsBibliothek*, the Bavarian state library, a massive blocks-long building on Ludwigstrasse, a major thoroughfare in the city filled with Sunday traffic. The public record's office and state archives lie behind the library, so Kreisler figures to spend his Sunday in research. It is the minutiae and trivia of an investigation, which most appeals to him. The little things that most investigators hate the most.

'Perhaps I *should* have been an archaeologist,' he thinks as he enters the building, the nation's intelligence conveniently located in one place. The bicycle riding takes care of his physical well-being. It is the library systems of Europe that he thrives on intellectually.

He goes from building to building for several hours, skipping the mid-day meal, devouring instead information. By the time he is done, he has located every Reichert and Dachs in Bavaria, called them all, then moved on to the local agencies for housing the elderly. That is how, after many phone calls, he locates Frau Maria Dachs, age 88, in a nursing home south of the city. For that drive, a car will be necessary. He doesn't own one. He doesn't even have a license. Calling Lotte and asking her to chauffeur him around hardly seems pragmatic at the moment. Hence, the phone call to Dov Birnbaum.

"It's Yom Kippur," Birnbaum tells him on the front stoop of his building. "I can't drive."

"Can I borrow your car?"

"I thought you couldn't drive."

"I've learned."

"You'll fill up the gas tank?"

"And put air in the tires."

"Apostate."

After all, what is there to know about an automobile? Turn the key, put your foot on the accelerator, turn the steering wheel the way you want to go. He's had lessons. Years ago. He needed to be able to pass a test for the police force. But he hasn't been behind the wheel of a car in a good year. Not legally, at any rate.

At three in the afternoon, belly rumbling from hunger, a cautious Kreisler, driving under the speed limit, makes his way south toward the Swiss border to the small city of Weilheim. In the center of town, in a four-story yellow structure built in the Fifteenth Century, Frau Dachs has recently been deposited like an unwanted baby in a basket. Kreisler presents himself at the main desk and explains the matter of his visit.

"A police investigation. Frau Dachs may have been the witness to something."

"That was never mentioned," a short woman in a nurse's outfit tells him.

"They may not have thought it relevant. Who brought her?"

"I believe her daughter." The nurse has to look through her records to make sure. "Yes, a Frau Reichert and a Herr Kaspers. Just yesterday, as a matter of fact."

"Yesterday. Herr Kaspers." Kreisler jots everything down in his pad. Very official-looking. "A description of Herr Kaspers?"

"I wasn't on duty then. I didn't see."

Kreisler grunts, disappointed. "Maybe someone else?"

"Is it important? The man's appearance?"

"In the case of a criminal act, one never knows what is important and what isn't. As for Frau Dachs...?"

"You may speak to her, I suppose," the nurse says, "but I don't know how much of any use you'll get out of her. She is addled. One of the other nurses just tried to medicate her, and she tossed the pills on the ground and swore at her. We don't mind, you understand. Those behaviors come with extreme age."

Kreisler notes everything down in such detail, the nurse may think she has just revealed the secret of eternal life. Then he follows her, chatting away about her own miserable existence, until they reach a dismally green day room lit by a single overhead chandelier. Frau Dachs is among a half dozen elderly women sitting in wheelchairs, mostly sleeping, occasionally groaning.

"That's her," the nurse says of a woman sitting by herself next to a radio playing an orchestral piece Kreisler recognizes as a Wagner opera. "Do you want me to stay?"

"Unnecessary," Kreisler tells her. "She may be more inclined to speak to me alone."

He does not come from a line of long-livers. Grandparents and parents alike all were dead before they hit fifty. This fact has haunted Kreisler since he was a youth abruptly sent to live with an aunt and uncle who were not overly enthused about taking on the responsibility of parenting someone else's child. It is one of the reasons he has never purchased an automobile but prefers to bike ride everywhere. For the circulation, the lungs, he stays trim and fit.

"Frau Dachs," he introduces himself, bending to peer into her face. "My name is Kreisler. Avi, if you wish. I've just come from Munich. I'm with the police."

She has been crying. This is evident to him by the trail of tears descending through the wrinkles of her cheeks onto a damp bib around her neck. He offers to wipe them off with a handkerchief, but she starts when he makes the approach.

"Wer ist du? Was willst du? Warum bin ich hier?"

"I'm a friend," Kreisler says. "I don't know why you're here. Perhaps you can tell me."

Frau Dachs spits in his face.

Unperturbed, he casually uses the handkerchief on his own cheeks. He is going to have to start shielding his face from these German hausfraus, he thinks.

"Anna Kirmair, Adolf Hitler's maid, says you saw something the other day. Maybe heard something. At Prinzregentenplatz. Do you remember anything?"

"I don't know where I am. Why did they bring me here? Who are you?"

Kreisler plows ahead. Throw everything at her and see if anything connects. That's his idea. Shock her into reality.

"Were they arguing? Herr Hitler and his niece, Geli? Did you hear a gunshot? Yes? You heard something? Something out of the ordinary?"

Frau Dachs's eyes widen suddenly. She fixes him with a look of confusion, fear, falls back into her chair, and covers her eyes with her arm.

"You heard something."

"I'm sorry, sorry, sorry, he shouts. Then out he goes, down the stairs. Out, out, out. Sorry, sorry, sorry. You should have seen the blood, Herr Winter. It made me sick."

Frau Dachs breaks down into great wails of terror, awakening all of the other wheelchair-bound patients and alerting the staff, who come running to her defense.

"That's enough, Sir, enough," the first nurse he met shouts. "You've frightened her. It's enough."

Kreisler backs away, eying the old woman. A witness she was, indeed, but what kind? What prosecutor would rely on her testimony? But if there was blood, lots of it, and he knows there was, then the killer's clothes must have been covered in it. And who cleans the clothes in that household? The maid. Did they throw them out, he wonders? Or are they still around, still stained? Hitler's minions didn't think of everything.

* * *

It is nightfall by the time Kreisler returns Dov Birnbaum's car, fully fueled with no nicks or dents, and unlocks the door to his own apartment. He isn't completely surprised to see Anni Leeuwenberg sitting on a chair by an open window, smoking her cigarette into the night.

"She found my IUDs," is the first thing out of her mouth.

"Is that what happened? I wondered." He yawns.

"Do you blame her for being upset?"

"No. Why did you leave them here?"

"Why indeed?"

Anni doesn't leave her chair but puts her cigarette out on the window ledge. Kreisler pulls a chair over and, sitting by her side, picks up her hand, studies it before kissing it and holding it up against his lips.

"It's been a long day," he says. He can smell the tobacco on her hand, but doesn't care. He's ready to jump into bed and sleep. She can stay if she wants, but no fucking tonight.

"My publisher Waldmann wants to see you tomorrow," she says.

"Early or late?"

"Whenever you can make room for him. He says it's time to go after Hitler, and he thinks you're the man to get it done. Avi?"

Anni waits for a response that never comes. Rising quietly, she finds a blanket to place over the sleeping detective. He is snoring softly, his head thrown back at an awkward angle against the back of his chair. Setting him in a more comfortable position, she gets her own blanket and curls up on the couch near him. *"Morgen,"* she thinks, tomorrow, *"beginnt der krieg."*

Chapter Ten

September 21

Kreisler doesn't remember how he got from the chair to his bed. All he knows is that when he wakes up, he is still wearing the clothes he got dressed in on Sunday, and he can hear a clattering of typewriter keys in the front room.

"Anni," he calls out.

"Breakfast is made," she replies. "I hope you like apple pancakes."

Kreisler sits up in bed and stretches. He sniffs but smells no telltale signs of breakfast having been prepared internally. "You cook?" he asks, stripping out of his old clothes.

"Seriously? I bought them at the café down the street. I borrowed money from your wallet."

Which lies open on the bureau next to his bed.

"You didn't take my notepad, did you?" he asks. His pants are on, but the rest of him is bare. It's only six in the morning, but it is a Monday, and he needs time to wash. Anni is sitting at the dinner table pecking with two fingers at the typewriter, his notepad open beside her.

"That would be a yes," she says. "But your scribbling is hard to decipher. Winter? Dachs? Weilheim?"

"It's a long story." He disappears into the bathroom. Soon after, Anni hears the flow of the shower.

As soon as he is out, she says, "How long is it? The story, I mean. You went to Weilheim?"

"A hunch," is all he tells her. "What are you typing? More Communist propaganda?"

"Hitler's obituary."

"You wish. Don't make it yours."

Kreisler, nevertheless, is grateful for the food and forks it down in a minute in his hurry to leave.

She remains behind, banging the keys. "You going to see Waldmann?"

"Later," he says. "I do have to put in an appearance at HQ. Would you do me a favor?"

He stops in the doorway. She ceases her typing. "You gonna kiss me first?"

He does, long and deeply enough to make him almost want to get to work late. Almost. "Your breath smells of tobacco," he says.

"Thanks for the compliment, Romeo. You trying to get me to quit?"

"They're not good for you, and if they're not good for you, they're not good for me." He grabs his things, including the notepad. His pistol, he straps to his waist. "The favor."

"Yes?"

"I promised the pathologist I'd claim a body before they cremated it."

"A body? Whose?"

"Klara Fries. Call the synagogue. Ask for Dov Birnbaum. Tell him a coffin is coming over. He doesn't have to know she isn't Jewish. We'll bury her in the Jewish cemetery."

Kreisler hurries downstairs, carrying his bike. On the sidewalk, he looks up toward his third-floor window. Anni's red head is poking out, looking down at him.

"Hey, Avi!" she had shouted to get his attention. "Winter, Dachs, Weilheim. I figured it out! Keep up the good work!"

"Thanks. Don't fall."

The last thing he needs is to clean up another defenestrated corpse. Anni's six-foot body would take up the entire sidewalk.

Pedaling through the Munich streets as if he is vying for the Tour de France, he feels rejuvenated. Being loved and loving in return is something that pulls him down from the clouds, smack onto the earth. It is a primal emotion, maybe **the** primal emotion, mother to child, lover to lover. When he was young, he had not viewed life from above, the skeptic more adept at critique than participation. Freud would say the loss of his mother and father at an early age was responsible for the walls and staging he has erected for his throne since then. He can't say. He doesn't know. In the past, he would not have offered to take care of Klara. He would have distanced himself from both Anni and Lotte. Now he finds that both women have reached into his heart and forced him to engage in the world in ways he isn't used to.

At the offices of Munich Homicide, the hope he is feeling evaporates the moment he sees the group of men exiting Fritz Langer's office. Among the high and mighty are Schwarz, the city councilor, and Franz Gürtner, the Bavarian Minister of Justice. Inspektors Sauer and Forster don't even glance Kreisler's way as they head to their desks. Langer signals him in.

"Where was Hindenburg?" Kreisler jokes. Langer doesn't laugh.

"You're off the case," Langer says. He points to a chair. "Despite Hitler's wishes. He doesn't run things here. Gürtner called this meeting first thing in the morning. He is aware of your religious background. What did I tell you, eh?"

"Am I off the Klara Fries case?"

"No. Not that there's much of a case to be made." Sitting in his own chair, Langer lights up a cigar. "You still insist it wasn't a suicide?"

"Neither is the Raubal case. Hitler killed her."

"Avi, don't make me do something I don't want to."

Kreisler shifts in his chair, anger rising, frustration jabbing him in the ribs. "Fine," he says. "Take me off. Sauer and Forster are good detectives. Just tell them that I have tracked down Frau Dachs."

"Who?"

"The landlady Reichert's elderly mother. She wasn't there when we got there. But she **was** there **before** we did. She saw what happened. She knows what happened. She saw Hitler in the apartment at a time when he was supposed to be in Nuremberg. They hustled her away so she wouldn't rat him out. Fritz, you don't like the man any more than I do."

"But I like my job, and I intend to keep it. You should want the same thing for yourself."

"So...."

"So, there are plenty of other murders in Munich that need the careful eye of a good detective like yourself. You've only been on the job for a short while, but you're already one of the best we have. Despite your being a Jew. Never forget that, Avi. You have a handicap, for good or for bad, and it will only take one mistake to kill your career."

"Despite my father's Iron Cross."

"Irrelevant."

"Despite his degrees in medicine and physics."

"You're tossing out platitudes."

"Despite everything. Everyone. Einstein. Freud. Mahler. Mendelssohn."

"Ditto. Trotsky. Sverdlov. Litvinov. Kamenev. You might as well paint a hammer and sickle on your forehead and march around singing *The Internationale*. Jews and Communists. That's all the people know. Traitors. Back-stabbers. Be a good German, and maybe you'll survive."

"Maybe." Kreisler stands, turns to go, then has a thought that makes him look at Langer curiously. "You joined the party, didn't you?"

"For political reasons only. Gürtner advised it. Once they're defeated, I'll pretend it never happened. You don't have that luxury."

"I suppose not." Kreisler reaches the doorway before again looking back. "Klara Fries was also pregnant. I suspect the father of her baby is the murderer. I also suspect he's one of Hitler's Brownshirt guards. We're going to bury her in a few days. Maybe you'll attend the funeral."

Back out on the street, Kreisler has no intention of backing out of the Geli Raubal investigation. He just isn't sure how he'll manage it. He needs allies, that's the most certain thing. Outside the police. Lotte and Anni. Dov Birnbaum. Hardly a phalanx of Roman military might.

He hops on his bicycle. Since Klara Fries's remains have not been claimed, he assumes that her family will be of little or no help. If he can even find them. If she has any. She must have had other friends besides Geli Raubal and David Sussman, now deceased. People with whom she might have confided regarding her pregnancy. Maybe Anton knows.

This gives him some direction. He will take up Anni's offer to meet with her publisher, Oskar Waldmann. First, a slight detour past a pharmacy. His pistol rubs against his leg as he pedals. He has never liked wearing the weapon. But after the encounter with the Brownshirts in Sussman's burned-out place of business, he isn't taking any chances. Even in daylight.

The pharmacy in question lies directly across from the Englischer Garten, a high-end store for a high-end clientele. Klara was moving in loftier status circles at the time of her death. He'll have to talk to Frau Becker, the landlady, again, to see if Klara was meeting her rental obligations on time or if someone, a male admirer, was covering her rent for her. It's a common enough practice in Munich. A wealthy businessman having a girl on the side for whom he shares his bank account.

The thought crosses his mind as he pedals to a stop before the pharmacy's large plate glass front window that Anton could have been helping her in some way. Could he be the father of her child? No. Kreisler instantly dismisses that notion and returns to an SA soldier as the main suspect. Someone who would have access to Geli Raubal and who would have the status within the party to both take care of her and to kill her and get away with it.

He leans his bike against a postal box and heads into the *Gartenstrasse Apotheke*. The store is so extensive, far larger than Sussman's, that it resembles a major department store selling clothes items off of racks and weaponry, pistols and ammunition, kept in locked cases. It is a lavish display of capitalistic opulence intended for customers not impacted by the Great Depression. National Socialist paraphernalia is obvious everywhere.

Women browse among the dainties on display. Men ponder the purchase of a pistol. Kreisler isn't ten feet into the store when a man brushes by him in a hurry to leave. They bump arms, causing the man to turn an irritated gaze at Kreisler, who immediately recognizes the man with whom he has become entangled.

"You," he says. The tall, bulky shape from Sussman's. The club-wielding SA soldier is now out of uniform, wearing the coat and tie of a successful businessman.

It is clear to Kreisler that he has been recognized, as well. The brief glare in the eyes is the giveaway. But the man merely wipes himself off, dirty Jew, and continues out the door. Kreisler is tempted to follow but figures that, since he's already been spotted, he wouldn't be able to track his suspect very far. Instead, he catches the attention of a girl dusting off a shelf of perfumes.

"That man who just left the store," he asks. "A customer?" He wasn't carrying any bundles. "Or an employee?"

"Herr Kaspers?" the girl says. "He manages the store."

Kaspers. Kreisler doesn't need his camera. He can visualize the face of Hitler's bodyguard from the Bratwurstglöckl restaurant and from Sussman's pharmacy. Now here. Interesting. More interesting is the pharmaceutical log kept here. Like the one kept by Sussman, the Gartenstrasse Apotheke lists all of the purchasers and purchases of its medications. There is no mention of a Klara Fries anywhere. Does this mean she never patronized this store after all, that Sussman's annotation was incorrect? That she never purchased medication here? Or is it possible, Kreisler wonders, that she didn't need to purchase her drugs here because the manager of the business absconded with them for her? Until she needed something for her pregnancy. Unwanted. So, he absconded with her life.

Kreisler pulls out his notepad and jots down his thoughts outside on the sidewalk under the warmth of the September sun. Last day of summer. A day that should be appreciated for its beauty, but is instead filled with thoughts of murder. Here's the conundrum: If this Kaspers was Klara's lover/collaborator, why would he be trying to blackmail Hitler, his purported boss? Where do his loyalties lie, if he has any? If he's not working for Hitler, who is he working for?

The problem with trying to hover above the chaos is that you don't capture the full scope of it. He is missing something that is probably right in front of him. Maybe Langer is right, Kreisler thinks, as he begins to bike to his next stop. Maybe he has kept himself above the fray for so long that he doesn't completely grasp his role in it. He's sure Lotte and Anni would concur. He'll have to ask Anton about his character in the love triangle. How does this all play out? Is he a German or a Jew? Is he a hero or a coward? A problem solver or a problem creator?

Der Weg, the Leftist newsletter Anni writes for, is published out of a warehouse that manufactures shoes. Herr Waldmann, the publisher, is not in the business of fitting leather onto people's feet. His brother owns the building and lets out the space to both the manufacturer and the newspaper. His brother is not a Communist, but Waldmann is, and somehow they get along. As long as the rent is paid.

"Anni told me you were coming today," Waldmann says, extending a hand to the detective. Waldmann is an old-time Red having served time in prison in Russia for the failed uprising against the Czar in 1906. Arrested with Trotsky. Exiled with Lenin. He is proud of these facts. He is sixty years old, thin as a plank, and just as knotted. All he knows is revolution. He will die fighting the fight.

"Is she here?" Kreisler asks. The back room of the shoe factory is loud and filthy. Noise from the factory is ear-piercing alone. Here, the presses are running the latest edition, adding to the cacophony that doesn't seem to bother the older man. Of course, he's deaf, so that helps.

"What?"

"Anni Leeuwenberg! Is she here?"

"Anni, my eyes and ears, mainly my ears."

Waldmann acts as if Kreisler is a seeing-eye dog, grasping his hand and letting the detective lead him to where he is pointing, a small room in the very back. Once the door is closed and the noise somewhat reduced, he offers Kreisler both a chair and a glass of schnapps.

"I'm so used to this *aufregung,* this commotion, I barely notice it anymore. You know my Anni well?"

"She never mentioned me before this?"

Waldmann moves aside papers on his desk so he can pour his drink without spilling any over his work. "She is a secretive woman, that one. About her private life, that is. Work, politics, I can't get her to shut up. What a brilliant mind. She belongs in America, not here."

"But you respect her." Love her?

"I do. As a father of a daughter. Here, drink."

Kreisler turns down the offer. "I assume she did tell you about what I have been investigating."

"Hitler."

"In part. There have been several murders, related, I think."

"Including this Geli Raubal suicide?" Waldmann downs his drink, pours another. "You sure….?" Offering the beverage.

"No, thank you."

"Because you're on the job. Good for you. A true professional. Among the cops in Munich, that is a rarity."

"I happened to meet Geli Raubal," Kreisler says. "Anni and I both did. Just before she died. I also was one of the first detectives on scene with the body."

"And your conclusions?" Waldmann finishes his drink and gets down to business, picking up the latest edition of *Der Weg*, which he shows to Kreisler. "My own conclusions."

Kreisler takes the newspaper being printed in the outer room that very moment. The front page headline reads, 'NO SUICIDE! MURDER!'

"You could be sued for this," Kreisler says.

"I could be shot for it, but so what? Anni tells me you like to spear the bull."

"She did, did she?"

"So do I. Here's the deal as I see it," Waldmann says, leaning across the desk, breath smelling of alcohol. "Guilty? Innocent? Who cares? Let the dirt fly where it will. If Hitler isn't guilty of that, he's guilty of everything else. I just want him to pay for something."

"Hitler is just one man."

"With him down, the whole fascist movement goes down with him. You don't appreciate the full scope of this," Waldmann says. "Hitler wants to be chancellor of Germany. Dictator of Germany. But in the last elections, his party lost a majority of their seats in the Reichstag. Hitler is playing up to the upper crust. He wants the semblance of legality. He has to downplay the violence in his own party while not losing the support of Röhm's Brownshirts. So, you can imagine what is going through his mind now when his own niece dies under suspicious circumstances in his own flat. You get my point?"

Kreisler skims the article. There is no byline, but he knows the style of the writer full well. The contents could only come from one source. "Where did you get this information?" he asks. "Cops?"

"We get many tips."

"How do you know they're true?"

Waldmann sips, enjoys his alcohol. "A theater critic will tell you that the truth is nothing but opinion. I'm advocating an opinion. Let the world decipher the truth."

"You don't vet your informants? You simply write what they tell you if what they tell you is what you want to hear?"

"My dear Constable Kreisler," Waldmann explains without a hint of regret, "the truth died with Darwin. We're no longer part of the animal kingdom. Don't you read the papers? We don't have to act on instinct, which is the only natural truth. We act upon what makes our lives happier. For Hitler, that means killing us. For us, it means killing Hitler. How's that for truth? Pure Darwinism. Kill or be killed, yes? You want to live, don't you? We might not unless we act now in whatever way is necessary. The enemy of my enemy is my friend. At least, for the moment."

Kreisler shifts in his seat, wondering if speaking to Anni's publisher was such a good idea, after all. He doesn't care for the direction the conversation is going. It makes him feel like a lonely soldier on a battlefield fighting for a hopeless cause, surrounded by a jeering mob of cynics.

"You claim one thing," he tries arguing back. "The Nationalists claim something else. If the truth doesn't matter, how do you know opinion does? Who will the people believe? You or Hitler?"

"That's where you come in." Waldmann's fist comes down on the desk, scattering his papers. "Dig up evidence. Make the lies what they are: lies. Convince the world of the truth."

"Which you just said doesn't really exist." Kreisler can't help snorting his doubts as he lowers the newspaper. "From what I've experienced, the world can be convinced of almost anything. Politicians lose elections, get assassinated all the time. Movements don't always die as a result."

"The Great War started with an assassination. The next one may die in its cradle if we act, Inspektor. There was no autopsy?"

"No."

"And you don't find that at all suspicious?"

"I do. Hitler is guilty. I don't think it. I know it. Fuck whatever you think of the truth. Geli Raubal did not shoot herself. But courts of law require proof."

"Not always," says Waldmann. He leans back in his chair, contemplating his prospective Lancelot. "You're not a religious man, I take it."

"Should I be?"

"Not in the Twentieth Century. I'm a Jew. Are you? I don't know. Anni hasn't spilled the beans on that one. She just says to trust you. But do I consider myself the chosen of God? Look at me. Do I look chosen? God created fifteen million light-years of planets and stars, galaxies and solar systems in six days? I don't think so. But, therein lies the problem for men like you and me, Inspektor. May I call you, Avi?"

"That's my true name, not an opinion."

Waldmann gives the detective the smile of a professor observing a top-notch student. "You see," he says, "before the collapse of empires, I was an astronomy student. In Moscow. When you assess the actual status of our world in the context of everything that exists out there, you tend to develop a skeptical view of everything that happens here. On earth. In Russia. Until it affects your family. Then everything goes out the window."

"Are you married? Have children?"

"The detective gets right to the heart of the matter. Don't peel the fruit. Get right to the core."

"*Do* you?"

"If I say 'no', will that upset your thesis?" At that moment, it appears to Kreisler that the publisher starts to reach for his bottle of schnapps before thinking twice about it and settling back in his chair. The sixty-year-old revolutionary notices the noticer noticing him.

"One day while I was at my studies," Waldmann continues, "the Russians sent their Cossacks through my native village and burned it to the ground. I had family. But they emigrated to America. Perhaps I should have gone with them. Princeton. Harvard. Could I have transferred my credits and become an Ivy League scholar? We'll never know. I chose to join Lenin instead and landed here. The intellectual heart of the Communist revolution before it became a reality. We tried here, in Bavaria, with Eisner. Oh, well, another assassination. Hitler was there, you know. At Eisner's funeral. I marched right behind him. He was a full-blooded Red in those days."

Kreisler has his notepad out in case Waldmann says anything that might be of value to his investigation. So far, pencil has not touched paper. "Is Stalin doing better than what the Fascists propose here? Is he your answer?"

Waldmann lifts his shoulders and shows the palms of his hands. In another life, he might have been a comic performer. But fate took him elsewhere. He sighs.

"It is a difficult life we lead, Avi, we realists. We are guests in an amusement park operated by lunatics. Only, the world isn't very amusing, is it? How does one maintain his sanity in such a place?"

"By doing good deeds," Kreisler says.

Waldmann can no longer resist the desire to take another drink. He does so knowing he is being watched and judged. Once he has gulped down his urge, he gets to his point.

"We intend to print everything we can to condemn the Fascists and their leaders. Truth? Opinion? Who gives a shit? Would you consider that a good deed? And you, if you are willing, will feed us the morsels of filth we need to end their game. Anni is committed to this. She will write whatever details you give her, perhaps with a colorful twist or two. So what? Being good doesn't ever get you good. If all the good men are frightened, there are no good men at all. That's my lesson in life."

Kreisler rises, putting his notepad away. "I might need some money," he says. He is satisfied. The goal's the thing.

"For what?"

"A trip to Vienna. The funeral of a young woman I happened upon the other day."

"Done. Anything else?"

"A good lawyer, if you know one."

Waldmann laughs, stands to offer his hand in partnership to the detective. "I know many good lawyers," he says. "Successful? No. Good. Yes." As Kreisler reaches the door, the publisher adds one last bit of advice. "Watch your back, Avi. I don't want to be paying for your funeral. Or Anni's."

Chapter Eleven

Adolf Hitler has many admirers but few friends. One of these is Heinrich Hoffman, a middle-aged man trained in photography by his father. His studio on Schellingstrasse in Munich is filled with photographs of the National Socialist leader for which Hoffman is paid a royalty on each. He has become a millionaire thanks to Hitler's patronage. Hitler allows no one else to photograph him.

Hoffman is, like Franz Schwarz, a member of the Munich city council. He has been married twice. His first wife produced a son, also named Heinrich, and a daughter, Henriette, age eighteen, called by her friends Henny.

It is Henny Hoffman Kreisler has come to interview, though he has brought rolls of film in to have processed. These are just a cover. Hoffman himself is too busy a man to assist him. When Kreisler enters the store that afternoon, having parked his bicycle outside, he sees a busy shop manned by two young women. One, a blonde showing off slender legs beneath a blue dirndl, is standing on a ladder dusting off shelves of photographs. The other, brunette, younger, is helping a family from behind a counter. The family consists of a father, mother, and daughter, a child possibly five or six years old.

Kreisler takes snapshots like this in his mind whenever he plans his memoirs, his life as a detective in Weimar Germany. Who knows what significance these scenes will have? His guess at the moment would be that one of the two young women employed by Hoffmann will be the key to his investigation. This may be true. But there is a third person in the studio who, ultimately, will play an even deeper role in his life.

He waits patiently as the father, mother, and daughter complete their transaction. The girl, he notices, is entranced in a book of astronomy, fully engaged in its contents. Having his own children is something he hasn't considered, even as his relationships with Lotte and Anni have blossomed. That would be really coming down from the clouds, he thinks. Having a child.

"She's into astronomy," he says to the daughter's mother. "That's not what I'd expect from a girl her age."

"Her psychiatrist says she's got a genius IQ." The mother, very young herself, smiles engagingly at Kreisler, pats her daughter on the head. The child continues to read. "Hana, say thank you to the man."

Hana gives a brief, curious glance up, mutters a soft reply, before returning to her book.

"She's shy," the mother says, before paying for her purchase and turning to go.

"Thank you, Fraulein Ziegler, Herr Marksohn." The girl behind the counter, having dealt with her customers, now gives Kreisler her full attention.

"Children," he says with a smile as a way of introducing himself. "I'm Inspektor Kreisler of the Munich Police Department, Homicide." He proffers his credentials. She is taken aback.

"Homicide?"

"I'm afraid so. This is the Hoffman studios?"

"Yes, it is. I'm my father's daughter. I mean, I'm Henriette Hoffman. Is it my father you're looking for?"

"Maybe." Kreisler's attention lifts toward the blonde girl coming off the ladder. At the word 'homicide', she had shared a look Kreisler interprets as 'Oops, we've been found out'. "We've had several mysterious deaths recently," he says to them both. You may have information that can help us solve what happened."

"You're talking about Geli, aren't you?" Henny Hoffmann asks. "We were informed it was a suicide. Such an awful thing. She was such a sweet girl."

"A good friend of yours."

"Absolutely."

"And yours, Fraulein…?"

"Eva Braun," the blonde says. "No, I wouldn't call her a friend, actually. An acquaintance, that's all."

Kreisler somehow doubts 'that's all' as the girl vanishes quickly behind a curtain at the far end of the counter, obviously uninterested in revealing anything else.

"Don't mind her," Henny says. She appears to be a bright, perky teenager, someone whom Kreisler can envision being a loyal companion to the vivacious Geli Raubal. "She was jealous of Geli," she whispers. "She's got a thing for Herr Hitler. I think it's kind of creepy."

Kreisler would agree, sort of like having 'a thing' for Jack the Ripper, except a part of him sees every woman of the lower classes these days as a gold-digger. Not that he blames them. You get by in whatever way you can. This is certainly not the case for Lotte or Anni. No gold in his future for them to squabble over.

"Herr Hitler is rather much older," he agrees. "Does he return the interest?"

"I don't think so. But you should see the way she fawns all over him whenever he comes here. Geli called her a monkey girl. It makes me want to pull her hair out."

Kreisler nods. He has his ubiquitous notepad out, ready to fill it with gossip of a useful sort. "I have to be honest with you," he says. "I don't believe Geli killed herself."

"You don't?"

"That's why I am interviewing everyone who knew her. Like yourself. A girl her age."

"Five years younger."

"Even so. Close enough. You accompanied her places?"

"We went to Obersalzberg a few weeks ago, before…it happened."

A customer enters the building, causing a bell to chime. Henny greets her, then calls for Eva Braun to assist.

"Who else accompanied you?" Kreisler asks. "Did she happen to tell you she was pregnant?"

The question, asked innocently enough, is not one the eighteen-year-old

Henny anticipated. Clearly, she doesn't want Eva to know, so she nods for Kreisler to follow her out onto the sidewalk.

"She did tell me," Henny says, looking about to make sure Eva is far enough away not to listen in. "I hate that girl. Ever since we heard about poor Geli, she hasn't stopped babbling about Herr Hitler and how she's going to marry him someday. What a slut!"

"Did **he** know about the pregnancy?"

"Not then. She was nervous about telling him."

"But he found out?"

"I guess. I don't know. Well, after all, at some point it was going to have to come out, wasn't it? It's not like you can hide that sort of thing forever."

"No, it isn't." Kreisler gazes through the plate-glass window into the photography shop, his interest fixed on Fraulein Braun. "Who else was aware of the pregnancy?" he asks. "I don't imagine it was common knowledge."

"Klara knew."

"Klara Fries?"

"Yes. She was with us that day. So was Elfriede, Geli's sister, and Julius and Martin."

"Brownshirts."

"Her Hitler doesn't let Geli out of his sight unless she's being accompanied by someone, like her mother. Or his guards."

"Their names, Henny? The Brownshirts."

"Schaub and Kaspers. They're nice. But…." Henny takes another look about to make sure when she speaks, no one else can overhear. "I think she had a fling with one of them. She's very flirtatious, Geli, my mother says. She definitely wasn't a virgin, I mean, even before she got pregnant. She must have loved the guy."

"The father of her child?"

"Yes. She was always very careful, if you know what I mean. My mother says I better not behave that way. My father is very old-fashioned."

Kreisler shares a conspiratorial nod as if his parents had treated him the same way.

"He wants me to marry Herr von Shirach. One of Herr Hitler's friends.

He's a lot older than I am," Henny says, "but my father says it's my obligation to Germany to produce children for our future. And Herr von Shirach is of noble descent, so it would be a good match."

"For your father."

"For the family."

All of this detail, this teenage prattle, may have been discarded by any other detective, but Kreisler finds it useful in putting together a complete picture of the world Hitler and his niece inhabited before they fought and she died. Waldmann and Anni, the journalists, would agree.

"I'm curious," he says to Henny. "Did you know that Klara was thrown from a window, that she's dead? It wasn't in the news. She was pregnant, too, and murdered probably because of it. Did anyone tell you that?"

This abrupt detail is part of the interrogator Kreisler's strategy. Throwing his subject off guard. Causing them to discharge information that they might otherwise have omitted had they been in greater control of their thought processes. Henny is not surprisingly dazed and shocked by what Kreisler has told her. She lets out a startled yelp that causes passers-by to notice.

"Her, too? You think Julius or Martin….?"

Kreisler pretends not to be aware of Henny's shock. "I believe there's a connection between Klara's death and Geli's." He moves in, hovers over the shorter girl as if protecting her from the world of her father. "I believe Klara was blackmailing Herr Hitler. When did you last see her or Geli? Did she tell you who the father of her child is? Herr Hitler? One of the Brownshirts? Or someone else?"

Henny is crying now. It can't be helped, Kreisler thinks. Women tend to react this way, at least in his experience. Perhaps he is mismanaging them. That wouldn't be startling. He puts an arm about the girl's shoulder and leads her to a quieter place beneath a tree, away from the nosy pedestrians. She blows her nose in the handkerchief he gives her.

"A Jew," she says when she is calmer. "An actor. In Vienna. And Herr Hitler knew."

* * *

Lotte is not the type of woman to act on a whim. This is not how she was brought up. It is not the way she was educated. It is not the way she is by nature. In her world, in her Prussian upper-class strata, she is expected to play a role in the family fortunes, to improve them through marriage with other aristocratic families, perhaps even higher on the social scale. Not that there are many families with a more prestigious lineage than the Leinsdorfs.

Hugo Leinsdorf, her father, manages a publishing empire that was founded by a great-grandfather in the Eighteenth Century. Her mother, Luisa, is a daughter of Prussian military royalty, descendants of a general who fought Napoleon. Lotte has an older brother, Karl, but he died in the Great War, leaving her the eldest remaining Leinsdorf child. She had a younger sister, too, Maria. Had. Maria was fifteen when she hung herself in her bedroom on her birthday. Lotte loved her sister. She keeps her portrait in a locket she wears around her neck. She doesn't know why Maria killed herself, but she suspects why. For the same reason, Lotte took to the drink.

Tonight, she feels inexpressibly lonely eating a late supper with her mother and father in the great dining hall of their mansion facing the Englischer Garten. Cooks prepared her meal. Servants deliver it to her place. Swabian ravioli. Veal meatballs with capers. Roasted onions and fondant potato. Anni Leeuwenberg would be disgusted if she saw what the Leinsdorfs had for dinner every night. Maybe that's why Avi prefers the tall, red-headed Communist.

When the wine is poured, Lotte takes a sip. Red from Burgundy. The wine has always been her downfall, the reason her relationships have always faltered. One of the things she loves most about Avi is that he has always taken her back. Always forgiven her. It is why she has never had any other serious relationship with any other man.

"Hoffmann intends to marry his daughter off to von Shirach," Lotte's father is saying when she realizes he is talking. Her head is spinning. This Burgundy is strong. "It certainly wouldn't hurt us if you would consider socializing with those people."

"Those people, Father?"

"The National Socialists. They support eugenics. The strengthening of the gene pool. Everyone is doing it now."

"If the Nazis win," Lotte says.

"They might. Hitler is gaining a lot of friends among the industrialists. Merging with them can only benefit us. It's not like you're seeing anyone seriously."

"How old are you now, dear?" her mother asks.

"Does it matter?"

"To a woman, it most certainly does. The child-bearing age is very important. Once a woman gets too old, the children she bears could end up, well, who wants to think of it?"

As the 'help' takes away the dinner plates in preparation for dessert, Lotte begins to disengage. She needs to find her own place. Now that she is managing the family book store, she certainly has the money to afford this form of independence, though a woman of her age and lineage living by herself would be looked upon as 'unusual'. Her plan had been to move in with Avi, but then she found Anni's lipstick and IUDs in his bathroom cabinet, and that hope vanished in a heart-killing instant.

"I am seeing someone," she says.

"Who? Not that policeman, I hope," her mother says.

"Just someone!" Lotte shouts. She finishes her wine. Then she rises from the table, stumbling over a leg of her chair.

"Charlotte, aren't you going to have dessert?"

No. No dessert. Even if they're serving plum dumplings.

"Charlotte. Lotte. Come back."

"No, no, no! I'll marry whoever the fuck I want!" Lotte doesn't know if she is just thinking these thoughts or has actually yelled them at her parents. She runs to her room, grabs her car keys, dresses in a warm coat, and heads outside. Where is her whim taking her? The one place she has never been. The one place she needs to go to. Anni's flat.

She doesn't want to end up like her sister Maria, that's the thing. At fifteen, by far the prettier of the two sisters, she had been affianced to a German manufacturer of automobiles. Ever since the moment she discovered her sister's lifeless body hanging by a belt from a light fixture, Lotte has fought the notion of suicide for many years, contemplated it during her worst times. Why didn't Maria say anything to her? Why didn't she give her beloved sister a chance to save her life? The death of Geli Raubal has been an unwelcome reminder of everything she has tried to suppress. Being pregnant. Having a child. Having a family. Feeling whole with someone she can truly love. Like Avi, who her parents know as an old university friend with whom she has been seen far too often to believe her 'just friend' stories.

She has told Hugo and Luisa that Avi is Catholic, not that he was raised by Jewish converts to Christianity. She has told them that he is involved with law enforcement and is a highly regarded, intelligent man in the city. They never questioned the friendship, but would never accept a marriage between her and Avi because he is not of their social class.

'I'm as big a coward as Avi,' she thinks as she drives through the city at night. She realizes she is tipsy from the wine and shouldn't be behind the wheel. But had she stayed a moment longer with her parents, she would have blurted out something she would surely have regretted. Something about hating them and everything they stood for. She should have left them years ago, but never found the courage.

Anni came into her life during her most rebellious phase when Lotte marched with the Communists, held up their banners, and chanted their chants. The constant violence on the streets between the followers of Lenin and those of Hitler and the right-wing Freikorps drove her back into the arms of drink and her parents. That, and the fact that she knew she could never be like Anni.

Tonight is the night to cease being afraid. Anni has been a friend, if a cool one. Now Lotte sees her simply as an adversary who must be confronted. If she has lost Avi to her Communist rival, the only reasonable option may be the very one she has struggled to avoid, Maria's way. Let her fucking parents figure out who to leave their wealth to without her.

Anni lives in the Bohemian neighborhood of Schwabing among cabarets and theaters. Artsy people are by nature rebellious people. Here change thrives, conservatism is scorned, people live, work, and party as if the Victorian Era never happened, as if classes did not exist, as if men and women were equal. The Nazis will change all of that, will drive the liberal thinkers out, will force them to emigrate or end up in the German version of the Russian gulags.

Lotte swerves crazily around beeping cars, barely noticing the men paired off with each other, kissing openly on the street, wearing women's clothing, dancing, or puking in the gutter. Women showing off their wares to bankers and businessmen who are out on the town without the permission of their wives. Communist banners proclaiming the rights of all workers.

She is trying to recall through the fog of her memory what building Anni lives in. Is it that way? Down that alley? By the neighborhood market or the barber shop? What finally sparks recognition is not the building itself, an old warehouse that rents out spaces to artists and writers, but a commotion on the street outside the building.

She has every right to be afraid of the Brownshirts. This is not their territory. They have no right to be here. This is pure provocation, an insult to freedom. Lotte feels anger rise. She grips the steering wheel of her Duesenberg and nearly drives into the group of men hurling taunts at an equally raucous gang of lesbians, coming from their local *kabarett,* who show no fear of the National Socialist thugs.

Coming to a screeching halt up and over the curb, skirting a beech tree, separating the opposing political camps like a wedge, she manages to stagger out from behind the steering wheel. The cool autumn evening helps to clear her head. So does the sudden, shocked silence of the mob whose attention has been forcefully turned to her.

"Sorry," she says, leaning against her door, her head throbbing. "I'm a little drunk." That is when she notices a big Red flag above the entrance to the warehouse and the number 13 in worn brass.

Bad luck, thirteen. She remembers thinking the same thing the last and only time she came here. With Avi and Anton. After one of his plays. A disaster that.

"Pardon me," she says to a burly Brownshirt who grabs her arm.

"I wouldn't go in there just yet," he says.

"Fuck you." Breaking free, she ignores the warning with an "I don't like

Hitler." Let her father and mother swallow that.

But the Brownshirt won't let go. It is only with the intervention of the lesbians, who come to Lotte's aid, that she is able to escape and push her way into the warehouse. Once inside, she immediately vomits, freeing her stomach of ravioli and veal meatballs. At least, her head is beginning to clear. Enough to realize that she is not alone at the base of the stairwell leading to the higher floors. A hooker is performing a service on a young man, fly unzipped. Pausing in her efforts to bring him to conclusion, she gives Lotte a helpful tip.

"Don't go up there, honey. Somebody's getting their ass kicked."

"Anni?"

"Who knows? But it's a freebie, if you ask me."

In that moment, Lotte jolts into total sobriety. "Anni!" Her mind goes blank except for images of brutality. Klara Fries was tossed out a window. David Sussman was found in a river. Geli Raubal was shot to death. Who knows what a band of drunken Brownshirts would do to a beautiful red-headed Communist?

"Anni!"

Lotte kicks off her heels, ignores the puddle of food waste on the floor, and takes to the stairs in her bare feet, cursing her dizziness and trying to remember which floor Anni lives on. That, as it turns out, is not an issue. She can hear the yelling from the floor above. The laughter. The loud male cheering. She has her purse with her, but that is hardly a weapon. Even so, she wields it with a mighty swing at a man standing guard in front of Anni's open door. He ducks the blow, but Lotte gets past him and darts into Anni's room.

"Anni!"

"Fuck her, Stenbach! Hurry up! Give us a turn!"

Anni's flat is not big. Just enough for a bookshelf, a writing table, a bed and bureau and a kitchen area. Lotte can't immediately see Anni for the crowd of men surrounding her bed. What she can hear, besides the men rooting their colleague along, are Anni's muffled cries and the hard slap of a hand across her face.

"Shut up, you Red whore! This is what you get! This is what you get!"

"Just throw her onto the street, Steinbach! Hitler wants her dead, not fucked."

"Fuck you, Kaspers! You had your shot. Now it's my turn!"

The focus is so intent on the beaten woman stretched out on her mattress, soaked in her blood, that no one sees Lotte. When she launches herself at the man called Kaspers, he is so caught off guard that he allows the much smaller female to trip him up and send him to the floor.

"Stop it! Stop it!" Lotte screams. "I'm a Leinsdorf! A Leinsdorf! My father publishes the People's Observer!" She uses her slender arms to power her way through the men to Anni's bedside where she is horrified to see her friend so mauled, bruised, and disfigured. Is she even alive, she wonders? "My great-uncle is Hindenburg. When he hears of this…"

The men back away. Only the man called Kaspers stands his ground. "You're lying," he says, rising to his feet. "Who are you? What right do you have to be here? Are you a Commie, like this cunt?"

Lotte's response upon seeing what these so-called men have done to her friend is to haul off and slug Kaspers in the mouth.

"That's who I am!" she shouts. "And when I tell Hitler how his boys handle women…. What do you think the press will do with that?"

Standing between the hulking Kaspers and Anni's bed, Lotte stares the much bigger man down.

"Kill 'em both," one of the men suggests.

"No. Not here. Not now.," Kaspers says, nursing his bloody mouth. "You better be who you say you are. Or this will happen to you. She better not write another article. Tell her that."

Kaspers swivels about and leaves, his men following. As soon as he is gone and as soon as Lotte can control her shaking, she bends over Anni, eyes swollen shut, naked from the waist down, breathing so softly her breaths are barely audible.

"Anni."

She gets no answer, then, heart pounding, goes into the kitchen area to run in a bowl of tepid water. Finding a ragged dishcloth, she wipes down Anni's face, removing all the blood, leaving behind the black and blue and scratches. Anni's fingers, she notices, are tainted with blood, but she suspects it might not be Anni's. Her friend put up a fight and gave as much as she could before she was overwhelmed.

"Now I know why Avi loves you so much," she says. "You're everything I'm not."

Unfortunately, the room is not equipped with a telephone. Removing Anni's skirt, she covers up her friend with a blanket and hurries downstairs for help. The Brownshirts have departed, but their lesbian enemies have stayed behind, aware that something bad must have happened in the building next door. It's easy to enlist their support, so that the next time Lotte hurries upstairs, she is not alone. By now, Anni has come to her senses and is trying to get herself into an upright position.

"Anni, no, don't," Lotte tells her. "What are you doing? Sit still."

"Call Avi."

"Not yet. You need a doctor. You should go to the hospital."

"I hate hospitals. Just get me into my tub and run next door to the cabaret to get some ice. I have painkillers over the sink."

"You can't stay here," Lotte tells her. "Not after this."

Anni nods, groans, lays back against her pillow. "Fuckers," she mutters. "I'll show them who won't write again. I recognized one of them."

"Anni, don't."

Anni falls into a deep sleep before she can reply, leaving Lotte at a loss.

"You're right," one of the women from the cabaret says. "They'll come back for her if she stays here. That's one feisty woman. She don't back down for nothing."

Lotte can hardly disagree. Now they'll all be in for it. As she heads out of the room to run in Anni's bath, she wonders if Anton might not be right, after all. A nunnery is sounding pretty damned good about now.

Chapter Twelve

Kreisler now has a number of reasons for traveling outside the country and heading for the elegant capital of Austria. Not only does he intend on attending Geli Raubal's funeral, he has now been equipped with two names, thanks to Henny Hoffmann: Geli's lover and Geli's obstetrician. If Waldmann wants names, he'll get names. If Anni wants to write Hitler's obituary, she can come along for the train ride.

He returns to his flat around midnight, with a full moon gracing the Munich night. Langer has dumped other cases on his desk, but Kreisler feels hopeful that he can wrap up his investigation within the week. He is closing in on Klara and David's killer and gathering enough information to satisfy Waldmann's readership. Whether or not he can prove beyond a doubt that Hitler fired the fatal bullet won't matter in the court of public opinion. Sullying Hitler's name may be enough.

"Herr Kreisler."

As soon as he enters his building carrying his bicycle, his landlord, Greene, confronts him in the hallway coming down the stairs from an upper floor.

"Herr Greene," Kreisler replies. "Aren't you up rather late? Rent isn't due yet."

"Not the rent, not the rent," Greene says. He is an elderly man who needs the handrail to maneuver the rickety stairs. "When are you going to put in that phone?"

"Soon. Soon, I promise."

"Well, you got visitors. They're not living with you, are they? I should take their phone calls, too?"

"I have visitors?" This could be good, or it could be very bad. "Male or female?"

"I didn't peek. I heard voices. My hearing…. But they can't live here unless you want to pay higher rent. I need to be informed of these things."

"So do I," Kreisler says. "Don't worry. I'll take care of it."

"The last thing I need is trouble."

Kreisler lets the old man pass before he jogs up the staircase. Two voices. Not waiting on the landing. Already inside his apartment. He can understand one voice. But two?

At his doorway, he leans his bike on the railing and takes out his Walther pistol. He's not taking any chances these days, but his door is locked, so he can't just push his way in.

"Hello?" He bangs on the door. For some reason, the picture that flashes through his mind is that of Klara Fries with an open window being hurled to her death. The hero tries battering down the door too late.

When Lotte unbolts the lock and shows herself, dried blood stuck to the strands of her hair, Kreisler raises his pistol as if he's going to take out whoever is responsible.

"Lotte, you've got blood in your hair." He reaches to touch it. "What are you doing here?"

"It's not me. It's not me, Avi," she says, wearily, a little too calmly for his liking.

"Not you?"

Then who?

Two voices, the landlord said.

"It's Anni," Lotte says. "It's a long story. Don't worry." She lowers his pistol and takes his arm.

"I shouldn't worry?"

"Not now, at least. We've just come from her place."

"She's all right? What is she doing here? What are you both doing here?"

Anni is lying in his bed, propped up on pillows, looking like she's just gone ten rounds with Max Schmeling. Two black eyes, swollen on the left side, a bloodied lip, and a bleeding nose. She is barely conscious but is able to react to his embrace and kiss before falling back onto the pillows.

"Fuck them!" Kreisler yells. "Who did this to you?"

"Brownshirts," Lotte says. "I was going over to her place to speak to her. About you. About us. And when I got there…"

"We need to get her to the hospital," Kreisler says, slipping his hands beneath Anni to lift her off the bed.

"She doesn't want to go," Lotte tells him. "We've already been through this with her. She wanted to come here."

"She could have a concussion, broken ribs. "

"No, Avi." Anni stirs, groans. "Tell Waldmann."

"What? What happened? The fucking Brownshirts? I'll kill them!"

Anni even manages a smile. "Such bravado. Call Waldmann."

"What is he going to do? Give you a glass of schnapps?"

"Just do me a favor. I can't go back to my place. Let me rest. Let me figure things out."

Before he can reply, Anni has fallen into unconsciousness again.

"We've already given her pain meds," Lotte says. I don't think anything is broken. But she was raped, so…"

"Raped?"

Kreisler loses his balance, drops to his knees beside Anni's bed. Rape is nothing new to him. He's been a street cop in Munich for a half decade before becoming a detective. Rape is a daily occurrence in Munich, sometimes prosecuted, most times ignored. But it has never happened to any woman he loves.

"She was lucky I happened by," Lotte says. "If I hadn't gotten there, they probably would have killed her."

"I want to know who did this. I want to know."

Kreisler caresses Anni's hand. Lotte remains standing, feeling awkward, looking every bit as beaten as Anni but without the notice or concern.

"The articles she writes for *Der Weg*. That's why they did it. She won't quit, Avi. You know that."

"She'll have to."

"She won't, and neither will you. Just do what she says. I'll take care of her as well as any doctor. You forget. I was pre-med. I don't think she has any broken bones. Just bruises. I felt her ribs. They seem okay."

"Internal bleeding? She could hemorrhage. You don't know."

"It's what she wants, Avi. You argue with her."

"I will," he says. "Later."

Decision made, he picks Anni's limp body up. "Your car is here?"

"You didn't see it? Parked right out front."

The closest hospital is only two miles away, five minutes by car. Kreisler isn't taking any chances. Anni is a stubborn woman who doesn't trust anyone in authority, including doctors. She is young, passionate, and thinks herself indestructible. This, at least, will prove her wrong about one thing.

Three hours later, four in the morning, they are back in Kreisler's apartment, nursing and nourishing Anni with a bowl of potato soup concocted by Lotte. Pumped up on painkillers, Anni is all mouth, stitched up though it is.

"Thank God I didn't lose any teeth," she says, slurping down her meal. "I can't go back to my apartment now. You think they fucked me up? You should see what they did to my place."

"Did you recognize any of them?" the detective asks.

"All Nazis look alike. It was dark. They caught me by surprise. By the time I knew what was going on, I just figured I was a dead woman. I can't go back there. I don't even know if I can go back to get my things. If anything's left."

"I'll go," Kreisler says.

"We'll go," Lotte corrects him. "I recognized one of the men. I heard names."

Lotte doesn't divulge what names or what face. She waits for Kreisler to give her some attention first. "I punched him in the face, actually. Rather forcefully, I thought."

"You did?"

"We're a team, aren't we?"

"Absolutely. By the way," Anni says, "I've arranged everything."

"Arranged?"

"For your girl. The funeral. At the Great Synagogue, with burial right after. Tomorrow."

"Tomorrow?"

"Avi, are you not capable of sentences of more than one word?" Anni finishes her soup, places it on the side table next to the bed. "You know us Jews. The quicker in the ground, the better. I would say the same for Hitler. Did you come up with any juice today?"

"Seriously? How about some sleep first?"

Kreisler can only gape at that lovely face, no longer quite so lovely. Apparently, she didn't get the Brownshirts' message. He glances at Lotte, but she still refuses to look at him, brushing out Anni's long red hair.

"I interviewed Henny Hoffmann, Heinrich Hoffmann's daughter. There's juice there. I also paid a visit to Klara Fries's other pharmacy, Lotte. I'm thinking it's almost time to go to the state prosecutor."

This at last gets Lotte to look at him. "Won't you have to get your bosses' approval for that?"

"Not necessarily. First, I'm going to Vienna if anyone wants to join me."

When two hands instantly shoot up into the air, Kreisler can only shake his head in wonder. He is a detective of the mind, not of the heart.

"You two, I am certain of this," he says, "will be the death of me."

* * *

Lebensraum.

This is a key element in the philosophy and policy of the National Socialists. It means Germany feels constricted, pressed in on all sides. In the west by France, which defeated Germany in the Great War and confiscated, as a result, Alsace-Lorraine. In the east, Russia and the Slavic nations. For the German race to attain the full greatness of its bloodline, it must swallow up more territory, east, west, north, and south, chew up the lesser peoples who currently occupy those lands, and repopulate them with Aryans.

Martin Kaspers is a Prussian German born in Latvia. His father was a Lutheran minister, his mother a dressmaker, and he was raised in a large family, the sixth of six children, the only son.

All appearances would indicate that Kaspers was a bright, energetic child, a capable student, somewhat introverted and bookish, with a love of hunting and sport. Girls appealed to him, and he, in turn, appealed to them. He is a rugged, blonde Aryan, after all, who could recite by heart Goethe and Rilke. His father wanted him to follow in his footsteps and become a minister. Kaspers, having raped and killed his first woman when he was fifteen, was honest enough with himself to discount that plan.

Instead, at eighteen, having earned his diploma, Kaspers was heading to university when revolution broke out in Russia and spilled over into his native Latvia. Chaos ensued as it will in wartime, and Kaspers was recruited by the German Freikorps to fight off native Latvian independence seekers. He has no problem with killing, so why not? Only, the Germans lost, and Kaspers took flight, emigrating to Germany, where he was ultimately introduced to the man, a fellow pharmacist, who months before ordered him to get as much dirt as possible on Adolf Hitler.

"You've been in a fight," this man says. He is a burly, broad-shouldered man cracking his knuckles as he negotiates a path between his desk and a window looking out onto a bright Munich morning.

Kaspers, a brawler himself, has placed himself in a chair out of the other man's way. His lip is swollen where Lotte struck him the night before. He says, "You wanted me to send a warning to *Der Weg*. That's what I did."

"To Der Weg. To Waldmann. You went after the woman, instead, didn't you?"

"Find the hole. Plug the hole."

"That's an ugly thing to say." Kaspers's superior sinks his hands in his suitcoat pockets as he views the traffic below.

"I never ordered you to blackmail Hitler. You gained access to him to get information, to spy."

"It was a way to provoke him."

"And to make a little money on the side?"

Kaspers remains silent.

"You like women," his superior says. He looks askance at Kaspers, perhaps regretting his decision to trust him.

"In my way."

"The wrong kind of woman, apparently."

"Which kind isn't?"

"The kind that doesn't commit you to a criminal activity. Two, in fact. First, the blackmail. Then, the murder. This brings the police into the mix. The key is to push Hitler. Not to involve us. He has his followers, but he isn't invulnerable. What makes Hitler so charismatic is also his vulnerability. I've learned this. I've seen this. Great oratory derived from some inner passion, which I, regrettably, lack. The oratorical skills, I mean. That's how he has won over the hearts and minds of so many people. But if they are made to see his true self…"

That can be said of anyone, Kaspers thinks.

"This is a game of cat and mouse," the other man says. "It takes cleverness, guile, which Hitler lacks. That is why he put me in charge of the organization. He invents the concept, then turns it over to people like me to make it work. For this reason, he will either fail or he will drive the party into the ground."

"He is not a true Socialist."

"He is a Jew-hater, pure and simple. And he can't distinguish between the two, Jews and Socialists. For him, they are one and the same. And the workingmen will suffer as a consequence. Who dies in wars? Working people. Hence, he must go, and I must be able to take his place as leader of the whole party."

Kaspers understands this. In part, he believes it. He doesn't like Jews either. Any more than he likes women. As for Hitler, he's just an Austrian fraud, about as Aryan as the niggers in darkest Africa.

"You didn't kill Fraulein Raubal, did you?" comes the unexpected question that finally upsets Kaspers. "For him?"

"No. Absolutely not. He did it."

"You're sure? People play both sides these days. I need to know you are with me."

"Of course, of course. Yes, I was there," Kaspers says. "Not in the room where she was shot. Outside. They argued. A shot was fired."

"By Hitler or by the girl?"

"I didn't see, but Hitler was beside himself with grief, still holding the weapon."

"Which you took from him and planted before you called me."

"Yes," Kaspers says, annoyed that he should have to repeat what he has told his boss many times since that morning. "I did what I could to control the situation. One of them called in Hess. I didn't."

Kaspers' boss, one of Hitler's inner circle, is relieved to hear the story repeated. But that doesn't clear up everything. "You killed the other one."

"She was talking to too many people."

"To Raubal?"

"Even so, I didn't kill her."

"Hitler did. Yes? In your opinion, at the very least."

"I have said so at least a hundred times."

At last, the broad-shouldered man finds satisfaction in the answer out of Kaspers he wants: a nod of the head, which elicits in himself an unapologetic cheer from the beast who would replace a monster.

"The Inspektor," he says. "This—"

"Kreisler. He's a Jew, though he tries to disguise it. His birth records are clear."

"Let him keep digging. Maybe he can expose Hitler." The idea has much merit. "Let him do the provoking. Let him take the brunt of the backlash. And let him die, if he must, along with everyone else in his orbit, so long as the blame falls on one man. Not on us."

Chapter Thirteen

Anni will move in with Kreisler even though his rent will go through the roof now. The landlord, Greene, is old-fashioned and doesn't like the thought of unmarried couples cohabiting. But he will accept their money. Maybe if Kreisler has his own phone installed...

Kreisler is not completely dense or thoughtless when it comes to affairs of the heart. In the few hours that remained before the next day was to begin, he slept on the couch while Lotte shared the bed with Anni. But he hears Lotte, first thing in the morning, awake before the others, on the landing outside the flat, smoking a borrowed cigarette, sitting on the top stair facing the floor below, weeping.

"Lotte?"

She glances up and behind at Kreisler, half-dressed, trying to stifle her tears. Smoking might help, but, being unaccustomed to the intake of poison, she utters a series of coughs that wrack her body.

"When did you pick up that habit?" he asks as he sits beside her.

"About five minutes ago. Am I doing it wrong?"

Kreisler takes the cigarette from her, studies it for a moment, takes a puff, then puts it out on the floor. "That's the only right way to do that. My uncle Fuchs smokes two packs of these a day. I can hear him coughing in Berlin."

Lotte smiles, wipes her eyes on her sleeve, brushes her bangs away from her eyes. It is the first time he notices a bruise on her forehead.

"How did you get that?" he asks, touching the fading mark. "You were bleeding. From your bout with the SA?"

She shrugs, turning her face away, a shy, flirtatious gesture. "I'm afraid that would have been too heroic of me. No, I banged my head on the steering wheel of my car. Too much wine for dinner. You know. But don't worry, I'm not going down that road again."

"I know you won't."

Downstairs, someone is hammering. Kreisler doubts it's Greene. His landlord is so old and decrepit, he can hardly lift a fork. Maybe one of the other residents is hanging something in their apartment, or Greene has hired a workman to repair the front stairs. An inexpensive workman.

Lotte says, "My parents want me to get married. They've got their eyes on someone like Baron von Millionaire. Worse, they'd be thrilled if I married a National Socialist. Imagine me: Frau Hitler. I ran out on them. Drunk. Some hero, huh?"

"You are a hero. You saved Anni's life."

"Only to have her—"

"What?"

"Nothing. I was about to be unsympathetic."

Leaning against the handrail, Lotte hides her face in her hands. Her breath is raspy. Perhaps from the tobacco. Perhaps from too much crying.

"I've had some crazy thoughts the last few days," she says, still in hiding.

"Such as?"

"I could marry Anton. At least, he couldn't become a priest then. I'd edit his plays, manage his career."

"Good luck with that."

"It was just a thought. A crazy one, like I said. I dreamed about my sister last night."

Abruptly, she begins to sob again. Hard, bitter tears. Kreisler thinks she looks so small next to him, fragile, that she might even break apart right on these stairs and leave nothing of herself behind. He takes her in his arms, holding the back of her head tightly against his shoulder.

"I'm sorry. I'm sorry. I promised myself all last night I wouldn't do this," she says.

"It's all right."

"No, it isn't. It's selfish of me. You and Anni make a fine couple."

"You're just tired. We all are. Hell, the whole world is."

"The whole world isn't us."

I don't care about the rest of the world, she is thinking. *Let it rot.* Slowly, her despair subsides, her loneliness, and she listens to the beating of his heart, pumping hard. He is sharing her moment of desperation, she can tell. But what, in the end, does it mean?

"I love you, Avi," she whispers so that at the very least his heart can hear her.

"Yes. I know."

"But you don't love me. Not like you love her. Who can understand it? How love forms?" And dies. Lotte makes an effort to control her emotions, pushing away from him. "I'll get over it," she says. "There must be one good Nazi out there who would make my parents happy."

"Probably more than I would." At least, she can joke, Kreisler thinks. "You could move in with us," he says. The notion born, flies from Kreisler's lips before he can hold it back. Whatever reaction he expects from Lotte, laughter isn't one of them.

"I'm not a prude," she says, chuckling, "but I'm no Mormon either. I'm used to my own bed, my own closet. Just promise me one thing, will you, Avi?"

He lets her kiss him then, lets her caress his face. Her eyes beam hope his way. "If something should happen, take care of me, will you? Don't let me linger."

* * *

Klara Fries was too young to die. But being dead, she deserves a place to rest. At least, that is Kreisler's opinion. But having three atheists and a lapsed Catholic like Anton conduct a service is asking too much.

Dov Birnbaum graciously took over as rabbi and coffin carrier along with

Kreisler, Anton, Waldmann, the publisher, Klara's neighbor Kurt, and two other members of Birnbaum's synagogue. The women aren't allowed to touch the coffin, though they can walk behind at a respectful distance. It is only at this mournful moment that Kreisler realizes how few male friends he has. Or, at least, how many friends he can count on to attend such a ceremony.

Frau Becker, Klara's landlady, has come escorted by Kurt. Kreisler breaks away from Anni and Lotte to have a brief conversation with her.

"Frau Becker, how nice to have you come. I'm sure Klara would have appreciated it."

"What else could I do for the poor child?"

"Her room," Kreisler says, getting to the succinct point of his greeting her. "Have you rented it out yet?"

"No. I haven't had the chance or the heart."

"It is as Klara left it?"

"As you left it, Inspektor."

"Good. Good," he says. "Keep it that way for just a little while longer if you can. I was not as efficient in going through the apartment as I should have been." Excitement at discovering the blackmail letter that evening had disrupted his train of thought. Very unprofessional.

"Oh, well, as you will," Frau Becker replies. "But I must have it back soon. I need the rental income."

"I may, in fact, have another tenant in mind."

The men are wearing yarmulkes. Lotte walks beside a still sore and limping Anni down a lane bordered by shade trees on both sides. The New Israelite Cemetery, built in 1908, is quite extensive and is surrounded by a wall over two meters high for the peace and protection of the occupants who, it is believed, will arise on the Last Day.

The only sound is Birnbaum's chanting a prayer that Kreisler would be embarrassed to say he's unfamiliar with. At the gravesite, set close to the wall, they lower the casket near a hole already dug, and Birnbaum finishes his prayer. Then silence as each of the celebrants looks to another one to say something out of respect for the departed.

"Well, I suppose it's my turn," Kreisler says.

"This was your idea, Avi." Birnbaum nudges him.

"Klara Fries. Let's give her a name. How's that for a start? If we can't afford a grave stone or plaque or something, she can at least know we know where she is and who she was."

Kreisler feels Anni move in beside him, Lotte, beside her. Anton, behind them.

"She was a free spirit," says Anton.

"She was an artist," says Anni.

"A singer," says Lotte.

"A child of God," says Birnbaum, "Praised be He."

"And she deserved better than this." Kreisler looks up and to his right. Waldmann has not joined them in the closing testimony. He has run into a stranger, a man in a long coat and a wide-brimmed hat that covers his face. They are speaking to one another in earnest fashion, eyes lowered to the ground, Waldmann wagging a finger, the other man nodding in rhythm.

"And she was a good person. Fuck what anyone else thinks."

After Kurt recites what turns out to be the concluding sentiment, a thoughtful stillness falls over the cemetery. Thousands of graves offer companionship to the newest member. Some are veterans of the Great War, Jewish artisans and professionals who saw themselves as German first and who died fighting the Jews of England and France. Politicians are buried here. Educators. Poets. Policemen. Every one of them, no matter their social status or social influence, a Jew.

"Well, I hope she wasn't anti-Semitic," Kreisler says and turns away to let the cemetery staff take over the business of lowering the coffin and its contents into the grave. "Not for me," he tells the others.

"Not for you, what, Avi?" Anni asks.

"A hole in the ground. Six feet of topsoil over a claustrophobic box."

"You'll be dead. You won't know a thing."

"How do you know that? Read Poe sometime. *The Premature Burial.*"

Anni grips his arm on one side. Lotte takes the other, Kreisler eying Waldmann and the secretive man still engaged in an intense discussion of some kind. Around them, on the far side of the two-meter-high wall, Munich goes about its daily affairs. From the trees, showing their first autumn colors, birds descend looking for food on the cemetery floor.

"When it's my turn," Kreisler says, "it will be on my terms. *Meine Ort. Meine Zeit. Meine Hand.* My place. My time. My hand. A quiet place out in the country, I think, overlooking a pond or lake. A summer day, preferably warm and sunny. A bottle of pills…. A pistol is too messy… and a bottle of water. A final salute to the world that really doesn't care, and that's that."

"You'd deprive us the pleasure of seeing you off?" Lotte asks.

"I'll take you with me, if you want," Kreisler says with a smirk. With a sudden motion, he redirects the trio toward Waldmann, calling out, "Hey, Publisher, you missed all the excitement. You had no words for Klara? She could be your ticket to Hitler's own demise."

Waldmann and his fellow conversationalist cease talking. They have moved toward a bench with a squirrel perched on the back of the seat. The squirrel bolts upon Kreisler's approach. Waldmann pokes his companion with an elbow, and the secretive man finally shows his face.

"We need to speak, Inspektor Kreisler," this man says, noting the two women. "In private, if it doesn't offend the ladies."

"It does," says Anni, "but we'll wheedle it out of him later anyway, so go ahead."

With a bow to his co-conspirator, Waldmann bids his adieu and escorts Anni and Lotte and Anton out of hearing distance, regaling them with an inappropriate joke. "Did you hear the one about the National Socialist and the orthodox rabbi going to a barbershop?"

The punchline disappears with the comic and his audience. Even though they have moved a distance away, the stranger directs Kreisler in the other direction as if the wind can carry his words to the others.

"You know that one?" he asks.

"The joke?" Kreisler looks around in time to see Waldmann cackle at his own humor. The ladies don't seem too amused. "I think it has something to do with the rabbi's beard and Hitler's moustache, if I'm not mistaken. More synagogue humor than cabaret. Not entirely my thing."

"It is hard to laugh at anything these days," the other man says. "My name is Glaser. Max Glaser. I'm a prosecutor in the Munich court. Your name, your work in particular, has come to my attention."

"Via Waldmann."

"And other sources. I've been an attorney, a prosecutor, in Munich for twenty years. I still have some friends on the force."

"More than I probably."

Glaser halts behind the thick trunk of a maple tree, much too dramatic, Kreisler thinks, for whatever this prosecutor wants to tell him.

"It is this Hitler business," Glaser says. He is even speaking *sotto voce*. Kreisler's alarm bells are ringing just as cautiously. "You're investigating the death of his niece, are you not?"

"Yes and no."

"They don't want you digging too deep, is that it?"

Kreisler keeps a steady gaze on the prosecutor. He isn't ready to surrender anything to a man he just met. "No one knows what to do about Hitler, in my mind. Is he rising? Is he falling? People don't know whether to cling to him as he goes up or jump all over him as he comes down. Are you the former or the latter?"

"Me? I'm just a prosecutor who wants to do his job."

"Hence, all this secrecy. You didn't want to meet me in your office."

"No, I didn't," Glaser admits.

"So, you're the latter," Kreisler concludes, the detective building his case. "You know Waldmann. He arranged to bring you here, I assume."

"He did." Glaser is a man of average height, average looks, middle-aged. He wouldn't stand out anywhere. Yet there is an intensity about his eyes, dark, feral almost, that belies everything else. He is a man on a mission. "Did Geli Raubal commit suicide as Hitler claims in all the media? Or do you suspect otherwise? Is that why you've been handcuffed by your own people?"

So, now we get to the point, Kreisler thinks. But how much should he reveal? Glaser could be friends with the National Socialists, just trying to pry into how much the detective knows that could be injurious to the star

Nazi.

"There are details to the case that suggest other solutions," is all Kreisler will say.

"Understood. My own contacts believe it wasn't a suicide. They won't tell me what they think happened. But that disquiet tells me a lot. That Hitler shot his niece, by accident or otherwise, does it matter? They had been arguing. She was pregnant."

"Who told you that?" Not the pathologist, that was certain. Kreisler steps into Glaser, now the interrogator, feeling blindsided.

"At a restaurant, The Bratwurstglöckl, I believe. Speak to the owner, Inspektor. He saw things. He heard things. It can be done, you know."

Now Kreisler takes a step back, wanting to create distance between himself and the prosecutor in case he decides, like the squirrel, to bolt. "What can be done?" he says, taking in Glaser eyeball to eyeball. "What's in it for you? Besides the law."

"Hitler can be taken down. The National Socialists can be taken down. It was almost done in Berlin in May. What was done there can be done here if we proceed with enough bullets in our gun."

An interesting way of putting it, Kreisler thinks. So thinks Waldmann, too. In which case, maybe Glaser is a socialist, and this is merely a political maneuver. An important one, maybe. But Kriesler's not close to accepting Glaser's commission. "You want to take Hitler down?"

"I do."

"Out of political rivalry?"

"Out of fear for the future of our country."

"Fair enough," Kreisler says. "Tell me what happened in May. In Berlin."

Glaser steps forward again, closing the gap. "Hans Litten is a prosecutor in the capital. A Jewish prosecutor. Contact him, if you want. Two workers from the Socialist party were stabbed to death by four members of the SA."

"Brownshirts."

"Fights like this between the two camps happen all the time. But Litten saw an opening. A brilliant and, I must say, a daring legal strategist. In front of the world, for hours, he interrogated Hitler, this Jewish attorney, no older than yourself, I would estimate, made him look foolish, dangerous. If he could link Hitler's violent rhetoric, the rules of destructive action he created for his party, then Litten could assert that Hitler was as guilty of the murder of those working men as the four men who actually did the killing."

"A neat trick. If he could pull it off," Kreisler says. But skepticism is his hallmark.

"If he couldn't, maybe we can," Glaser insists. "A second trial. A second interrogation. Not so coincidental anymore. Especially when the death involves Hitler's own niece, in his own apartment, with his own gun, after he has had, as we all suspect, grotesquely inappropriate relations with her."

Glaser is practically drooling with eagerness to put Hitler on the stand. Kreisler may be similarly persuaded, but he needs time to think. After what Anni just endured, can he risk dragging her and Lotte into something that could turn out very bad?

"Litten was unfortunate," Glaser says. "The judge on the case caved in to pressure. He cut Litten off. But there were other investigations all through this past summer. Hitler perjuring himself on the witness stand. I'm surprised you didn't read it in the papers. It made Hitler look culpable, and that is the last thing he wants as he courts the highbrows and working people of Germany. He wants the appearance of legality to make his rise, and he is busy all the time undercutting himself. Just a little shove, Inspektor, and down he goes."

Or down we all go if we fail, Kreisler thinks. Violence out in the public is troubling enough for a man who wants the crown. But if that violence was of his own doing against his own flesh and blood? In his own residence.

"His world is turning upside down," Kreisler says, making Hitler ever more dangerous.

"Yes. Absolutely. Whether or not he is guilty of Geli Raubal's demise," Glaser says with the eagerness of a cat about to pounce on dinner, "becomes irrelevant if the public suspects he is guilty. Waldmann has told me you are working with him."

"Well," Kreisler demurs, "let's not go that far. Herr Waldmann likes telling jokes."

"But this time let the joke be on Hitler. I can bring this case to trial if you can give me more substantial evidence to go on," Glaser says. "Just enough to let me bring the case before a jury. Win or lose, I don't care. Talk to the owner of the restaurant. Put Hitler in that room with Geli Raubal. Make it clear beyond a shadow of a doubt that he pulled the trigger, and we will save Germany. Perhaps all of Europe."

Kreisler is the sort of man who will not attach himself to any cause without excruciating deliberation. It is what has kept him since the loss of his parents from affiliating with any political group, religion, philosophy, or deep personal relationship. Hence, Anni and Lotte. A change has come over him since he has become a detective or since the world has begun to shove back and insist he become involved or become hopelessly irrelevant. He is only twenty-eight years old. But youth can no longer be used as an excuse. Geli Raubal, Klara Fries, David Sussman were all younger than he is, and now they are, along with his entire family, excepting the Fuchses, gone. So might the rest of Germany be if he doesn't act.

"The Bratwurstgröckl, you said." Kreisler gives in to Glaser's request. "All right. Tomorrow I'm going to Vienna. Geli Raubal is being buried. I'll get back to you if I come up with anything."

"Wonderful!" The prosecutor can't help himself, lifting his voice in excitement before remembering where he is. "As Caesar said, '*Alea iacta est.*' The die is cast. Good luck, Inspektor."

Yuh, Kreisler thinks. *That and a million marks will buy me a gravestone.*

Chapter Fourteen

It has been decided that only Lotte will accompany Kreisler to Vienna. Anni is not fully recovered from her assault. Her apartment was destroyed in the attack; everything, including her clothes, was damaged. So, during the day after the funeral, Lotte goes from store to store buying Anni a new wardrobe, perfectly working class. While Kreisler and Lotte are entrained for Vienna, tomorrow, Anni can start writing her own account of the SA attack and have it ready for Waldmann to print the next day.

The National Socialist press has already flooded the streets of the city with a counter-attack article penned by Hitler himself, condemning the left-wing press for spreading lies about his darling niece and himself. The right-wing propaganda machine run by Gregor Strasser and Josef Goebbels strikes out with rhetoric that seems to corroborate the opinions of lawyers Hans Litten and Max Glaser that Hitler's oratory intentionally propagates violence. The nation is titillated by the news. Munich is rocked by it.

In the evening, after an afternoon of rest, Anni is up for dinner at the Bratwurstglöckl, though the presence of Brownshirts and Schutzstaffel on the street and even in the restaurant causes her to lean heavily on Kreisler for strength. Fights break out wherever SA men confront members of the Communist or Socialist parties.

Anton was wary about bringing the women outside. He'd been handed a flier on his tram ride over calling for a protest march on behalf of Hitler. It was the two women who convinced Kreisler he needed to speak to the owner of the restaurant as soon as possible.

"It is as if madness has taken hold of us all," the owner, Herr Klintsch, tells them. He has seated them himself center-stage, and has to speak over the singing of a young cabaret performer who has the small crowd clapping to her melody. "I've hired two additional cops to keep the peace in here. Last night, a broken chair, a broken chandelier. All the politicians talk unity. This is not unity."

"Not all of the politicians talk unity," Kreisler says. "You were here the night Herr Hitler and his niece argued, I've been told. Hours, perhaps, before she killed herself."

"A terrible thing. Suicide. Yes, I suppose that must be the case."

"You must tell me everything you saw and everything you heard. This goes to motive," Kreisler says. He shifts his chair closer to that of Klintsch, briefly isolating himself from Anni, Lotte, and Anton. Even so, protecting them from retribution may be impossible. Anni won't back down anyway. Neither will Lotte anymore. As far as the Nazis are concerned, Kreisler thinks, if Waldmann and Glaser are right, we will all be considered witnesses to the crime of the century. All in line for termination.

"Will this go to trial?" the restaurant owner asks. "I won't be called on to testify, will I?"

"It is a suicide," Kreisler lies. "No testimony will be required."

"You're certain? I have a wife, children."

"On my word. Who else heard or saw this argument? Staff? Were Hitler and his niece by themselves or accompanied by guards?"

Cautious despite his surroundings, Klintsch looks about. He abruptly straightens in his chair when his gaze fixes on the entrance to the dining room. "Well, that one," he says, nodding toward the maître d' who is chatting with a man and woman. Both are familiar to Kreisler. The man is tall, Aryan, and brutish. The woman, much younger with a similarly Aryan appearance.

"The SA man, the pharmacist," Kreisler says. "We bumped into him at Sussman's pharmacy, Lotte. One of Hitler's personal bodyguards."

"That's the one I punched in the face!" she exclaims. "The one who..."

Kreisler has to keep Lotte from rising in her chair, afraid she might give everything away by pointing and hollering at him. Whatever murderous rage Kreisler himself might feel, he has to suppress. He's not a little bit surprised to recognize the young woman he's dating.

"He's robbing the cradle with that one," Anton says.

"Eva Braun."

Kreisler watches the pair as they are conducted to a table in a private room. Eva, however, with a tug and a pleading look at the SA rapist, apparently causes a change of plans, and they are seated only a few tables away, facing the stage and the singer.

"She loves to sing, that one," Klintsch says. "She's here occasionally with Herr Hitler. He is tolerant. Perhaps when Fraulein Raubal is out of town."

"Was."

"Pardon?"

"Was out of town," Kreisler corrects the restaurant owner. "She's dead lest we forget that, Herr Klintsch."

"Of course."

"Be that as it may," Kreisler says, keeping half an eye on Klintsch and the other half on Eva Braun and her escort for the night, "the argument between Herr Hitler and Fraulein Raubal. What do you remember?"

Like Kreisler, Klintsch's focus shifts. Stuttering, he starts to leave his seat as if he has changed his mind and no longer wants to tell what he knows. Kreisler takes hold of his arm and brings him back.

"So, the SA man…"

"Herr Kaspers?"

"Yes, him. He was there."

"The shouting was so loud, people in the dining hall could hear them. My waiter panicked and brought me in to see if I could calm things. Herr Kaspers had already intervened. He was standing between them, trying to get them to stop. But Fraulein Raubal was insisting she was going."

"Home?"

"No, no. To Vienna. I believe that is what she said. And, and…"

The words that Kreisler can see Klintsch intending to say next get stuck in his mouth. A bite of some meal that is utterly distasteful but that he can't spit out onto the floor without offending his guests. Until they have to be released or Klintsch will choke on them.

"'You're pregnant?' That's what he said. He shouted, I should say. Herr Hitler. Then lunged at Fraulein Raubal. Herr Kaspers protected her, and she ran out crying. He had to stay with Herr Hitler until he calmed down. Herr Hitler was remorseful. I was shaking, but he told me to run out and fetch her, bring her back because they hadn't finished their meal. Herr Hitler even apologized to me. I'll never forget that night, Inspektor. Especially after what happened to her after that."

"An unfortunate situation all around," Kreisler sympathizes. But it is the last recollection that Klintsch lays on him that is most disturbing.

"By a Jew, I distinctly heard Herr Hitler whisper to Herr Kaspers as I was leaving. A Jew. My God, I thought, he will surely kill her now." Klintsch glances toward the table occupied by Kaspers and Eva Braun as if to check whether or not they heard his revelation. Both are smoking, watching the singer, Fraulein Braun moving in time to the music, Kaspers surveying the dining hall until his gaze falls directly on Kreisler.

Without missing a beat himself, Kreisler raises his stein of beer and toasts the SA man, Hitler's guard. "I thank you, Herr Klintsch," he says. "You've been most helpful. You have given me work to do."

Klintsch is grateful to be able to vanish then. "So, a Jew," says Anni. "One of us. Worth killing for?"

"It would seem so," Kreisler says, setting down his beer and offering a smile to his companions as if nothing has transpired here other than a pleasant conversation with the restaurant staff. Geli killed for being pregnant by a Jew. *But*, he wonders, *who pulled the trigger?*

* * *

Vienna lies four hundred and four kilometers from Munich. By train, that would take Kreisler at least six hours, and he intends on leaving for the Austrian capital as early as possible. No later than six in the morning. By car, the ride will take about four hours if the traffic is light. So, by car it is with Lotte at the wheel. Anni will stay behind, but with an assignment if she is up to it.

"I am."

"I have dozens of photographs from my crime scenes," Kreisler tells her. "Have Henny Hoffman process them at the Hoffman photo studio. Henny. No one else. Tell her it's important and needs to be done right away. Her eyes only. For Geli."

"You trust her?"

"More than HQ."

Hitler has his own coterie attending the funeral of his niece. It is protocol and a wise political gesture. He prefers the drive by automobile to the train out of the busy Hauptbahnhof, but he will not travel with Geli's mother or sister to Vienna's *Zentralfriedhof*. They have preceded Hitler by train, accompanying the casket with Geli Raubal's body.

Hitler wants to avoid the crowds, all too well aware, thanks to the left-wing and right-wing newspapers publicizing where the leader of the National Socialists will be going today, of the national spotlight he is in. He is less fearful of the jeers from the Communist throngs who would hound him than he is of the shouts of support from his own people. How can he smile and wave and reply to the 'Heil Hitlers' when the weight of the world is on him? He knows what he did. They don't.

Julius Schreck is driving him to Vienna. He replaced the former chauffeur Emil Maurice, who had a fling with Geli, who was never the good little girl Hitler wanted her to be. Heinrich Hoffman sits in the back seat with Hitler, but will not be allowed to take any photos of the service. Gregor Strasser and Heinrich Himmler drive with him, as well, a show of National Socialist celebrity. Ernst Röhm, the head of the Sturmabteilung, follows in a second car with Rudolf Hess, Baldur von Shirach, and Franz Gürtner, the Bavarian Minister of Justice, Kreisler's ultimate boss. Women are noticeably absent in the assemblage.

By the time Kreisler arrives at the *Zentralfreidhof* with Lotte at the wheel, the funeral service has begun, conducted by Father Johann Pant. Dr. Müller, the Munich pathologist, said that Geli's mother not only took responsibility for arranging the funeral and selecting the site but also paid the full cost. Hitler didn't contribute a pfennig. The good Father has been apparently told that the Munich press got it wrong. Geli did not commit suicide. That report was a horrible blunder. She was killed by her own hand, yes, but in an accident as she was cleaning one of her own pistols.

Kreisler has to consult a map of the cemetery to locate the funeral. Angela Hitler obviously didn't restrict her purse for her eldest daughter. An intimate crowd has gathered around plot 9 near the Luegerkirche, a beautiful church in the very center of one of the largest cemeteries in the world. Whether or not it is meant as a slap in the face to her half-brother, Frau Hitler is telling the world that her child was someone special who belonged spending eternity with the most notable of Austrians. The Hitlers are not German. They are Austrian. Will Adolf end up in such a place? Not likely.

Lotte maintains a restraining grip on Kreisler's arm as they take the path toward the church. She'd prefer not to be spotted and become the central focus of everyone's attention. This is Geli Raubal's day. Her last one above ground.

"Are you sure you want to talk to Hitler? Will they even let you?" she wonders, gripped by worry.

"Look at the architecture of the church. Middle Eastern influence, I think. St. Peters meets Ancient Egypt.".

"That's not an answer."

"No, but it's my in." A flowered circular plaza fronts the church. Geli's funeral is being conducted beneath trees to Kreisler's right, a much more sumptuous and dignified setting than the one he had provided for Klara Fries. "Hitler is essentially a very lonely man, a misfit. He knows it. He tries to hide it, but he lives in fear of being found out."

"Herr Freud."

"I'm just saying. There is a human surviving within the monster."

"And you can befriend the man who killed his niece?"

Kreisler breaks his professional detective guise briefly to give Lotte a kiss on the cheek and a hug around the waist. "Well," he says, "maybe there's a monster surviving within *this* human, too."

He starts forward, bringing Lotte with him. The backs of the mourners are to him, a line of SS and SA guards at the very rear, competing even here for

Hitler's favor. Kreisler took the time that morning to dress in his mournful best. Lotte is a sight in black. Even so, they garner suspicious looks as they break ranks and push into the small gathering of Nazi dignitaries. Hitler, himself, wedged in between the photographer Hoffman and his chauffeur Schreck, seems distracted and catches sight of the interlopers.

"Stay with me," Kreisler whispers to Lotte. "We'll be safer together."

"Safer? I thought you said…"

Few of the gathered are paying attention to Father Pant as he intones a prayer, "Oh, Angela, may the Lord embrace you passionately in His palm, until we meet again in Paradise."

How can any of these people say they believe in God, Kreisler wonders, when what they truly worship is power? They are not saying good-bye to a fellow human, a lamb of God. They are working their way up the ranks of authority in the hopes of becoming gods themselves.

Perhaps there is an elaborate lunch prepared for after the service, either in the church or elsewhere nearby. Hitler's men are probably quite hungry, and hunger always transcends compassion. Hitler is no role model for them, fidgeting, restless, longing, no doubt, to be away as quickly as possible, back to the political grind, the exciting, ego-indulging rallies. He will be haunted by Geli Raubal's death for some time, but not forever.

Kreisler intends to intercept the man he assumes is Geli's killer on the way back to his Mercedes. With Lotte in tow, he figures he can get close enough to identify himself, point out the beautiful architecture of the church, and grab a few moments to speak to the would-be chancellor of Germany.

He is, in fact, maneuvering his way through the clot of uniformed Nazi henchmen when, for some reason, his attention is diverted. Perhaps it is the cigarette smoke, puffed into his face by an SA guard, that causes him to turn his head. In that moment, he catches sight of something that immediately has his guard up.

A young man, quite out of place, is moving like a Semitic shark through enemy Aryan waters. What a fool, Kreisler thinks, wearing a yarmulke no less at a Nazi funeral. Is the man crazy? Is he suicidal? Does he want to end up right beside Geli Raubal?

Then it hits him. Abrupt and stupefying. This man is not out of place at all.

"Stay here, Lotte," he orders her.

"What? Why? Where are you going?"

"That man over there. He's carrying a pistol."

"How can you tell?"

Kreisler doesn't have time to explain that this man, perhaps in his early twenties, has his right hand thrust inside a coat pocket. The arm is trembling. But it is the look on the face of the man that tells Kreisler he has every intention of shooting Hitler.

"That's the father of Geli's baby," he whispers before abandoning her and moving to get to the young man before he can make the mistake of his life.

Hitler's black-clad, red arm-banded sentinels have noticed him, too. Kreisler has one eye on them and one on the man he is certain fathered the doomed child of Geli Raubal. Before they can tackle the assassin, Kreisler swoops in.

"Don't be an idiot!" he says, latching onto the startled young man and forcing him back, unconcerned about anyone he has to shove out of the way in order to move Geli's Jewish lover out of harm's way.

"Let me go!"

"Give me the gun!"

Kreisler doesn't care if the man obeys his order. Tightening his grip on the arm, he causes the man to cry out in pain and release the hidden weapon. Kreisler is able to grab it and hide it within his own coat before the first of the Nazi guards intervenes, ready to pummel the intruder.

"Who are you? Who are you?" they shout, violence their first instinct. "Let us have this man!"

They are like cockroaches on the crust of a discarded piece of bread. Geli's lover is thrown to the ground. Kreisler is pushed aside. The beating begins. Fists. Feet. Boots. Claws. It is Lotte's shout and intervention that causes the thugs to hesitate. But it is a shout from one of their own, Ernst Röhm, that makes them stop the punching and kicking. Only then does Kreisler have the opportunity to show his Munich police credentials.

"I'm a cop! I have him. There are two Jewish cemeteries here. He probably just got lost."

Even so, Röhm orders his men to search the bruised creature lying on the ground, now in tears, harmless as it turns out. They find no weapons on him.

"I've come to Vienna to pay my respects," Kreisler explains, "to Herr Hitler and to his niece. I've been investigating her case."

"And this man, this Jew?"

"A nobody. I'll take care of him, find out what he was doing here. You should return to the service. Herr Hitler, I'm sure, doesn't want any bad press coming out of this."

Röhm is smart enough to pull his troops away, clever enough to have put on a good show for anyone who thinks he is trying to challenge Hitler for leadership of the party. As soon as the SA and Himmler's SS have backed off and returned to the funeral, Kreisler pulls Geli's lover to his feet, yanks the yarmulke off his head, tosses it on the ground, and stamps on it. Then he throws a mean punch to the young man's jaw before picking him up again.

"This is all for show," he says, speaking calmly. "I'm Jewish, too. I could have hit you harder. That was a crazy thing you just tried to pull off."

"What crazy? He killed my Geli!"

"Keep your voice down." Kreisler maintains his act, dragging the man over to a stone bench and plopping him down. "Your name," he says. "What is it?"

"Chaim Lerner."

"You're an actor?"

"What?"

"An actor? A singer?"

"An actor. How did you know? Did you know Geli?"

Kreisler looks around. Lotte is hurrying over, calling his name. "It figures, that's all. You're no Othello, I'll tell you that."

"What?"

"Shakespeare, for the love of God."

Lotte comes up, breathless, just in time to play Desdemona to Lerner's melodramatic fated Moor. "Avi, is he all right? What just happened? Those men—"

"We're fine," Kreisler says, feeling the stolen pistol in his pocket. "Did you really think you could get away with shooting Hitler? In front of all of these soldiers?" He shakes Lerner for the benefit of those watching.

"I…I…I don't know. We were in love. She wanted to run away and come to Vienna, so we could live together, have a family, raise a child."

"As a Jew?" The cynic in Kreisler rises to the surface. He can see in the soft look in Lotte's face that she buys Lerner's desperate, demented wish. "Look, you're lucky I was here," Kreisler says. "I'm telling you, frankly, it wouldn't have worked out. Not that I doubt your sincerity."

"Geli was coming! She *was* coming," Lerner shouts to the point that Kreisler has to smack him across the face. The SA are only meters away still. "I swear it!" he claims with a much lower voice. "To Semmering. To meet me there. She was really going to leave him this time. That's why he killed her."

"So far, only a theory," Kreisler says. "A girl such as Geli Raubal does not marry a Jew." But a point is made that intrigues him. He feels the pistol hidden in his coat. It is a small revolver, not like Hitler's heavier Walther that was discovered in Geli's room, presumably the murder weapon. "Did Geli know how to use a gun?" he asks.

"She was learning. She was afraid of the violence in Munich and felt she needed protection."

"She used a Walther?"

"I don't know."

"Or something like this?" Kreisler indicates the weapon in his pocket. "Small. A woman's weapon."

"Yes, more like that," Lerner says. "I bought it for her. I don't know names."

Unlike this actor, Kreisler is a pro at hiding his emotions. He will give nothing away. But his excitement is building. "She owned her own gun?"

"Yes. Two of them. One, I gave her. One, I think Hitler gave her."

"Then there was no need for her to leave her bedroom, travel to Hitler's room, steal his gun and use that to shoot herself when she had her own more convenient suicide device? It makes no sense." Sauer and Forster left this out of their final report to Justice Minister Gürtner.

Kreisler curses himself for not having had the opportunity to do a more thorough search of her room. Sauer and Forster took over that responsibility before he or Fritz Langer could explore her drawers or closet. Not that Langer would have been any more ethical. If the other detectives did their job, then maybe they discovered the weapon that Geli would have used if she truly intended on shooting herself. Those weapons would now be iron fragments in some Munich scrap heap.

"She liked shooting," Lerner adds. "She told me she was getting very good at target practice."

So, presumably, had she shot herself, Kreisler thinks, *she would have done a better job of it.*

He dismisses Lerner then, placing a hand on his back and pushing him away with an admonition to stay away from Hitler and to live a longer life. To Lotte, he says, "Glaser will like this. Hitler's gun was at the crime scene. The only person who would have brought it in was Hitler himself."

"Probably. But not positively," Lotte argues back. "Who else in the household had access to his gun?"

"What are you: his attorney?" Kreisler's attention has turned back toward the service, which is breaking up. "The important thing is, she had other pistols at her disposal to shoot herself. She didn't use those but, for some reason, grabbed Hitler's weapon out of his room, brought it back to her own, locked the door so no one could get in, then shot herself. Why? To place the blame on him?"

"To make him feel guilty," Lotte says. She's a woman, after all. That's what she would have done. You loved me. You discarded me. But you will remember me forever in guilt.

Hitler is leaving now. Everyone is heading toward the line of vehicles that brought them to the cemetery. The appearance and interrogation of Lerner was unplanned. It is Hitler Kreisler is here to see.

With a brusque, "Let's go", he pulls Lotte along as he goes after the National Socialist leader before Geli's uncle can make his escape.

"Herr Hitler! A word!"

Hitler is like a magnet drawing around him uniformed guards of the

Sturmabteilung and the Schutzstaffel. Kreisler recognizes other Nazi luminaries. He had spotted Hess outside Prinzregentenplatz 16 on the day of Geli's murder. Forming a brace around Hitler is Strasser, the Berlin party chief, and Himmler, formerly Strasser's underling, now leader of the feared Schutzstaffel. Strasser is dressed as a civilian, Himmler in his full military regalia.

Kreisler ignores them both. "I apologize for the disruption," he says. "I roughed up the Jew and sent him on his way. He was confused, lost, not worth a moment of your time. Particularly, on a day like this."

"Did you get his name?" Himmler demands to know.

"I didn't think it mattered. Such a small man."

Unlike the men protecting his flanks, Hitler seems disoriented. Is it possible he feels a modicum of guilt? Is it possible Geli Raubal is a migraine headache pounding away inside his head? Is it possible, under the bewildering circumstances, he doesn't even remember Kreisler? Strasser attempts to hand Hitler a lit cigarette to calm his nerves, only to have Hitler lash out at him and knock the cigarette to the ground.

"You know better than that, Strasser. To hand me such poison." Hitler seems, at least, jarred out of his troubled reverie, enough to notice Kreisler. "Tobacco is the Red man's vengeance upon us, Inspektor," he says. "We will pass a law someday outlawing it."

Strasser tries to apologize for the gaffe, but Hitler waves him off and strides toward his Mercedes. Kreisler grabs Lotte and follows, though it is hard to get a word in edgewise with all the retainers vying for position.

At the open-air car, Hitler does pause. It is as if a thought has come to him at that moment. He does recall Kreisler, and he wants to make a point.

"The world we live in is mathematical, Inspektor. Geometric. Cubes. Spheres. Pyramids. You, as a former architectural student, will appreciate this. Speer does. Never one of my best subjects, though, geometry. Straight lines I can draw. For the more complex work, I leave it to men like Speer, Strasser, if he stops smoking." Hitler climbs into the back seat of his Mercedes. "You are making progress on the other case?"

"The other case?"

Kreisler is thrown, not certain to what Hitler is referring. It was his intention to put Hitler in that awkward moment of vulnerability. Now, surrounded by Jew haters, in intimate conference with their leader, he is not sure how to respond.

"You know the one I mean." To Kreisler's surprise, Hitler, at that moment, leans over and signals for the detective to come closer. "They think I don't know that someone among my friends, someone even here today pretending to mourn my niece, is out to ruin me. I know better. I always know better. Find out who it is, Inspektor. You will be appropriately rewarded."

Once Julius Schreck is behind the wheel and Himmler and Strasser have joined Hitler, the Mercedes leaves the cemetery. Kreisler doubts that Hitler will give his niece a second thought after this. He can't help notice the stares aimed his way by Hitler's henchmen, though. They will give him second and third thoughts, no doubt.

Especially if Langer tells them I've got Jewish blood.

"Can we go now?" Hanging on his arm, Lotte pushes the hidden pistol up against his hip. "This place scares me," she says. Her anxiety is obvious to Kreisler, her body reacting to the chill breeze of intimidation and fear that Hitler leaves in his wake. "You were very brave."

"So were you."

"I was being a mother hen. Let's just get out of here. You must be hungry. I'm starved."

"Me, too," he says.

Trying to be the better actor, unfazed by what his life is becoming, he takes a final look at the resting place of a twenty-three-year-old girl who should be on her way to a singing lesson or a dinner date with Chaim Lerner. He says, " I never liked cemeteries. Even less now."

As they return to Lotte's automobile, they pass one of the Jewish sections of the Friedhof. It is a moment that, at some date in the future, Kreisler will recall as portentous. Like his father and his uncle, he has never given his religious heritage much thought. Amongst his own now, he feels history wrap around him. Ghosts of the past, sleeping here now, waking up just to eye an unbeliever pass by? Or spirits of the future, warning him that, distance himself from them as much as he tries, the worst is yet to come?

* * *

"Did you really mean what you said before?" Lotte asks him in the Duesenberg. They are driving south of Vienna, a hundred kilometers to the small village of Semmering in search of Geli Raubal's obstetrician. It is a honeymooner's trip through lovely Alpine country. Not the appropriate vista for what is on Lotte's mind. "To that boy. That a marriage between a Jew and a Christian can't work?"

"Not with that Christian, Hitler's niece." Kreisler leans back in his seat, yawning, glad to have Lotte do all the driving. "Hitler would have sent his dogs after them. He'd have chased Lerner down, murdered him, and dragged Geli back to Munich, where she probably would have ended up shooting herself anyway."

Lotte takes a turn off the main highway, Kreisler acting as navigator. "I didn't know you felt that way, Avi," she says, eyes switching from his face to the road and back. "So, were we doomed to fail from the beginning? Did I ever have a chance with you?"

"Oh, Lotte, don't ask that. Not now."

"I'm just curious, Avi, that's all. You can be such a cynic. One wonders if it's possible to have a relationship with you."

"One?" Kreisler gives her another instruction. "I'm a Jew only because my parents were," he says after a moment. "I don't practice it. I don't think about it. I have nothing against it. My religious feelings, or yours, has nothing to do with our relationship. Before, now, or in the future. You can pray to Osiris for all I think it matters."

"I don't."

"Whether or not anyone would be happy married to me for any length of time, Lotte, I don't know. Who really knows such a thing? You might be happier *with* a Nazi."

He makes his remark as a joke, but Lotte isn't laughing. "And Anni. Are you leading her on, too?"

"Lotte…"

"No, seriously, Avi. It isn't fair to her. If you have no intention of marrying her, you need to tell her. Now. Are you that selfish a man that you can't be honest?"

"Every woman wants marriage?"

"Not everyone." Lotte sighs. "Maybe Anni doesn't. I do. Does that make me hopelessly conformist? Unappealing? Wanting to have my own babies? Geli Raubal's funeral hit me harder than I thought it would. And Klara's."

"That's the world we live in, Lotte."

"So, we can't be happy? You and me? I feel so much older today than I did just this morning."

"You and me both."

Kreisler eyes the mountainous scenery ahead to avoid the plea in Lotte's eyes. Semmering is a village of only five hundred people during the off-season, when wealthy tourists have returned to the city. If his directions are correct, the man who would have helped Geli have her… son? daughter?… has an office in the middle of town, a nice little hide-away from members of the government who might look askance at his practice.

"We'll see, Lotte," he tells her. "Can that be enough for now?"

"We'll see?"

"Where the road takes us."

Well, at least it's not a 'no'.

Even in Semmering, there are National Socialist signs. In the moments before Lotte can park her car, Kreisler is shaken once again, as he was at Klara's funeral, by a sense of dread that he can't explain. He would blame the Jewish God if he believed in the Jewish God. Rather, he views history as one cemetery after another. If history is consistent, then the road ahead for all of them is uncertain at best, dark and unlivable at worst.

"Do you want me to come up with you?" Lotte asks as he opens his door.

"Of course. Why would I leave you here?"

Doctor Yankel Abramovich is lying in wait. Before Kreisler can even reach for the knob to 'Dr. Abramovich Ob-Gyn', the door is flung open by a frenetic old man, a Groucho Marx impersonator down to the disgustingly odorous cigarette.

"I've been expecting you," he shouts, poking the cigarette in Kreisler and Lotte's direction. "I can explain everything."

"Doctor Abramovich?"

"*Ihr seid die Polizei?*"

"Well, I am the police," Kreisler says, sharing a confused look with Lotte, who Abramovich scans head to toe. "We're here to talk to you. As a doctor."

"Not to arrest me?"

"Should we?"

"Probably."

Abramovich lets them into his office, peaking out the door to make sure no one else is preparing to leap at him from the corridor beyond. Stiffening his back and crushing out his cigarette in a tray on his desk, he takes a seat, offering two other chairs to his unexpected guests.

"Who died?" he says to Lotte.

"My dress?"

"Black. You were at a funeral? Not mine, I hope."

"Geli Raubal's," Kreisler says.

Abramovich reacts to the name with a jerk of his head and a nervous reach for his cigarette.

"Maybe you should open a window," Lotte says. The air is so filled with tobacco that she has to wave away the cloud of smoke still lingering around the desk.

"Of course. Certainly. Geli Raubal," he says, struggling to lift the creaky sash of the window behind him. "Did Lerner send you? Such a tragedy. I can't help but feel somehow responsible, though I never thought she'd commit suicide."

"It happens," Kreisler says.

Abramovich resumes his place on the opposite side of the desk. Kreisler can tell by the doctor's inability to look him square in the eye that he is still uneasy about something.

"When you came in first," the doctor says, " I apologize if I appeared rude...Frau? Fraulein?...but I thought maybe you were in the family way."

Lotte smiles, glances at Kreisler, who merely turns red.

"I suppose it was reasonable to think that way. You are an Ob-Gyn. But you also perform—"

"The other thing?" Abramovich puts a finger to his lips. "The Social Democrats have been trying to loosen the law for years, but we live in a very Catholic state. Five years, I could get. You're sure you're not here to arrest me?"

"For terminating pregnancies?" Kreisler says, straightforward. "That's not why Geli Raubal was seeking you out."

"No, no, absolutely not. She wanted the baby. Lerner wanted the baby. I get so many actresses coming to me for my services that I wasn't certain at first. You know actresses."

"Not many," Kreisler says, sensing Lotte's gaze on him. "How far along was she?"

"Two months, not noticeable yet. I didn't ask whether or not they planned to marry. I can say in my opinion that Fraulein Raubal was ecstatic about being a mother. Suicide was the last thing on her mind. That's why I was so surprised to hear about it."

"I think many people were," Kreisler says.

"She was so intent on having a healthy child, she quit drinking alcohol, stopped all of her medications, stopped smoking. Like me, she was a heavy smoker, but with quite a bit of fortitude. I must say, she was able to stop cold turkey, as they say. Perhaps it was her youth."

"Yes, perhaps." A thought passes through Kreisler's mind, too quickly to catch but it is something, he is certain, he wants to retrieve. He looks at Lotte, rubbing his chin in thought. "So, Hitler, we just learned detests smoking, wants to outlaw it. Geli stopped smoking for pregnancy reasons."

"So?"

Kreisler ponders this, still not sure where this is leading. "I need to see those photos once Anni has them processed and get back into Klara Fries's apartment."

"You've thought of something?"

"I don't know. Maybe. Dare I say, a smoking gun?"

Abramovich, at least, has no issues with smoking. He considers lighting up his old cigarette again, relieved that he is no longer facing immediate arrest. Instead, he pulls out a pack of cigarettes and offers them around.

"The SA sells these things," he says. "Did you know that?"

"You buy from the National Socialists?" Kreisler asks.

"That's how they make their money," Abramovich says. "My family used to be in the tobacco business. That's how I got hooked. The SA doesn't require membership fees, so they make most of their money on the sale of cigarettes. I like the Trommlers, the best. Three and a half pfennigs a pack. The Sturms are the most expensive. I stay away from those. Heavy in nicotine. Addictive."

"And you aren't addicted?" Lotte asks. "Doctor?"

"Well, I'm an ob-gyn, not an oncologist." With a grin, Abramovich politely accepts the well-earned criticism. "If Hitler abolishes these," he says, "then he's done one thing right, at least."

Chapter Fifteen

Japan has invaded Manchuria, and Anni Leeuwenberg isn't happy about it.

"Are you completely serious?" Kreisler asks her. He and Lotte have just returned from Vienna. It is late afternoon, and both are exhausted, Lotte immediately heading into the bathroom to make herself appear more presentable, Kreisler sinking into the nearest chair.

"The march of Capitalism goes on unabated," Anni says. Her face still shows the bruises of her assault, so she looks as if she has just come back from the Manchurian frontlines herself. She has thrown on one of the new dresses Lotte purchased for her at a high-end department store, so she hasn't refused the benefits of Capitalism quite yet.

"Can you at least sit down?" Kreisler begs her because she is marching much as the Japanese army is, though in the confines of Kreisler's small flat.

"The working man is always pushed around, Avi, that's the thing you don't realize. Or react to."

"Hitler's a socialist."

"I hope you're not serious. You should read my article on Germany's political parties and what they really stand for."

Yawning, Kreisler looks around the room, curious. "Did you get the photographs?" he asks. "Have they been processed?"

Without breaking stride, Anni points to the kitchen counter. "The Socialist wing of the National Socialists is trying to claim they represent the working man. They don't trust Hitler because he's coming across as a true lackey of the German industrial class, the Aristocunts."

"Anni. Really."

"I meant the Aristocounts. What did I say?"

"You know what you said."

Anni doesn't disagree. Instead, she pauses in her rant to stand beside Kreisler at the counter, giving him a quick peck on the cheek.

"How did it go?" she asks. "You and Lotte get along?"

"As well as Romeo and Juliet."

"Give it time, Avi."

"I have. I will." Kreisler opens the brown envelope that contains the finished crime scene photographs. He's not sure what it is exactly he is looking for, but he is confident he will know when he spots it.

"You found the boyfriend?"

"We did," Lotte answers, joining them with wet hair and a towel wrapped around her torso. Her clothes have been discarded. Anni takes note. Kreisler, enrapt in the black and whites, does not. "Avi saved his life. He was going to shoot Hitler."

"Good for him. Not good for Avi. Why didn't you let him do it? You would have saved me the trouble."

Kreisler's attention abruptly moves from the photographs. He pulls Chaim Lerner's pistol from his pocket. "By the way," he says, then notices at last Lotte essentially naked. "Make yourself at home."

"I will."

"And take this pistol." He hands it to Anni, who continues to ignore the sexual tension of the room. "I think it's a Walther PPK. In case. Just don't go tearing through the Maginot Line with it."

Anni takes and hefts the small firearm, getting the feel of it in her palm. Then she hands it to Lotte. "I don't need it. But Lotte can do some target practice in the apartment. If we can find the appropriate target." With a wink.

"Take it outside, ladies," Kreisler says.

Grabbing the envelope with the photos, he resumes his seat at the dinner table. Anni sits opposite him. Lotte goes into the bedroom to dress. With almost insufferable diligence, Kreisler examines each shot, up, down, right, left, side to side, corner to corner. Pictures taken from outside Klara's building, the bloodied body, and the gawking crowd. From inside of her flat, each room. Then, the Geli Raubal crime scene, outside and inside, as many photos as he could take before Sauer and Forster interrupted him.

"You'll lose your eyesight that way," Anni says.

"I just wish I had had more time. Sauer and Forster are good detectives, but they'll go along with a cover-up. There's no way Geli Raubal killed herself. The trace of the bullet. The landing point of the gun. The positioning of the body. Wait a minute."

Abruptly, Kreisler leaves the table and goes to the kitchen to scrounge through the drawers until he finds the tool he needs. A magnifying glass.

"You find something?" Lotte asks. She has given up trying to entice him with her body to stand behind Kreisler's shoulder and share in the investigation. Anni leaves her place to peer at the photographs on his opposite side.

"Maybe," he says. "Just before we were taken off the case, I asked Dr. Müller, the pathologist, to help me lift Geli's body so I could snap a few photos of her torso. I didn't have the chance to inspect it any further."

"So?" both women ask.

"So, I didn't notice that little thing beneath her left leg."

"What is it?"

Kreisler takes a harder, deeper, longer look through the lens. "The killer also didn't notice it, or he might have picked it up and gotten rid of it."

"What, Avi, what?"

With the smile of discovery that Sherlock Holmes might have appreciated, Kreisler makes the reveal. " A cigarette butt."

"That's it?"

If either Anni or Lotte had been expecting a momentous revelation on the scale of a Biblical prophet, they didn't get it. But Kreisler is beaming.

"Remember," he tells them, "Doctor Abramovich told us Geli had quit smoking to protect the fetus. And at the cemetery, Hitler had a fit about one of his men smoking. He said he'd ban tobacco if he could. Which means? Ladies?"

The light comes on. "If it wasn't her cigarette butt or Hitler's," Lotte says, "there had to be a third person in that room."

"But not necessarily the killer," Kreisler says. "It could have been someone helping Hitler cover up what he did. Someone who was there when Geli and Hitler argued, fought, and she was killed. A guard. His chauffeur. Someone always around him. Someone Frau Dachs might have seen. Someone who does smoke."

Which could be almost anyone, except that Kreisler is pretty sure he knows who that someone is. A man out on the town with Eva Braun.

"It's a much smaller list in any case," he says.

"Find out the brand of cigarette," Anni suggests.

"A good thought if we had the actual cigarette butt to study, but we don't. Yet. Oh, if only I had a degree in chemistry."

* * *

There's nothing anyone can do to uncover Klara Fries's killer tonight. By the time Kreisler is through poring over the photographs, it is after midnight, and he can't keep his eyes open any longer. Once again, he surrenders the bed to Anni and Lotte and submits to intermittent sleep on the sofa. He dreams, provocatively enough, of having a threesome with Anni and Lotte and is, therefore, mildly upset when he is awakened in the early morning with a persistent knocking on his door.

"Jesus Christ, Fritz!" he says when he opens the door to his apartment. Langer is waiting there on the landing. He isn't alone. Detectives Sauer and Forster have accompanied him.

"You need to put in a telephone," Langer tells him, obviously put out.

"This is *why* I don't have one."

Kreisler opens the door wider to let his fellow cops inside. As soon as they have entered, Langer looks up to see Lotte and Anni peering around a corner at the intruders.

"Oh, I'm sorry, Kreisler." Langer tips his hat to the two members of the fairer sex. "I thought I woke you up. I stand corrected."

"Why are you here, Fritz?" Kreisler asks. He fell asleep on the couch without having undressed, so he is still wearing the clothes he wore to Vienna, minus the suitcoat and shoes. His hair is mussed, and his eyes red and blurry. The other three detectives, he notes, are dressed for another round of murder investigations. He shoos Lotte and Anni back to the bedroom.

"You've created quite the stir," Langer says. "And I don't mean your lady friends. Good work, that." As he speaks, he moseys into the room and glances at Kreisler's crime scene photographs still laid out on the dinner table. He begins to browse. "You were in Vienna?"

"Yes."

"Without notifying me."

"Part of my investigation. You'll get the full report."

"I'm sure. " Langer continues to sift through the black-and-whites, taking some interest in them. Sauer and Forster remain dutifully silent. "You spoke to Hitler again."

"Briefly."

"Elucidating?"

"He spoke of banning cigarettes, Fritz. Bad news for you, if he does."

Langer picks up the photograph of Doctor Müller posing beside Geli Raubal's body, rolled over to reveal what lay beneath, something a rushing Kreisler had missed the first time. "His people waxed poetic about how you may have saved his life from some armed gunman."

"A young foolish boy who was not armed."

"A Jew?"

"That was my impression. I was in Vienna following up on the Klara Fries murder. After the funeral, I met with Geli's obstetrician. Like Fraulein Raubal, Fraulein Fries was pregnant."

"I see." Langer turns to his other detectives. "Sauer, give us some light, will you?" Once the overhead is on, bringing illumination to the room, Langer lifts the Raubal photo so he can get a better look at it. "There's something beneath her knee," he says.

"Yes."

"Care to explain? It's hard to make out."

"The remains of a cigarette." Kreisler looks to his fellow detectives waiting patiently in the background. "You fellows might be interested. The obstetrician, who was also Fraulein Raubal's doctor, told us she had stopped smoking to protect her baby. Hitler hates tobacco, blames the Apache for it. Which means a third person who does smoke was in that room *before* it was opened up by Hess, or whoever the hell broke into her room."

"You're saying she didn't kill herself?" Sauer asks, breaking his silence. Langer immediately shushes him.

"No one is saying that." Langer is clear about that fact. "Maybe it was there before the incident. Maybe one of the maids smokes and dropped it there, careless. Whatever the cause, the final report has been issued and given to the Bavarian Minister of Justice."

"Gürtner."

"Yes."

"Who attended Fraulein Raubal's funeral with Hitler?"

"Irrelevant. The case is closed. Ruled a suicide, it will stay a suicide."

"Even if we can prove otherwise?"

"And why would we want to do that?" Langer asks with a very weary intonation. "Stick with the Fries case. How is it coming along? People are dying every day. I need you on these other cases. You said she had the same doctor as Fraulein Raubal. Was he helpful?"

"I'm closing in on the answer, I believe," Kreisler says, causing Langer to turn a sharp look his way.

"Really?"

"Perhaps the very same man who dropped that cigarette under the remains of Fraulein Raubal."

Langer is pressed to come up with a legitimate and believable response. Kreisler's unanticipated revelation appears to him to be some sort of challenge thrown in his face in front of the other detectives. Kreisler is staring at him as if he is the guilty party, daring him to justify another verdict of suicide.

"The same man," Langer mumbles. "An unnecessary complication."

"A dangerous one," Kreisler says. "Which brings me to ask: why are you here tonight, Fritz?"

"Because, Kreisler, you have become Death himself. There's been another murder."

***

Another murder connected to the investigations of both Geli Raubal and Klara Fries. This is certain. How could it be otherwise? First, a young pregnant woman determined to have her child against the wishes of her over-controlling uncle. Second, a friend of Geli Raubal, also a blackmailer of her uncle. The first may have been accidental. The second was not. The first involving the cover-up of a powerful German politician. The second, perhaps the cover-up of a cover-up. Now, third, Kreisler is afraid, the witnesses are coming under fire.

This early in the morning, the Bratwurstglöckl Restaurant is closed. It is in the alley behind the establishment that Herr Klintsch's body has been discovered, lying face down on the gravel beside his car. It is quite evident immediately to Kreisler that the man whom he had interrogated only the evening before has been shot in the back of the head.

"You know this man?" Langer asks him, as they stand over the corpse.

"Herr Klintsch," Kreisler says, "the owner of the restaurant." He crouches to take a closer look.

"No cigarettes this time?" Langer asks. "That exonerates the Camel."

Doctor Müller, the pathologist, has also arrived. "A single shot behind the right ear," he says. "Fairly straightforward. No suicide, this one."

"Very funny," Langer says. "You met him?"

"I talked to him about an argument Hitler had with Geli Raubal the night she was killed," Kreisler says. "Very loud. Very contentious. She was pregnant, not with his baby, and she fully intended on keeping it."

"So, she killed herself out of distress."

"No, she was killed because, while Hitler is likely infertile or incapable of meaningful sex, the father was Jewish."

"The kid at her funeral?"

Kreisler won't say. "You've already decided the case, so there's no point in going over the facts if you have no interest in pursuing them," Kreisler does say. "Hitler loved his niece. This much is plain. His sexuality…."

"Don't, Kreisler. Not in public." Langer moves his newest detective away from the body and away from detectives Sauer and Forster, who are doing what Kreisler would otherwise have done: taking photographs and notes.

Once alone, up against the brick wall of the neighboring building, Kreisler forces his boss to listen.

"Despite what you might think, Hitler is a very isolated, secretive man who adored his niece. He couldn't bear the thought of her loving someone else, getting pregnant by him, let alone considering marrying him, let alone a Jew. She had to die. It was the only way. She was killed with his gun. She had two of her own pistols she could have used on herself if she had chosen to. But the unfinished letter on her desk is clear proof that she was planning a trip to Austria, which, in Hitler's mind, would have been the final insult. Maybe it's second-degree murder, an accident. They were fighting over the weapon, and it discharged. But that is when the cover-up began."

Langer raises his hands, has to fend Kreisler off. The younger policeman is getting too heated, too close to the truth. "And what do you hope to gain by all of this?" he speaks in a low but harsh tone. "Look what happened to Klintsch because you've been digging in a minefield. Consider who else you've spoken to. The maid? The landlady? You? Your girlfriends? Any one of you could be next. I can tell you this, Kreisler. It won't be me."

"Then let's bring him in," Kreisler says.

"Who?"

"The SA man. Kaspers. Question him. Light a fire under his feet. Let him sweat. Maybe he'll make a mistake, give everything away."

"To what end!" Langer exclaims. He is beside himself with frustration, hopelessly over his head, lost in a political maze that has no beginning and no end. He sees his career, recently upgraded, now torn to shreds.

"To get to the truth!" Kreisler shouts back. "The people of Germany don't want a psychopath running their country. How many cases can you slip under the rug? Someone killed Herr Klintsch. Are we to ignore this one, too?"

Of course, they can't, and Langer understands this. All credibility for the Munich Homicide Division would be shot.

"All right. Look," Langer says. "I'll put Sauer and Forster on this, not that they'll have much luck. No witnesses. But if you think Kaspers is the man responsible for Klara Fries and Klintsch, then get me proof! More than what you have. Put that fucker on the scene with the weapon in his hand. And do it fast, before he acts again."

Chapter Sixteen

"I want you both to leave the city for the time being."

Kreisler is dead serious when he returns to his flat, his two cohabitants already up and waiting for his return. Steaming tea has been brewed, toast with jam on the table, but Kreisler is too hyped up to touch food or drink. Mind already in another location with other people, he hurries into his bedroom, undresses, and hops into the shower, unmindful of the women watching every move he makes.

Only when he exits, still wet, does he issue his order.

"I have no intention of going," Anni says. "I don't know about you, Lotte."

"I'm not going either. Why should we? We didn't witness anything."

"You were raped, for the love of God," Kreisler exclaims at Anni. "You're publishing articles, written by you, about how Hitler is guilty. And you and I were seen by Kaspers in Sussman's pharmacy. He must know we're closing in on him."

"Let him come," Anni says. "We have windows, too. Only this time he'll end up on the sidewalk."

"You're too blasé for your own good, Anni."

How can they be so calm, Kreisler wonders, toweling himself dry before searching for a change of clothes?

"Here's the thing," he says to his two stubborn friends. "Kaspers, if he is Klara's killer and the restaurant owner's killer, is not Geli Raubal's killer. Hitler is, of that there can be no doubt. Kaspers, I could shoot, and who would care? Not the Munich Homicide Division, obviously. Hitler, they would have a problem with. Hitler, I need to bring to court. That is where the prosecutor Glaser comes in."

"And Waldmann," Anni says. "I can crank out as many articles as we need, pointing the finger at Hitler and tying his rallies to the violence Kaspers and the SS and Brownshirts commit every day. That's Waldmann's point. That's what that prosecutor up in Berlin was trying to do."

"Hans Litten. Who failed, and now Hitler is even stronger."

"But that was before Geli Raubal was killed."

Lotte's point is a justifiable one. A Hitler tied to sexual improprieties with his niece and subsequently to her suspicious demise could mean the end for him. And for his National Socialists.

"We're not afraid, Avi," Anni says. "We're long past that."

"We want to get even. We need to do the right thing."

How can he resist their earnest determination to be part of his life? Still, Kreisler has to make the effort to dissuade them, for their own good.

"But there is something more to this than simple murder. If that's all it was, if Hitler were not involved, no one would care. If I may be allowed to exaggerate a bit, or not, these deaths have national implications. Waldmann suggested it. So did Glaser. But it has nagged at me from the beginning," Kreisler says. "If Kaspers was involved with blackmailing Hitler, why would he try to eliminate anyone who could tie Hitler to Geli Raubal's death? Why help with the cover-up? And who would be pulling his strings? Kaspers is a nobody in the party. What does he have to gain by doing all of this?"

"We could follow him," Lotte blurts out. "If you're too busy. See where he goes, who he talks to."

Anni seconds the motion with a slap on her friend's back. "Great idea, Lotte."

Kreisler may instantly reject the casting of Lotte as Holmes's Dr. Watson, but Anni's quick to add her own name to the drama. "Teamwork," she says. "We'll take turns. You can't be everywhere, do everything, Avi. We'll arm ourselves."

"You don't even know how to shoot that Walther."

"As long as it has bullets in it, I'll figure it out."

"Me, too," Lotte says. "So, it's settled. We'll meet up here, tonight, and share what we've learned."

"Fine. Suit yourselves." Kreisler throws up his hands in exasperation. "Now you know why I'm not married, Lotte."

But when the initial annoyance and concerns over their safety passes, Kreisler leaves the apartment feeling weirdly at peace. Almost happy. What he had lacked for so many years, what he had never realized he needed so much in his life, is family. And there they are, Anni and Lotte, seated at the dinner table, plotting out their day, as he shuts the door to his flat. Whatever else they might be or might become, for right now in this important moment in his life, they are just that: family.

His day is also plotted out. Hitler's best architectural friend, though he may be, he knows the gatekeepers will never allow him back into Prinzregentenplatz 16, and neither Sauer nor Forster have anything new to add. Their report is final and conclusive: Angela Raubal died of a self-inflicted gunshot wound to the chest. But he does intend, when he can, to re-interview each of the members of the household staff to see if anyone besides the dotty old Frau Dachs can place Kaspers in the apartment the night Geli died. First, he intends to return to Klara Fries's apartment, to which he knows Frau Becker will grant him access.

Frau Becker is more than happy, even anxious, to let Kreisler into the formerly rented unit. "You should see the place now," she tells Kreisler as they make their way up the stairs, her key chain jangling from her hand, her voice trembling with anger. "I don't know who got in or how they got in…vandals…and tore the place apart. I can't afford a workman to come in and make all the repairs it needs now before I can rent it to someone else. Unlike a lot of folks, I do keep a respectable building."

Kreisler's shoulders sag with disappointment when he sees the damage Kaspers…. It had to be him…inflicted on the residence. Carpeting lifted up, shades taken down, cabinets thrown to the floor, clothes tossed about. Kaspers should have thought of that the night he killed Klara, Kreisler thinks. He must have panicked. Maybe David Sussman caught him leaving, and that was what landed him in the Isar. But now it is Kreisler's turn to see if there is anything of value salvageable for his investigation.

"Frau Becker," he says as the landlady mutters her misery behind his back, "do you know if Fraulein Klara ever had guests over, regular ones, boyfriends, girlfriends, any familiar face?"

"Well, you know, I try to mind my own business," she replies.

"As you should. But I'm thinking in particular of Angela Raubal. Do you know who I mean? Adolf Hitler's niece."

"The girl who just killed herself. Like Klara. I read all about it in *Der Weg*. I curse Herr Hitler. Yes, when I saw her photograph in the newspaper, I recognized her at once. A pleasant girl, the one time I spoke to her."

"She was unaccompanied?"

"Yes. I believe so. Really, I don't know. We live so far apart. Could she have walked here by herself? Maybe they waited outside for her."

Kreisler doubts Hitler ever let her go anywhere without an escort, mother, sister, or someone else. Beginning to assume he has come all the way here on a fool's errand, Kreisler drifts into the bathroom, Frau Becker trailing in his wake. Here, too, the cabinets had been searched, emptied, contents strewn across the floor.

"I'm going to start throwing things out and sweeping up the first chance I get," Frau Becker says.

"Not just yet, please."

Kreisler stoops and picks up a bottle of pills from the Sussman Pharmacy. Anti-nausea medication. Kreisler remembers the brand name. What is most illuminating are the pill bottles labeled for Angela Raubal.

She couldn't well bring them to her apartment under Hitler's watchful eyes, he thinks, *so she stored them over here.* This would have been difficult if she had been accompanied here. He wonders what else she might have stored with Klara.

"What about a man?" Kreisler asks. He has brought a picture taken of Kaspers. Not one from the Bratwurstglöckl but from the scene on the sidewalk on which Klara Fries landed in death. He points to a face in the crowd. "Ever seen him?"

"Oh, yes, that one," the landlady affirms. "Is he the one? You know, the one you think...?"

"I'm just trying to find out if he was a regular visitor to Klara's rooms. Do you know?"

The possibility that she might have helped harbor a killer causes Frau Becker to turn away with a sob. She can't speak for several minutes as she stumbles out into the hallway. Kreisler follows after her, but not before pocketing several of the pill bottles belonging to both Klara and Geli. Maybe Kaspers left fingerprints that would place him here.

Then again, if Frau Becker could identify him…. He just doesn't want her to get killed, too.

"He was here. He was here," she manages to speak between her hand-wringing tears. "Loud. Always loud. Even when he said, 'Auf Wiedersehen, Frau Becker.' You'd think such a man, a killer, would know how to be quiet."

"He's SA."

"I should never have let him in, never have allowed him access to the poor child. If Herr Waldmann knew…."

"It isn't your fault," Kreisler tells the old woman. Too late for Klara. Too late for David. But not necessarily too late for her. "Do you have any relatives outside the city, Frau Becker?" he asks.

"Why?"

Lie. "I'll find someone to do the repairs. Maybe he can go through the entire property. Just leave me a list of work you'd like done, and I'm sure he'd be happy to do it."

"For how much?"

Kreisler is thinking Dov Birnbaum is just the person to ask to do God's work. "For next to nothing, I can assure you. Go away for a week. Two at the most. He gets the job done. You return to a castle on the Danube."

Suddenly, the dark clouds of death part. Frau Becker is beside herself with delight. "I always wanted a castle." A smile perches on her face until something catches her eye on the carpet in the main room. Then she grunts with disgust, bends to take a closer look. "Do you think he did this, too? That *ungeheuer?*"

"What, Frau Becker?" Kreisler asks, following her gaze.

"How disrespectful." She indicates a charred stain in the rug, shaking her head. "Don't put your damned cigarettes out on my carpets."

* * *

Joseph Goebbels, the National Socialist Party propaganda minster has, with Hitler's approval, declared this a day of support for their leader, under fire from the left-wing Communist Jewish press. In Munich, Berlin, and elsewhere across the nation, party members and supporters are being asked to attend rallies and march in protest against any effort to criminalize the death of Geli Raubal.

In Munich, Hitler speaks for two hours outside Nazi Party Headquarters, berating his enemies, after which the local SA marches through the streets of Munich singing their new national anthem, the *Horst-Wessel-Lied*.

'*Die Fahne hoch*! Raise the flag!

The SA marches with a calm, steady step.

Comrades shot by the Red Front and reactionaries

March in spirit within our ranks.'

Horst Wessel had been an SA member killed by a Communist two years before. At least, that is how the story went. Never mind that he was an SA provocateur fomenting trouble in the leftist neighborhoods of Berlin under the orders of Herr Goebbels. For the SA and the National Socialists, Wessel, a former construction worker, has become the emblem of their cause.

'Clear the streets for the brown battalions,

Clear the streets for the Storm Division man!

Millions are looking upon the hooked-cross full of hope,

The day of freedom and of bread dawns!

For the last time, the call to arms is sounded!

For the fight, we all stand prepared!

Already, Hitler's banners fly over all streets.

The time of bondage will last but a little while now!

The moment Anni hears the first note of that hated tune, she pulls Lotte into the nearest store and places a phone call to *Der Weg* and its publisher Waldmann.

"Oskar," she says. She has to raise her voice. The connection is bad and the noise level on the street is high. "Close up shop. Lock up and go home."

"I can hardly hear you."

"I said, lock up and go home. Get everyone out. The Brownshirts are on the march and they're gunning for trouble."

"Coming for trouble, is that what you said?"

"Hitler's pointed his finger at you, do you understand? Get out now!"

On his end of the conversation, Oskar Waldmann can hear exactly what Anni is telling him to do. Will he do it? Absolutely, not.

"Don't worry about me," he says from blocks away. "We're armed. We'll fuck up anyone who tries to get in. It's you who should stay off the streets. Where are you?"

She and Lotte are peering out the plate-glass front window of a candy store directly across from the pharmacy owned by Martin Kaspers. This is downtown Munich, but they might as well be in an American ghost town. The streets have cleared of pedestrians and shoppers. The air crackles in the way a battlefield does before the first shot is fired.

"Oskar," Anni swears at her boss. "Don't be stupid. You, we can do without. The presses we need. Lock up and get out of there."

"Stay safe, stay away," is all Waldmann will say in response. Then the line goes dead, and whatever is going to happen will happen.

"Well?" Lotte asks at her shoulder.

"That *meshugana* is going to get himself killed."

Lotte looks out the window to catch two young boys running in the direction of the marchers. They are armed with sticks which will snap in two with the first blow and leave them defenseless.

"There's nothing you can do, Anni," she tells her friend. "Kaspers is probably off goose-stepping with all the other Brownshirts. I just hope Avi isn't out there somewhere."

Oh, he is, Anni thinks. And before Lotte can stop her, she is out the door.

* * *

Kreisler turns left when everyone else is going right. Or right when everyone else is going left. He prefers the center position from which he can view the traffic coming and going, so that he can choose the path no one else would think of.

If everyone else is on the street marching to Hitler's tune, then Hitler's apartment will be bereft of guards and open to infiltration. So, that's where he is heading.

There is no point in trying to contact Anni and Lotte. He can only hope they have made the sensible decision to stay at home. Anni, of course, won't. She'll grab the closest implement and wield it out on the street alongside the burliest German Cossack. That will leave it to Lotte to influence Anni's behavior to see the sense of living to fight another day.

Kreisler gains access to Prinzregentenplatz 16 when he tips his hat and says, "Remember me?" to the building landlady, Frau Reichert.

It is hard to focus when his mind is torn between the here and the there. Anni is a biblical female warrior, a defender of everything that she loves, fearless in defense of her beliefs. This is why he loves her. She takes 'stand by your man' literally. To the death. Lotte is more patient, steadier, reliable. The type of woman who prefers being in the background but who he knows will always have his back. That is why he loves her. If he could only explain that to both of them.

"No one is here today, Inspektor," Frau Reichert tells him. Her attitude, he can immediately see, is one of reluctance, even fear. "We thought everything was taken care of."

"It is, it is, Frau Reichert," Kreisler says. He is ever affable in situations like this, where he expects push-back. "But I'm investigating another murder, two, in fact, that may have a connection with the terrible suicide of Fraulein Raubal. If I may just have a moment of your time. The entire staff's time, if possible."

Frau Reichert turns to stone in the entrance. "Who is it?" comes from behind her. A man's voice. Herr Winter. "Oh, it's you," he says when he sees who is blocking the doorway.

"You're going out, Herr Winter," Kreisler says.

"I was going to."

"The march for Herr Hitler?"

"Uh, no. Supplies. Why? Why are you here? I thought—"

Kreisler plants his foot in the entryway. "Everyone thinks the same thing," he says, exhibiting disbelief. "I don't understand it. A pregnant girl, in love, with plans to vacation in Austria, to have a child, to start a family, suddenly just shoots herself in the chest with a gun belonging to someone else when she has two of her own guns five feet away. How are these facts so easily dismissed? Then there is the letter."

"What letter?" Frau Reichert asks.

"Does it matter?" Kreisler says. "People have already made up their minds. Even the priest, Father Pant, who conducted Geli's funeral service. I spoke very briefly with him. He was told it was an accident. How else, in good conscience, could he perform a service in a Catholic cemetery for someone who is officially recognized by the Munich Police as a suicide? Hitler himself says it. But I digress. Your testimony has helped solve the problem, a suicide it is, and, regrettably, condemned that poor young lady to an eternity in hell. Father Pant may have been misled. All of Germany may weep for our little Geli. But down there," Kreisler points toward Satan's burning pit, "they know when someone is lying, you see."

The gasp that Frau Reichert lets out, a sob, tells Kreisler that she is a woman with a guilty conscience. Winter himself, perhaps a believer in the majesty of Christ, is taken aback, though he reacts with more composure.

"She did what she did," he says. "None of us saw anything. None of us were involved."

"But you are," Kreisler interjects. "The moment you concocted a tale of misery leading investigators, good men all, to believe Geli committed such a heinous act. Led them to believe that she was capable of taking not only her own life but that of the baby she was carrying, you became involved. Two souls condemned to eternal damnation. For what?"

Kreisler now stands his ground and waits. He hears two things: Frau Reichert's crying and the distant rumble of a mob marching to the beat of evil.

Then comes from the back hallway, a third sound, a quiet voice, shamed perhaps by Kreisler's words. "She didn't do it," this voice says. "She was arguing with him when the gun went off."

The maid, Anna Kirmair, steps into the light.

"You saw this?" Kreisler asks. His heartbeat quickening, he fumbles trying to pull his notepad from his coat pocket.

"No. We all just heard it."

"All of you? Are you sure there were no witnesses, someone who saw what actually happened?"

Now is not the time to let up on these people. Loyal to Hitler they might be, but if their souls are at all decent, they will crack under Kreisler's continued pressure.

"Herr Hitler was so agitated," Frau Reichert says. "I saw him come out of Fraulein Raubal's bedroom. He was shrieking, unrecognizable. I've never seen…my mother…"

"Frau Dachs."

"She was so scared, she passed out right at my feet. I had to take care of her, didn't I? My own mother. How did I know what Herr Hitler had done?"

"You talk too much, Maria," Winter says. He tries to push Kreisler out of the way, but the detective refuses to budge. "You have to go now, Inspektor. You put us all in danger. It is over, all over."

"Yes, in the here and now, Sir, it may well be," Kreisler says. "But down the road, when the Kingdom calls to you, you might be forced to think otherwise." Kreisler takes a hold of the man's arm, looks deep into his blinking guilt-ridden eyes. "I can see you're a good man, a man with a conscience. A working stiff just trying to do right and provide for his family."

"It isn't easy these days. Since the Jews stabbed us in the back."

"Indeed, Sir. All I am asking is what happened after. Once the deed was done, other people intervened. Hess. Von Shirach. They told you what to say, what to do, yes?"

Winter can only shrink back and try to slam the door on Kreisler's shoe, but Kreisler moves too quickly and is inside the building before Winter can act.

"Who else was there when Hitler shot Geli? There was at least one other person there, someone who was smoking, an SA man, perhaps. Give me a name."

Frau Reichert wipes her face on her apron. She has calmed down enough to risk peaking at the homicide detective. "*Oberstleutnant* Kaspers. He was out in the hallway smoking. Yes, I remember now. How shocked he was, how agitated. Herr Hitler was too *verstört,* too distraught, to do anything himself. The *Oberstleutnant* looked in the bedroom and came out cursing, cursing, at us! What did we do? He throws his cigarette down in anger, then goes into Herr Hitler's office to use the telephone. "

"He was yelling," Anna Kirmair says. "What do we do? What do we do?' I heard that."

"He was speaking to his boss," Kreisler says.

"I don't know who he was speaking to. But once he hung up, he was calmer. He told us there were people coming over. Important people who knew what to do in situations like this. We shouldn't worry. Then he told us to go to our rooms, and he would handle everything. We did as he asked. What else could we do? We were all so frightened."

Kreisler can hardly manage his pencil as he jots down Frau Reichert's and Anna Kirmair's words verbatim. Will they be willing to testify if Prosecutor Glaser calls on them to appear in court, in public, before the nation's press? This is not his problem. It is Glaser's.

He attempts the impossible, though, managing to pacify his own nerves while hoping to assuage theirs.

"Say nothing to Kaspers," he tells them. "Your secrets are safe with me. Pretend I wasn't here. The most important thing is to protect the reputation of a young woman who, I think we can all agree, was worthy of our compassion."

Now, he thinks, closing and putting back his notepad, *is the time to contact Glaser, to bring the matter to court.*

And to arrest *Oberstleutnant* Kaspers for obstruction of justice, if nothing else. Under cross-examination, attacked by a competent prosecutor like Hans Litten or Max Glaser, perhaps Kaspers will give up the boss, will undermine the party, will save Germany.

But Kreisler hasn't even dropped the notepad into his pocket when his own brilliant take on the Raubal/Fries case slaps him in the face.

That's exactly what Kaspers wants to have happen! To undermine Hitler. Kaspers is a mole. Schutzstaffel. Sturmabteilung. He wears many uniforms. All the wrong ones. He wasn't covering up for Hitler. He was trying to incriminate him. Blackmail was one thing. Intentional. A money grab. The killing of Geli Raubal was unexpected. When it happened, maybe Kaspers saw the opportunity to destroy Hitler. What was the first thing he did after confronting a hysterical Nazi Party leader? He called his master. He got instructions. He called people in. To deal with the problem? Or to take advantage of it? In which case, Kreisler needs to know who was there in the apartment before he and Fritz Langer arrived. Everyone.

"One last thing," he tells the landlady, the butler, and the maid, clearly making his stand. "I want all the names of the people who spoke to Herr Hitler. Who talked to you? What did they tell you to say and, lastly, when they arrived, who spoke to Oberstleutnant Kaspers?"

* * *

There is actually one other thing they can do for the police detective. Allow him to use the house telephone.

"Herr Hitler has one in his office," Frau Reichert says. "There's one in his bedroom, and there's one in the pantry we use to make orders."

"The one in Herr Hitler's office will do," Kreisler says.

Following her upstairs, down a hall, and into Hitler's primary work area, he closes the door on her, locks it, then heads to the large desk with the portrait of Hitler and the Nazi flag overhead. An iron bust of Hitler takes up one corner, a rather egocentric paperweight holding down handwritten notes that Kreisler takes as the first draft of a speech.

Hitler keeps his desk clean. There are noticeably no photographs of anyone. On the desk. On the walls. For someone who desired to be an architect, Hitler keeps things simple. Like his drawings. Absent of humanity. If he possessed any framed pictures of Geli, they are gone now. In the trash with any other telltale evidence that she meant anything to him.

Kreisler keeps a record of important phone numbers. He won't need Anni's anymore since she's moved in with him. He has Lotte's and Anton's, and he has his work numbers, with the most recent additions being those of Max Glaser and Waldmann at *Der Weg*.

The first person he calls is the prosecutor Glaser, who picks up, breathless, on the sixth ring.

"No time to talk!" he yells into the phone.

"You don't even know who this is," Kreisler says.

"All right. Who is it?"

"Inspektor Kreisler, and you'll never guess where I'm sitting right now. Behind Adolf Hitler's desk."

Now Kreisler has the prosecutor's full attention. "You're kidding, right?"

"I can smell his cologne. Why do you sound like you've just swum the English Channel?"

"We're under siege here. The Brownshirts protesting. Somehow they found out we're investigating the Raubal case, that we aren't satisfied with the verdict of suicide. We've had to barricade the doors. I hope you've found something worthwhile, Inspektor."

"Oh, I have, Sir, if you dare call his household staff as witnesses. I have their testimony about what they saw and heard."

"Bring it to me," Glaser says. "When you can. Not now. They'll rip you apart, those bastards."

"Right now, I'm gazing at a speech he intends to make in…Berlin, it appears…next week. Just glancing through the first couple of paragraphs, I'd say he's on the attack."

"When isn't he ever? How did you get in?"

"Charm."

"Nobody else is there?"

"Not in his room. I've locked the door. I don't know how much time I have. I wanted to let you know—"

"Search his drawers."

The prosecutor's order startles Kreisler. "You have a warrant?"

"Fuck the warrant. I told you what is going on here. You'll never get another chance like this. Bring me whatever you find."

At that moment, the connection with Glaser goes dead. Hopefully, the same isn't true of the prosecutor, Kreisler thinks, hanging up Hitler's phone.

It's not about proving a case against Hitler, he knows. It's about making him look as bad as possible before the German nation. From outside the office, Frau Reichert is banging on the door.

"Herr Inspektor! Herr Inspektor! "

"It's all right, Frau Reichert. Just give me a moment."

Unfortunately, Hitler rightfully trusts no one. All of the drawers are locked, no key is visible, and Kreisler has no intention of tearing apart the office. There is little on top of the desk to warrant great interest. But on the far side of the large room, there is a second, smaller desk, one used by his personal secretary, a Frau Schroeder.

While he can imagine an anxious Frau Reichert standing just outside, ear to the door, he takes a stab at searching the secretary's desk for any valuable bit of information he can grab.

"One minute, Frau Reichert!" he calls.

"But it's Oberstleutnant Kaspers, Inspektor. He's coming. He'll be furious if he finds out I let you in."

Shit, Kreisler curses to himself. There is a secretarial notepad on Frau Schroeder's desk. He whisks that into his coat, then hurries to the door. In pushing it open, he nearly knocks Frau Reichert to the floor.

"Hurry!" she tells him. "One never knows about these people. They can be so hateful."

"You'll be fine. I just needed to make a call. I made it. Now we can all go about our business."

Unless the Brownshirts destroy the city. Anni and Lotte had better not do something stupid, he thinks. He had meant to place a call to Waldmann at *Der Weg,* too, but time ran out. He has reached the downstairs hallway when Kaspers bursts into the Prinzeregentenplatz foyer, outfitted in his brown SA officer's uniform and backed by two other stormtroopers.

Kreisler doffs his hat and says, "Heil Hitler."

Kaspers says nothing but gives Frau Reichert the glare of a displeased goblin.

Once on the street, Kreisler lets out his own muttered curse. His bicycle has been kicked into the roadway and stomped upon until it is no longer a viable means of transportation. He doesn't have to speculate very hard to figure out who is responsible. Rather than turn about and get into it with Kaspers, he hurries on foot in the direction of the office of the left-wing newspaper.

Anyone out of the street now is there for one of two reasons: either to join the Brownshirts in their protest march or to attack them in force. Sensible people wait for the sun to come out rather than get caught in the storm. Neither Anni nor Lotte are among that group. Neither is Kreisler.

The closer he gets to the ominous sounds of conflict, the faster he picks up his pace. He is not in the best of shape for a twenty-eight-year-old cop, however. To catch his breath, he pauses in the entry of a bank. Anxious customers huddle inside. It is an opportunity for him to pull out the stolen secretarial notepad and flip through the pages.

Meetings, rallies, rallies, meetings. Hitler's schedule is an onerous one. From one end of the country to the other. Hamburg to Bremen. Berlin to Dresden. He is shoring up his alliances, building his bridges. He has a meeting with Paul von Hindenburg, the president of the nation in a week. No one is happy with the current government, and Hitler is vying to become the next chancellor, second in power in Germany only to the venerable von Hindenburg. If necessary, Hitler will run against von Hindenburg in the next elections.

Hitler does not like visiting doctors, dentists, or anyone in the medical field. But Kreisler finds other interesting calendar notations in the book. Dinner with Fraulein Braun on the first of next month. A week in Obersalzberg for Oktoberfest. A photoshoot with Heinrich Hoffman. A meeting to resolve the issues with Berlin.

The latter entry piques Kreisler's interest as it hints at what Glaser and Waldmann both inferred. That there is dissent among the National Socialists, especially those in the north, in and around Berlin. A rift. A precarious divide at a time when the next elections are around the corner, and Hitler is calling for absolute party unity. The leader of the northern branch of the National Socialists has been Gregor Strasser, who attended Geli Raubal's funeral, who Hitler's household staff placed at Prinzregentenplatz 16 on the day that Hitler would like to forget ever happened.

The possibility is worth looking into, and Kreisler literally runs with it as he jogs toward the offices of *Der Weg*, into the maelstrom.

Chapter Seventeen

Anni and Lotte can go no further. A full-scale riot has broken out in Marienplatz, and the police have been called in to quell it. Nazis and Communists have been at each other's throats for years, but it seems Geli Raubal's death has sparked something different. A nerve has been struck. An outrageous act has been committed, and someone should pay for it. One side blames Hitler. The other points a steady finger at the Reds and the Jews.

Anni feels for the small Walther in her pocket.

"Maybe we should turn back," Lotte suggests.

"I have to get to the press."

"Why? What good can you do?"

"I can get a story, an accurate one, a bird's eye view of what Hitler's *Juden krieg* is like."

They have to move southeast toward the Isar to reach *Der Weg's* building. Darting along the sidewalk whenever an opening appears, the two compatriots make their way in small chunks of ground over the course of an hour before they reach Waldmann's brother's warehouse. Here, the damage has already been done, lamppost lights shattered, torn signs littering the streets, blood with the accompanying bodies, some moving, some not, leaving a replica on the streets of the 1919 uprisings orchestrated by the Freikorps against the Jews, Communists, and other German turncoats. Over three hundred political assassinations were carried out in those terrible postwar days of revenge.

The Waldmann shoe factory has been breached, the main doors thrust outward and off their hinges, shards of glass coating both the exterior and interior of the building. Anni removes the pistol as she moves into the plant, Lotte at her heels. They are not dressed for sport or battle. Grime and grease coat the bottoms of their dresses and their shoes. Much as they try to avoid bodies, they can't.

"We gave as good as we got," a fellow reporter tells them once they find him in the back offices of the building, hiding in a closet with a female secretary. He has a gash over his right eye and a fat lip. The young woman has wet herself, so Anni avoids a hug.

"Have you seen Herr Waldmann?" she asks.

"Not since we ran in here. We called the *polizei.* They never came."

"Waldmann would never leave his post," Anni says, directing Lotte back into the main room where the presses produce the weekly newspaper.

The clean-up hasn't begun yet. Footwear of all kinds lies in and out of boxes ready for shipment, now vandalized. Casuals, boots, high heels. There will be more than a few happy hausfraus tonight wearing something they couldn't have afforded on their own pfennig. The survivors, beaten and angry, are arming for a counterattack.

"You gonna join us, Anni?" asks an old man who runs the presses. He has located a wrench and is swinging it about like a great ape threatening to protect its territory.

"Alfred, you will only kill yourself doing that," Anni tells him. "Help me look for the boss."

The boss is not in the building. He is out back in an alley facing the river. Not actually facing it, though. Back to the river, he is hanging, a chain wrapped around his neck, from a light post. He has been stripped of all his clothes and beaten to a pulp first. Then the hanging. Since they have no immediate way to take him down, Anni locates the nearest wounded Brownshirt and shoots him twice in the head.

"Anni, for God's sake!" It is the only thing that Lotte can think to say.

Anni's response is to grab Lotte by the arm and drag her out of the building. "Let's go," she orders.

"Where?"

"To meet Avi. It's time to take matters into our own hands."

"What do you mean?"

"What do you think I mean? If I have my way, Hitler won't even stand trial."

They had planned to meet back up with Kreisler that evening anyway. But they haven't even gone a block when Anni retches, sags against a yellow postal box, and empties her stomach.

"They sicken me," she cries. "Fascists. Killers. Waldmann was my friend."

"I know. Come on."

Anni has not let go of the Walther. Because it has gained the attention of people on the street, Lotte takes it from Anni's weakened grip and hides it in her purse. Anni doesn't fight her for it.

"You brought a purse?" she says.

"Well, see, it came in handy."

* * *

Kreisler arrives home after dark, with the police out in full and the streets cleaned of all violence. He is looking thoroughly disheveled with a hole in his pants at his right knee. Yet, as enervated as he feels, the moment he steps through the door into his flat, he perks up.

"Lotte! Anni!"

Two reasons to survive anything. Hugs and kisses would be nice. Just having them in his life, though, will suffice. Limping home after getting sucked into a melee of SA Brownshirts going after a perceived Commie leaving a perceived Commie bakery, he bears the scars of battle with the excitement of recounting his tale to the two women he is devoted to. There is much to tell. After leveling one or two with his fists, he resorted to using his Walther to scare the remaining hooligans off. Then, well…he made his way to *Der Weg*.

"Anni! Lotte! Your knight in rusty armor is back!"

But he doesn't get a response. Not from Lotte. Not from Anni. No hugs. No kisses. Just silence. An awful, ominous silence.

"Hey! Ladies!"

Oskar Waldmann. There is every reason in the world for him to be scared for Anni. He was there when Waldmann's body was taken down from the light pole. He saw what the Brownshirts did to Anni's publisher, her friend. Nothing is beyond them.

He comes to an apprehensive, hyper-wary stop in the middle of the front room. He had burst into the flat without having to use a key. The door was wide open. Fine, if Anni and Lotte were still seated at the desk, going over his photographs, ready to leap up from their work to greet him as he had imagined they would.

But they don't.

Because they're not here.

And they didn't bother to lock the door behind them.

"Lotte? Anni?"

He does his due diligence, gun drawn, searching the remains of the apartment, though he knows he will not find them here. At least, he thinks with profoundest relief, he finds nothing else. Bodies. Nor does he spot any blood. In fact, the apartment looks no different than it did when he left that morning. No overturned furniture. No opened drawers with contents strewn over the floor. And no open window with two angelic bodies lying dead on the sidewalk.

Get a grip, he thinks. They went out, who knows why, to buy dinner for everyone, and simply forgot to secure the apartment. Still, he takes the stairs down two at a time and bangs on Herr Greene's door.

Greene is too slow to answer. When he does, he is wobbly from sleep. Kreisler isn't sympathetic.

"My two friends," Kreisler yells at him. "Have you seen them? Did they leave my flat?"

"So, now I'm your Zuhälter? Your pimp?"

"They're not upstairs."

"Neither am I. Believe it or not, Herr Kreisler, I trust you. You always pay your rent on time. For five years running. You're my best tenant. But upstairs I wasn't. I didn't see anyone come in. I didn't see anyone leave.

Until now, when I see you. Do you need to use my telephone?"

"Can I?"

"You need to ask?"

Kreisler doesn't bother calling Munich Homicide. It is late in the evening, and Fritz Langer won't be there. Kreisler doesn't know the evening shift of detectives, but he does know Langer's home phone number.

"Kreisler? What?"

Langer sounds as fatigued as Kreisler feels. Too bad.

"Pick up Kaspers!" Kreisler hollers as if he's the boss. "We need to pick him up tonight!"

"Are you out of your mind? Were you out in all that shit today?"

"He may have kidnapped Charlotte Leinsdorf. Do you know who she is? Who her father is?" Mentioning Anni the Communist will only cause Langer to hang up.

On his end of the conversation, Langer tries brushing the cobwebs of sleep away so he can counter his inferior's disobedient attitude. "Leinsdorf? What is he? A member of the Reichstag?"

"A publisher. A rich one. Who will put your name in his newspapers if something happens to his daughter? Kaspers will kill her. That is what he does."

Langer is fully awake now. "You need a warrant," he yells back. "A warrant. Do you have one?"

"He's a plant, Fritz! Working for one of Hitler's enemies. He was there when Hitler shot Geli Raubal. He was there not to cover things up, but to implicate Hitler. We're in the middle of an internecine Nazi struggle for power. It's not Hitler behind all these murders. It's someone else."

Whatever Kreisler might think, this is not what Langer wants to hear. "How do you know all this? How do you know he even kidnapped her? What proof do you have? She's an adult. She could just be out somewhere. If she was caught up in the riots today, that's on her. Call me in the morning. Don't bother me about one of your *Freundinnen* tonight!"

Langer breaks contact, leaving Kreisler squeezing the receiver in a quivering hand, staring into the mouthpiece, threatening to hammer Herr

Greene's kitchen counter with it. Restraint wins out. A warrant? Langer wants a warrant?

Okay, then. I'll get one.

Kreisler next calls the number the prosecutor Glaser gave him, a home phone number. A woman picks up.

"Yes?"

"May I speak to Max Glaser, please?"

"Who is this? He isn't here. Leave us alone."

The woman hangs up on him. Not a good sign. Now he's at a loss as to what to do. He's standing like an idiot in the middle of his landlord's apartment, shaking like a baby, tears of rage leaking from his eyes.

Herr Greene takes the receiver from his hand and places it gently back in its cradle. "If I might make a suggestion," he says. "I couldn't help overhear. I can see you're upset. Go upstairs. Perhaps your two lady friends just went out and will be back soon. All this commotion for nothing."

"Not for nothing, Herr Greene." But Kreisler can't move, can't use his usually fruitful mind to work out what to do next. "You didn't see what I saw today."

"You're in love," Herr Greene says. "With two women? What a miracle. But you must be patient. Go upstairs, clean yourself off, make yourself presentable, and wait. An hour, at least. In the meantime, let me make a few calls on my own telephone."

Kreisler finally lets the dam break. Perhaps it's the old man's unexpected kindness, the words of a father he never had. He is sobbing as Greene conducts him into the hallway to the stairs.

"I'm a veteran, you know," Greene says. "You may not think it to look at me. Seventeen years ago. A captain in the infantry. *Der Stahlhelm.* Iron Helmets. I'm one of them. I know people."

His landlord is right. Maybe he jumped to too frightening a conclusion and should just give Anni and Lotte an hour. One hour. No more. He will not envision them as Waldmann hanging from a lamp post.

Back in his apartment, he showers, gets a change of clothes. In his heart, he knows they will not be coming back. Not on their own. But he will do as

Greene suggests. One hour. No more.

To make the time go by, he returns to the spread of evidence still on the dining table. To his trained eye, it does look like someone has gone through the photographs and messed them up. Maybe Lotte and Anni, but he is quick to notice that the photo with Kasper's face is missing. So, too, other photographs he remembers were there before.

One thing that was not taken was the thick pharmaceutical register he and Lotte had taken from Sussman's Apotheke. Stuck within its nearly three hundred pages, Kreisler finds a black and white photo that one of the ladies must have stuck in, perhaps as a sort of bookmark. Turning to that page, Kreisler takes the photo and immediately sees the item in the ledger that either Anni or Lotte drew a black circle around. This is a snapshot he took of the Nazi membership ledger containing Klara Fries's information and membership number: 2344. Why he missed this before, Kreisler doesn't know. Perhaps because the name Martin Kaspers, Nazi Member number 2343, hadn't been relevant to him at the time. But it was relevant to either Anni or Lotte.

'*Good work, my dears,*' he thinks. Klara and Kaspers registered together. As a couple? Certainly, not by coincidence. Was Klara playing Kaspers, or was he using her? Or both? In the end, the only membership Klara Fries belongs to now is that of the dead.

Kreisler glances at his watch. Fifty minutes gone. He's not waiting the other ten. But where can he go? If Kaspers was here, perhaps looking to do some harm to Kreisler rather than to the two women he found, where would he take them? What would he do with them? What good would they be to him?

The answer to one of the questions lies on the pharmacy ledger page, in which the Nazi membership list containing the names of Klara Fries and Martin Kaspers had been placed. He happens to look at it as he is putting on his evening coat and reloading his Walther pistol to head into the night. It is the very page that registers Klara's picking up her anti-nausea medication with Sussman's note that she did not want her former pharmacy to be notified. The Garten Apotheke. The pharmacy Kaspers manages.

Kreisler has no way of knowing whether or not this is where Kaspers would take his hostages, but it is a beginning. Taking the stairs down, he nearly runs over Herr Greene.

"Where are you going?" Greene shouts at him as Kreisler heads to the exit. "I've made some calls."

"To a pharmacy. On Gartenstrasse."

It is only when he hits the street that he remembers he no longer has a working bicycle. The pharmacy is a hike of several miles, but he has no choice. Ignoring Greene's shout from the doorway, he begins his race, not even knowing if the finish line is the right one.

As he goes, he sees Waldmann again, battered and strung up, dehumanized. He sees the bloated body of David Sussman pulled from the river. He sees Klara Fries in pieces on the sidewalk of Frau Becker's apartment building. He foresees a future where such butchery is a daily matter so prevalent that people, pedestrians, pass by such scenes, eyes averted, unwilling to believe what is happening right in front of their own doorsteps. What can a homicide cop do in such a world other than surrender to the improbability of it all?

As he approaches the block on which Kaspers' pharmacy is located, Kreisler has to slow down, if for no other reason than he is out of breath. But he must also surveil the premises, make sure he doesn't give his presence away, make sure he is even in the right place. He glances at his watch again. It is just after one in the morning. He's made surprisingly good time. He plants himself beside a tree within sight of the pharmacy and waits.

After only a few minutes, he is rewarded for his patience and logic. Several cars are parked in the front. When the door to the pharmacy opens, Kreisler can clearly see two men come out and approach an automobile bearing a Nazi emblem. The glow from a neighboring streetlight reveals Kaspers. The other man is familiar to Kreisler, but it takes him a moment to place Gregor Strasser, the Berlin region head of the National Socialists. He attended Geli Raubal's funeral service. Hitler slapped the cigarette out of his hand. There is no love lost between the two Nazi leaders. But where are Lotte and Anni?

Only one way to find out. Brazen it.

Kreisler leaves the protection of the lime tree and heads straight across the empty intersection toward the parked car and Strasser and Kaspers. His gun is drawn when he confronts them.

"Herr Strasser," he says to the man he presumes is Kaspers' boss. "We met at Geli Raubal's funeral."

Strasser is as large a man as Kaspers but several years older, undistinguished in looks, professorial, and, apparently, a man who has no problem contradicting Hitler on party policy. "I don't remember you," he says. His eyes are fixed on the gun Kreisler is holding.

"You offered Herr Hitler a smoke. He rejected it," Kreisler says.

"I don't recall that either. You have a gun. You are pointing it at me."

"Your man here is a murderer," Kreisler says, redirecting his Walther at Kaspers. "He threw a young woman named Klara Fries out a window. He drowned a young man named David Sussman in the Isar River. And I think you are probably aware of his involvement in the murder of Angela Raubal. Am I wrong in any of this? Now I believe he has kidnapped two friends of mine. I want them."

Strasser, wisely, does not shift a glance toward his underling, barely recognizes his existence not five feet away. "Herr Kaspers and I are both in the pharmaceutical business. This is how we know one another. He was a student of mine in Berlin."

"And now you are here."

"Outside a pharmacy."

"Which is closed for the night. I'd like to take a look inside, if it wouldn't be too inconvenient."

"It would," says Kaspers. He speaks to Strasser. "He's a Jew."

"I'm a homicide detective. He's a killer." Kreisler frisks Kaspers and comes away with a small revolver. Strasser is weaponless. Satisfied that the enemy is unarmed, Kreisler waves his gun toward the entry. "Inside."

Strasser, still without looking at Kaspers, turns and walks back to the pharmacy. "Hitler is your enemy, not me," he says. "What he will do to your people if he ever has the power will not be pleasant. I am your friend."

Kreisler's pistol is his opinion-maker at the moment. He chooses silence over dialogue. A good interrogator knows to keep his mouth shut and let the culprits hang themselves.

Kaspers opens the entry to the store. While it is dark up front, Kreisler notes a light in the far back.

"What will you do?" Kaspers asks. "Arrest me? Good luck. See what good it did your friend Glaser. Another Jew."

Glaser? The name casually tossed out makes Kreisler's hand shake. The woman who answered his call to the prosecutor was frightened, said he wasn't home. Then, where was he? With Oskar Waldmann? Dead? Strung up for opposing the Brownshirts, for daring to confront their leader? Still, Kreisler will not be drawn in.

In a storeroom at the back of the store, Anni and Lotte are waiting for him. Lotte is the first to cry his name and run to him. Kreisler is so ecstatic to see that they are both alive, he drops his guard.

"Avi! Thank God! You found us!"

"Lotte, wait…"

Before Kreisler can even ward her off, he is smothered in Brownshirts, three of them coming out of the darkness to overwhelm him and relieve him of his weapon. Struggle is pointless. The numbers are against him. But that is when Anni strikes back. Apparently, Kaspers forgot to check her clothes or confiscate the small pistol Kreisler had given her from the boy Lerner in Vienna. Clever enough not to engage in a shootout, she merely changes places with Kaspers and sets the barrel of her gun against the back of Strasser's head. At six feet, she is more than level with the National Socialist strongman.

"*Meine Herren,*" she says, "*wir haben eine Pattsituation.*" We have a stand-off.

The way Anni stands with a straight arm and a stiff hand and a steady trigger finger proclaims her readiness to do whatever she has to do to secure her freedom. The bruising on her face, given her by the very man Kreisler intends to arrest, only enhances her image.

"The Communist has balls, I'll give her that," Kaspers says. He has his own pistol, too, lent him by one of his fellow Brownshirts, and points it at Kreisler. "As you say, Fraulein, a stand-off. What now?"

Be brazen. Like always.

Kreisler steps forward, right at Kaspers, unmindful of the handgun aimed at his face. "You surrender," he says, "and take your chances with the court. After all," he glances at Strasser, "isn't that the whole point? To get publicity? To tell the world, in full view of the German public, what Hitler did to his niece? You were right there, Kaspers. After Hitler shot the girl, he was in a panic. He turned to you, his loyal SA bodyguard, and asked for help. He didn't know what to do. You did. You called Herr Strasser."

"It came as a shock to all of us," Strasser says, feeling the muzzle of Anni's revolver against his head.

"An opportunity nevertheless opened up for you. My God, you must have thought," Kreisler says. "Hitler has handed you his career, his party, his very life. Right in your hands."

Even now, Strasser, his own career, party affiliation, and life, in someone else's hands, remains cool. "I see what you are trying to do, Inspektor. Yes. Clever. Bring us all down. Hitler. Me. The works. Yes? But I advised Franks to do nothing. What you cops found was as we left it."

"No, mein Herr," Kreisler barks. His finger, indicting Franks, lacks only a trigger. "You advised him to corrupt the scene. Make sure Hitler takes the fall. His relationship to his niece was already the scuttlebutt of the party. Now, you have this. The act of an enraged, mentally unstable cuckold. Who would want such a man as the leader of any political party, let alone the president of any reasonable nation? Who wins out of a situation like this? You, Herr Strasser?"

"I don't see how…."

"And by making sure the world finds out about it, in court, in depth, the whole bloody mess, you will end Hitler's career. And, dare I say, boost your own. Unless, of course…."

Now Kreisler lowers his trigger finger and opens up a palm in warm friendship to the very man he knows is a serial murderer.

"Unless Kaspers turns on you and takes you down, too. A death sentence revoked as a reward for betraying everything he stands for."

Kreisler moves closer to Kaspers halfway between the two Nazi leaders.

"The blackmailing was the mistake, Oberleutnant," Kreisler says. "It led to murder, and that, Herr Strasser, will fall on you if Kaspers testifies. So, then, what do we do here? Who is the true enemy? Me? The law? These two innocent ladies, although the one holding the pistol on you, Herr Strasser, isn't as innocent as she looks? Or your own minion, whose greed and penchant for raping and murdering women has led us all here tonight? I know what I would do if I were you."

"Trust you?" Strasser asks. "If you know so much."

"Kill them all," is Kaspers' solution. Well, why not let the Communist bitch blow Strasser's brains out? Then kill her. And the cop. Strasser will be dead, and Hitler will be made to take the blame for all of it. Any lie can be made truth.

Only, Kaspers' solution is interrupted by a shout from the front of the pharmacy and a sudden slamming open of a door leading into a back alley.

"Polizei! Polizei!"

Kreisler is startled. Kaspers freezes. His associates try to flee but are intercepted by members of the Munich Police Department. And who should be in the lead but Fritz Langer, holding his own Walther and confiscating that of Kaspers?

"Inspektor Kreisler," he says, "would you tell your girlfriend with the red hair to lower her pistol, or one of our fellow officers will have to shoot her, and such a shame that would be. You would be left with only one bedfellow."

"Fritz?"

"You're surprised? After the phone conversation we had? Thank your landlord. Herr Greene and I are both veterans of the Great War, both members of the Steel Helmets."

Langer has Kaspers put in cuffs and led outside to the alley. With Strasser, he takes an apologetic stance, allowing the Nazi official to leave the front way with one of his men.

"Really, Fritz?"

"Politics," Langer explains. He doffs his hat to Lotte, who has found Kreisler's embrace, and Anni, who has handed her gun over. "Ladies. I trust the rest of the evening will be more pleasurable."

"Fuck…"

Before Anni can complete her complimentary remark, a gunshot rings out from the alley. It is the final violent crack of reality in a day that has been filled with bloodshed and death. Kreisler's immediate reaction is to push Anni and Lotte out of harm's way. Langer doesn't react at all. That is the giveaway.

"Kaspers?" Even the cynical Kreisler is stunned by what he knows has just happened.

"Politics," Langer responds, indifferent to his underling's shock. What is one more body after all? "Be well, Avi. Say nothing. You're a hero."

Epilogue

August 2, 1934

I n three years, murder has not stopped in Munich. Murder has not stopped anywhere. It is hard to read any newspaper these days, though it is something Lotte insists she and her two roommates, Kreisler and Anni, do, just to know what is happening in the world.

It isn't easy. Less than two months before, the Nazis unleashed their Night of the Long Knives. It was not, or should not have been, a surprise. The Socialist wing of the National Socialists had long disagreed with Hitler's political vision. So, on a warm late spring night in early June, one hundred and fifty members of the SA were killed. Ernst Röhm was one. Gregor Strasser was another. Kreisler could have told them to watch their backs, but who listens to a Jewish atheist?

Herr Greene is happy to have the two ladies living in his building. In the old days, when he was much younger, he had an eye for the ladies and they for him. He is a widower now and appreciates whenever Lotte or Anni look in on him. It has been a tough few years for Anni. Hitler banned all trade union activity. Though Waldmann was dead, she took over the reins of Der Weg and has been publishing and writing articles for it ever since, though the KPD, her party, has been banned from politics since the notorious fire at the Reichstag in '33.

Hitler is now chancellor of Germany with only one man between him and total power: General von Hindenburg, now eighty-six years old. A man of such importance no longer cares if Kreisler was an architectural student or not. Briefly, Kreisler wore the helmet of a German hero thanks to his having destroyed the men who were trying to frame Hitler. Kreisler rejected the crown. Hitler has become too powerful. It is as if every attempt to assassinate him physically or spiritually only makes him stronger.

The Gestapo came into being a year ago under Strasser's former aide, Himmler. Goebbels has conducted a mass book-burning of over twenty-five thousand titles considered unpatriotic, Communistic, or simply too Jewish. All local governments have been handed over to the Nazi Party. And the Reichstag passed an Enabling Act giving Hitler the complete power to enact any law he chooses without involving the Reichstag.

What next is, of course, a question that should be on everyone's minds.

On Lotte's thirtieth birthday, the friends decide to celebrate despite everything. Anton, who has fulfilled his promise to join the Catholic ministry, meets them at a favorite Italian restaurant, the Osteria Bavaria. He has no income. Neither does Anni, who survives on the income Kreisler gets as a cop, and Lotte earns from her bookstore.

"They were in my store again this morning," Lotte says over linguini. "I told them, we have eliminated all controversial books, but they still found a dozen, among the children's books, for God's sake, and wrote me up a warning. The crap I have to carry now, it almost makes me want to close the store entirely."

"You and me both," Anni says. "I'm going to have to shut down pretty soon." Lotte has cut out the wine. Anni has picked up the habit, but only when Kreisler treats them out for dinner. "I am down to two other writers. I can't pay anyone. We used to be a weekly. Now I'm a monthly. I don't want to put young kids at risk of being beaten up just to hand out my shit. I mean, is it worth it anymore?"

"You should get out," Anton says. "Get out now. Isn't that what that prosecutor, Glaser, did? Cut out for Austria?"

"I know too many people," Kreisler says. "I'm respected in the office. As much as Langer snips at my heels, he won't get rid of me. He knows I'm his best detective."

"You're too good," Lotte says.

Once the meal is done, their waiter offers a dessert menu. Kreisler orders cheesecake, the four can split.

"Well, I am to be ordained in October," Anton says. "October 19th to be precise. You're all invited, in case you forgot or didn't think you would be. Even the Jews among us. I promise no crucifixions. Post-election, you will no longer be my friends. You will become my flock."

"Sorry, Anton," says Anni. "Baaaa is not in my vocabulary."

"Do you even know any Latin?" Lotte wonders.

"Of course, I do. *In principio erat verbum.*"

"*Et Deus erat Verbum.* Congratulations, Father Maier." Kreisler gives his friend a pat on the arm.

"Even so, fellow sheep, despite your duly noted sarcasm, this will allow me to perform weddings for those so inclined."

"Who would those be?" Anni asks, licking her fingers clean of cheese filling. She is just a little drunk.

"I have to be blunt? Though I must say, your current arrangement continues to puzzle and amuse me. Who would I be marrying? In what order? Would the Church even allow such a thing?"

"We don't care," says Lotte. "As long as we're happy, fuck the world."

"Hear! Hear!" Anni raises her glass of Burgundy with a laugh, losing precious droplets of red wine on her skirt as she giggles. "See how much we have converted our Lotte, Avi. A subversive among the elite."

"What about children?" Anton asks. "You can't have children without being married."

"Says Saint Anton."

"Give it time, Father," Kreisler says. For neither the time nor the place, he intuits, is quite right. For those living and breathing, though, he raises a glass. "A toast to us. To the survivors. One is for cheesecake, sweet and tart. Two is for the wine that comes à la carte. Three is for lovers who share one heart. Four is for friends who fate will never part. Cheers."

"Bravo for the poet."

Glasses clink. Smiles dominate. Happiness can exist sometime, somewhere. One can hope, at least.

* * *

That evening, word finally reaches Munich that Paul von Hindenburg has died of lung cancer. Hitler now rules Germany. As the four friends leave the Osteria Bavaria, the sun is literally setting on Germany. Kreisler walks hand in hand-in-hand in hand with Anni and Lotte, and Anton. He is, as Fritz Langer says, a great detective. But even he ignores the meaning of the reddening sky.

If the four friends are to survive the coming years, they will need more than fate to intervene.

Acknowledgments

I would like to show my appreciation to the ladies of Level Best Books… Verena Rose, Shawn Reilly Simmons, and Deb Well. I began writing over 50 years ago. These wonderful ladies have opened the door that had been held shut to me for a half-century.

About the Author

Born in Portland, Maine, Peter Clenott is a graduate of Bowdoin College. He currently resides in Haverhill, Massachusetts, and works for an anti-poverty agency. Of indeterminate age, Clenott claims to have told fellow Bowdoin graduates Henry Longfellow and Nathaniel Hawthorne they would never make it in this business.

AUTHOR WEBSITE:
   https://peterclenott.squarespace.com/

SOCIAL MEDIA HANDLES:
   https://www.facebook.com/peter.clenott.1
   @PClenott

Also by Peter Clenott

The Unwanted

Hunting the King

The Hunted